30 DAYS

LANCE CLARKE

Manor Cottage
Books

First published on ebook Kindle April 2012. This edition published March 2017 by Manor Cottage Books.

The catalogue record for this book is available from the British Library
ISBN 978-0-9957595-0-3

Cover design and typesetting: Jake Arden Communications
Cover image: Shutterstock

Acknowledgements

I want to acknowledge the gentle shove, given me by my lovely late-wife who simply said, "…get on with it…!" To Brenda Aldred who researched Indians, tin mines and other necessary detail. But also, to my editor Jake Arden, who turbocharged this edition. Others, too many to name, have also contributed in one way or another.

I first sketched the idea out in the George Bush era after reading of the involvement of Carl Rove, who masterminded the progress of both father and son to the White House. The inspiration also comes from a fine American Lieutenant Colonel I worked with in NATO, whose loyalty and standards I admired; we disagreed on some political issues, but I was always able to lean on the fact that Europeans have history on their side.

It is, of course, pure fiction; but as with so many stories like this, it leans on fact and raises uncomfortable questions.

Lance Clarke, March 2017

What readers say about 30 Days

"Lance Clarke has written a page-turning, white-knuckle ride of a political thriller. Thoroughly enjoyed it."

"Fast-paced, exciting, thought-provoking. Definitely going to read more by Lance Clarke. Well-thought out, highly descriptive, exciting and, yes, even educational. I'm not crazy about politics but this author made things relevant and interesting, and very believable! If this was made into a movie, I think it would be a hit because it has all of the elements that Hollywood loves: violence, sex, intrigue, humor, love..."

"The more I got into it, the harder it was to put it down."

"Exposes paranoia in US political circles and government agencies. Good holiday read."

Also by Lance Clarke

Laka Stvar
Know Thyself
Not of Sound Mind

PART ONE

THE ARIZONA GAMBIT

"....to secure these rights, Governments are instituted by men,
deriving their just powers from the consent of the governed."

American Declaration of Independence

Chapter 1

April 2008. Special Agent in Charge, Dan Quantock sat at his desk in FBI headquarters on Pennsylvania Avenue scrolling through his inbox looking at the latest reports on his herd. The herd, who often behaved with bovine stupidity, were US senators and their families and Dan's job was to protect them from predators, rustlers and themselves. Of today's red flag messages, the most urgent was the case of the teenage daughter of the Senator for Wyoming who was claiming she had been sexually assaulted by her Afro-American, female soccer coach. Black predatory lesbians in Wyoming, thought Quantock, times were definitely a-changing. But the girl's fundamental Christian mother wouldn't see it that way and was more likely to blow the suspect away with an assault rifle than follow due process. She was also very close to President Jake Brannigan.

He forwarded the email with instructions to his trusted subordinate Jim Rook. Next on the list was the knucklehead Senator for Kentucky, who had decided the time was right to sponsor a bill outlawing halal meat for being cruel to animals and had succeeded in earning an Iranian death fatwa and uniting not just Shia and Sunni across the world in outrage, but also Jews worried that kosher rules might be next. The man needed his skull seriously rapped, as well as protected from some home-grown Muslim extremist looking for a target. Quantock fixed his gaze on the photograph of his President on the wall. Senator Knucklehead was another Brannigan crony so Quantock needed an agent on the case who carried a big stick but spoke softly. Another case for Jim Rook. He kept his eyes on Brannigan. There was something Slavic about the stern heavy face. He could have been related to Boris Yeltsin. He cracked a smile. Maybe he was a Russian plant. Real name Brannigofsky. That would explain things.

Quantock's Blackberry pinged. It was a text message from Alvin Studebaker, a CIA buddy and chess partner. "C5." Alvin was playing the Sicilian Defence. Quantock stood up and ambled over to the chess board set up on a side table. He regarded the disposition of the pieces and smiled. "Alvin, you think you're sly," he whispered as he moved his knight, "but so am I." He texted: "Nd5."

Quantock was tall, six-foot two-inches in his socks, and lean. He was forty-one, but thanks to his gym work still had the body of a thirty-year-old. He wore his thick jet-black hair short in a buzz cut and his face was angular and chiselled with a strong jaw. He wasn't handsome but women used to be attracted by his twinkly grey eyes. He glanced at the photograph of his wife and son which hung above the chess set. It had been taken at the christening in 1992 and they both looked radiant. The anniversary of their death was two days away. His eyes clouded at the thought, forcing him to blink.

He walked to the window and peered through the anti-blast blinds. It was a glorious spring morning and shiny red, white and blue tulips were standing to attention in the flower beds on the sidewalk. He poured a cup of coffee from the pot he kept on a corner table and flicked on the TV. The CNN headlines were being broadcast. The President's gamble on a troop surge in Iraq appeared to be paying off and jihadi terrorists were being taken out left right and centre. But the economy was nosediving and the collapse of the housing market bubble was accelerating.

In Texas, federal agents and state troopers, backed up by SWAT teams, had ended the siege of the fundamentalist Mormon Yearning Church of Zion without resistance and four hundred and twenty-six children at risk of sexual abuse had been taken into protective custody. Quantock was glad. Fifteen years ago, almost to the day, he had taken a bullet at the Waco siege, which had been an unmitigated disaster for the FBI and a nightmare for him. Seventy-six men, women and children shot, burnt, crushed or gassed to death. But all of the hard work which had been put into fixing the problems in the Bureau in the late 1990s and again after the intelligence failure of 9/11 was now in danger of being wasted if President Brannigan won another term in office. Outsourcing American manufacturing, military and CIA functions was bad enough, but handing over federal law enforcement duties to private sector agencies such as Blackwater was madness. Utter madness. But no one paid attention to what Quantock had to say. He reached for his pill box and gulped down a tablet with a slurp of coffee. "Count your blessings Dan," he said. "Count your blessings."

The phone on his desk rang. "I've got Senator Kinz on the line, sir," his secretary said. "I'll take it," said Quantock with a grin. He liked and respected Randolph Kinz, the Senator for Arizona. He was civilised, erudite, honourable, honest, a Vietnam war hero and a true patriot. "Senator Kinz, you son of a gun, how are you?"

Chapter 2

"Ginny! Come to the kitchen and help me make baklava!" Mrs Angela Grivas shouted. Ginny put down her book and obeyed. She sat at the old pine kitchen table as her mother unrolled thin sheets of filo pastry.

"Here!" Mrs Grivas ordered. "Take this and start brushing in the oil." Ginny loved cooking with her mother and learning the intricacies of Greek cuisine. The kitchen was always brimming with pots of herbs and fragrance. Basil, bay leaves, thyme, oregano, rosemary and sage. Plump bulbs of garlic and strings of onions hung from the walls, next to dried red peppers. A huge bowl of luscious red tomatoes sat on the sideboard. Her mother's face was lined and her black hair was greying but she was still beautiful. She was also still the same dress size as when she got married. Ginny's size.

"Tell me about your new boyfriend?" her mother asked.

Ginny giggled. "Mom, you are so lame. I don't have a boyfriend. You know that."

"You could be keeping him a secret. But you can tell me anything."

"I don't have a boyfriend. I'm not looking for a boyfriend. I'm a good Greek girl who takes her college studies seriously."

"You don't want to leave it too late. All the best fish will be caught."

"Thanks Mom. I'll take that under advisement."

Senator Nick Grivas padded into the kitchen and regarded them. "Baklava. Good. Make sure you use lots of pistachios and go easy on the walnuts," he growled. The women ignored him.

The Senator went to the espresso machine on the counter and noisily made a cup of coffee, switching on the TV as he did so. Fox News had an item about a picket of an abortion clinic.

Ginny grimaced. "I think that is so outrageous. Women don't have abortions on a whim. It's a major decision. They need support not abuse."

"What are you talking about girl," her father snapped. "You're 19. What do you know about abortion?"

"I believe women have the right to choose what happens to their bodies," Ginny retorted.

"And what about the bodies of the babies? Abortion is murder."

"No, it's not. It's legal in this country. It's legal in Greece."

Her father violently wagged his forefinger. "Don't you dare talk to me about Greece. You know nothing about Greece. The communists brought in abortion. And you know why? To reduce the Greek population. To keep Greece weak. You're meant to be intelligent. Go read a book about Greece."

"Let's not argue," Mrs Grivas said.

"Yes, let's not," said Ginny angrily. "I'm going to my room."

Ginny sat on her bed and punched a pillow, repeatedly. She couldn't stay here any longer. Her father was a tyrant. Her mother was weak. She never confronted him unless it was about his drinking or gambling, and then she was like a gorgon. That was acceptable for a Greek wife. Arguing with your husband about politics was not. The summer term was fast approaching. She needed an escape. Maybe go to Greece and study some history about the place. That would help her grades in her politics major. Her anger dissipated.

She stood up and looked at herself in the full-length mirror. Even though she was wearing sweat pants and a t-shirt and was without make-up, she looked okay. Her black curly hair was long and lustrous. She smiled coquettishly and caressed, squeezed and lifted her fulsome breasts. Maybe she would meet a nice Greek boy. That would please her mother and piss off her father – big time. She would do some research. She got her laptop and sat on the bed with it propped against her knees. First, she needed to check her Facebook updates and then her email messages. There was an email from Uncle Randolph. Senator Randolph Kinz wasn't really her uncle, but she liked him so much that's what she called him. He was in many ways her mentor. Uncle Randolph didn't have any children of his own and informally adopted a whole brood of kids, all the offspring of other senators. Every summer he threw a huge party for them all. But his message wasn't about this year's party. It was an invitation to meet up to discuss a very special and secret project which might require a month away from home. Serendipity! She emailed him back.

Clem Johnson heard his answerphone recording and sat bolt upright in bed, his head throbbing from a hangover. He'd spent the previous night at a friend's apartment smoking dope and drinking beer and watching a DVD box set of Frank Capra movies. Clem thought Capra was a master. There were very few directors these days who could get close to matching him.

Clem had staggered back to his apartment in Greenwich Village at 3am. It was now almost 10am, his mouth tasted like glue and his eyes were sticky and hard to open. He rolled out of bed and stumbled to the bathroom where he poured a glass of water which he drank in one swallow. After brushing his teeth, he went to his living room and pushed the glowing red button on the phone. He recognised Senator Randolph Kinz's cultured voice on the message. Kinz wanted to meet him to discuss a special project which needed someone passionate about film and politics.

Kinz was a Republican and Clem did not agree with his politics but he enjoyed the lengthy chats they had every now and again. The Senator believed that the American dream was almost Darwinian, that capitalism was a way of life as old as the history of man, and although it had evolved beyond mere trading of clay pots, it was up to governments to control it.

Against Clem's statements about capitalist greed, Kinz conceded that the position the US held in the world was a monopoly based on self-interest. But he stubbornly contended that this was a price that had to be paid. Capitalism was like a giant house of cards that had to be continuously re-stacked to avoid a total collapse that would be in no one's interest. The most repetitive statement that Kinz made was that he believed in his heart that the DNA spiral that formed the American psyche, its very heartbeat, was the spirit of its people. People who, throughout history, had come to the country to work hard, be ingenious and push back boundaries. Along the way some of their peers would have been exploited, but equally their struggle to survive gave them character. It was indeed very Darwinian he had said, somewhat earnestly, but in the end the best plants push up to meet the sunshine – and that was the truth of it!

They found more common ground when it came to movies and Kinz had introduced Clem to Capra. Clem tried to persuade Kinz about Tarantino's genius, but the Senator, although gamely wincing his way through the violence of Reservoir Dogs, could not be persuaded. He also thought that Michael Moore, one of Clem's heroes, was a fat, grandstanding, liberal smartass. But they did share a love of Ford,

Copolla and Lucas. Kinz was also very supportive of Clem's decision to study film and video at New York's School of Visual Arts and had helped persuade Senator Bill "Bubba" Johnson to allow his son to follow his own path. Clem had kept Kinz updated on the progress of his four-year degree. But he had kept quiet about his deepening involvement in radical politics. Clem was part of the Stop the War group at the School of Visual Arts and made a video of the marches and protests, which had continued since the invasion of Iraq. The video had been posted on Indymedia and received lots of favourable comments. Clem was also active in Peoples Global Action. He had been too young to take part in the Battle of Seattle, but was certain other historic events would happen soon and he would be there with a video camera.

Chapter 3

Quantock sat back in a comfortable studded, green leather armchair regarding a silver-haired, distinguished, Southern gentleman with a twinkle in his eye. They were in the spacious living room of Senator Randolph Kinz, at his elegant house in Washington.

"Do you know the story of Julius Caesar, Dan?" Kinz asked.

"Some," Quantock replied, taking a sip of coffee. "He was a military genius. Conquered Gaul and Britain. Veni, Vidi, Vici. Crossed the river Rubicon with his army to get political power. Ignored the warning to beware the Ides of March and got whacked by Brutus and other senators. What I can never figure is where was his close protection? Why didn't he have bodyguards?"

"He did," Kinz said. "But they threw in with the conspirators." He took a sip of coffee. "Do you think Caesar was a good or a bad leader?"

Dan thought for a moment. "On the whole, I'd say good. His legacy lives on. We owe the modern calendar to him. The army still teaches his military tactics to trainee officers. His legionnaires loved him."

"How do you know that?" Kinz asked.

"It's written down, isn't it?"

"Yes. Under direction from Caesar and later by his nephew Emperor Augustus. History is written by the winners. The losers don't get a look in. Then Shakespeare did a PR job on him. Made out he was decent but flawed. In fact, he was a ruthless, power-hungry, money-grabbing, cruel son of a bitch. Brutus and Cato were right to fear what he would do to Rome if he became a dictator."

Quantock smiled. "He sounds a bit like POTUS."

Kinz grinned slyly. "If you were writing Brannigan into a history book, what would you put?"

Quantock took another sip of coffee. "He claims to personify the American Dream. The great grandson of poor Irish immigrants who escaped the famine and worked like slaves to build a business from nothing. Their sacrifice enabled Brannigan to go to Yale. Made valuable contacts as a member of Skull and Bones. Went into the oil business with his buddy Dubya at the right time and made a killing. Then moved on to run Halliburton. High flyer in the Grand Old Party. Helped clean up Watergate. Reagan loved him and gave him the job of supervising the contra arms deal with Iran to free the hostages. Papa Bush was also dependent on him. His work with Storming Norman Schwarzkopf ensured that Saddam's army was annihilated in 1991. Held back from invading Iraq in order to give Saddam a final chance to come onside. Didn't make the same mistake in 2003."

"What about Vietnam?" Kinz enquired.

"Unlike you Randolph, he was a draft dodger. But he's more than happy to talk like John Wayne. Also, happy to torture terrorist suspects."

"And what do you think he will do if the wins the election?"

"Try to finish the job of making the business of America business. In the process, he will sell off or destroy every valuable American institution and Federal service. American society will return to the social conditions of the Wild West. Of course, he will ensure he has a healthy sum of money for his retirement in 2012."

"And what do you want, Dan? Where will you be in 2012?"

"I don't know."

"You puzzle me, Dan, sometimes. You're straight out of the Illinois boondocks. Hell, you even look like Lincoln. You aced college and were destined for greatness in the Bureau. Earned a medal for your bravery at the Waco siege and had some sort of mental breakdown. But you recovered and brought the Oklahoma bomber to justice. After taking down Timothy McVeigh, you got the job as Special Agent in Charge in Arizona and provided a good service for me and the citizens. Then some rich coke and booze-addled punk killed your wife and son in a car crash. And you lost it. The punk went on the lam and you tracked him down to a Palm Springs hotel. He fired at you and you fired back. Seven times. Seven bullets. Same number as the years you had been married. And there were no witnesses."

Quantock remained expressionless. But his eyes hardened. Then he smiled. "But you saved me."

"Yes. The President was under pressure to throw the book at you. But I persuaded him otherwise. Sometimes shared Western values are useful. You're flawed but decent, Dan. The punk deserved to die and sometimes there is something to be said about frontier justice, when all other avenues are closed. How do you find riding herd on me and other senators?"

"Riding herd?" Quantock questioned.

Kinz chuckled. "Don't play innocent. I know more about you than you know yourself."

"The job's fine."

"But it must get boring. Being a babysitter can't be your only destiny."

"What alternative do I have?"

"Help me with a very important project to safeguard the real American Dream, not Brannigan's grotesque nightmare."

"What sort of project?"

"I'm calling it the Arizona Gambit. What does the term gambit mean to you?"

"A chess attack where you are prepared to sacrifice a piece or pieces to kill the king. With respect Senator, before you go on I need to remind you that I am still an FBI man."

Kinz laughed. "I'm not planning to kill anyone. Metaphorically maybe, but not literally. But sacrifices will need to be made." He looked at Quantock probingly. "I'd like to see the gambit more in terms of the need to check a tyrannical king. "*The accumulation of all powers, legislative, executive, and judiciary, in the same hands, whether of one, a few, or many, and whether hereditary, self appointed, or elective, may justly be pronounced the very definition of tyranny.*" Who said that, Dan?"

"James Madison," Dan said with a smile.

"Yes, indeed." Kinz said. "Why don't we continue our discussion over dinner? My boy Pablo cooks a mean T-bone steak."

Quantock took a cab home. Kinz's gambit was mad and the risk of failure extremely high. A small group of the teenage offspring of a number of senators with whom Kinz was friendly was being recruited for a secret project at a hidden location. They would be supplied with food, accommodation and the facilities to make a top-class video: a state-of-the-nation address from the younger generation to their parents. They would explore what was right and what was wrong with America and what could be done to put things right.

Kinz had forensically outlined the details of the plan as he cut through his steak. The kids would have 30 days to make the video. Kinz would fix the distribution and broadcast of it on national TV just before the election. What the teenagers wouldn't know is that the outside world had been told that they were being held hostage by jihadi terrorists. Kinz was certain that Brannigan would seek to make political capital out of the event and would calculate that a hard-line populist response would be a vote winner. Kinz predicted a savage escalation of military action in the Middle East, with possible strikes against either Syria or Iran or both. There would be a witch hunt against Muslims at home. "Are you with us, or are you with the Muslims?" Brannigan would say. He would rekindle the rage which had engulfed America after 9/11 and would not be able to resist supersizing it. Then Kinz would prick his bubble. The kids would appear on national TV all fresh and excited and politically motivated only to be told that Brannigan had used them as pawns in the war against terror and in his election campaign. They would be outraged. So would the media. So would the American people. Finally, they would realise how much they had been duped. It would be a gigantic wake-up call and in their righteous anger the people would sweep Brannigan away.

Brannigan would lose the election and America's first woman president would be sworn in. But the Republicans would still control Congress for the next two years and the new president would screw up. Meanwhile the Grand Old Party would find a sensible, honourable, decent candidate to win the 2012 election. Quantock had asked: "Like you Randolph?" Randolph had replied. "No Dan. My time serving this great democracy will be up. It will be my retirement present. Now here's what I want you to do."

Quantock had told Kinz that he thought the gambit was mad and reckless. But then, Kinz's hero, General Patton had been mad and reckless and he had delivered the goods in WWII. Sometimes desperate times needed desperate and very bold measures. Quantock accepted the mission after getting assurances that the money was no object and that the Bureau would be protected from any fall out.

But now in the cab, his mind whirred through the contingencies. What if the "kidnap" went wrong? What if some have-a-go-hero used a gun? What if the kids breached the cordon sanitaire and got word out to their parents or friends? And it went viral on social media? What if Brannigan acted with intelligence and restraint and kept things on the QT? How would Kinz persuade the kids to give up a month of college study? Would the cover story he intended using on the parents be watertight?

A gambit needed sacrifice. Quantock didn't doubt that Kinz was willing to sacrifice himself. But he had used the plural. Sacrifices. Were the kids to be sacrificed as well? The media would have a field day on them. Muckraking for sex, drugs and political deviance. They would go through their MySpace and Facebook accounts with a fine-tooth comb and then hang them out to dry.

Brannigan was a master of the dark arts of media manipulation. What if he dodged the silver bullet and the blame landed on the Bureau? Was Dan a sacrifice?

What if? A line from Shakespeare came into his mind. He was sure it was Julius Caesar. Mark Anthony? No. It was Brutus.

"There is a tide in the affairs of men, which taken at the flood, leads onto fortune; Omitted all the voyage of their life is bound in shallows and miseries."

Kinz might be the ship owner, but Quantock was the captain of this voyage. Every contingency had to be covered. Every detail nailed down. The project had to be a hundred per cent ship-shape and Quantock fashion.

Quantock didn't feel like being on his own. He got the cab to drop him at Slim's Diner on Georgia Avenue. It was an old fashioned diner with a chrome serving-counter and red-leather booths, frequented since time immemorial by taxi drivers. Other people were welcome of course, but the raucous language, shouting, insults and general playful mayhem meant that they were unlikely to go there for a quiet doughnut and coffee. Slim had long since died. He had founded the place in the 1930s when the food was simple and filling and the coffee cheap and plentiful.

As the country's fortunes changed so did Slim's. A business consortium now ran the diner as part of a chain. Although retro, the equipment was state of the art and a wide range of drinks, including beer, and foodstuff was served. The most important element though was the staff and they bantered and controlled the unruly clientele with skill and humour. Tonight was unusual. The waitresses were grumpy and the customers were more truculent than usual.

Two Guatemalan taxi drivers argued about whether President Brannigan was a friend or foe of Latino Americans. This irritated a booth nearby who thought that there were more important things to worry about like the Chinese taking over. A large fat truck driver sat by the doorway. He always ate dinner at Slim's and was renowned for his double portions. His booth was crowded with what looked like a bucket of coffee and a dustbin of doughnuts, each one despatched in only two bites. The noisiest area was in front of the wide-screen wall-mounted TV.

As Quantock waited for his coffee and slice of Slim's famous cherry pie, he watched a panel discussing a vote in the House of Representatives for the government to issue a formal apology to black Americans for enslavement and racial segregation.

"That is political correctness gone freaking mad!" a white customer shouted.

"What about the red Indians?" another customer hollered.

"Fuck the Indians, man. They've got motherfucking casinos. It's time for the black man to get some compensation. A hundred thousand in dead presidents will do me!"

"Hard working people are losing their jobs and houses and our kids are dying in Iraq and this is what our representatives are jerking off to. Fuck this."

"Hey, I'm a hard worker, man!"

"Fuck you!"

The TV panel moved on to discussing a US census bureau report that the dominance of white people in America was being whittled away. Hispanic, Black, Asian and Native Americans would be a majority in the proportion by 2050.

"Goddamn!" Screamed Mr-Political-Correctness-Gone-Mad. "Say goodbye to the white man."

"Ha, ha, ha! Pay me my compensation cracker boy. Or you'll be my bitch soon."

A punch was thrown. And the diner erupted into what appeared to be a race war. The waitresses fled behind the counter. A couple of men tried to urge calm and they were punched to the ground. Some diners fought and others simply vented their rage by breaking furniture and windows.

There were sparks of electricity as lights were ripped from walls and the TV shattered as a coffee jug hit it square in the middle of the screen bringing the panel's platitudes to an explosive end. Quantock reached for his gun, but remembered he wasn't packing. He dodged the fighting and escaped to the sidewalk where he rang 911. A chair came smashing through the plate glass window, followed by a bucket of doughnuts.

Kinz was right. America was on the edge of a precipice. He heard sirens and walked home.

Chapter 4

Kinz arranged to meet Ginny at the Lincoln Memorial. He bought hot dogs and sodas which they consumed sitting on the steps of the columned temple overlooking the Reflecting Pool.

"How are your mom and dad?" Kinz asked.

"Fine," Ginny said, taking a slurp of Dr Pepper.

"They must be very proud of you."

Ginny looked into the distance toward the Needle. "Mom is."

"And dad?"

Ginny adjusted her hair, still looking away. "He's fine."

Kinz put his hand softly on her shoulder. "Ginny, you know I see you as the daughter I never had. You can say anything to me. Anything. It will stop with me." Ginny turned her face to him. Her lower lip was trembling. He continued. "I know how difficult your dad can be sometimes. Hell, let's tell it as it is, he can be a son-of-a-bitch. His moral certainty and passion can sometimes get the better of him. But I know he loves you."

Tears welled up in Ginny's eyes. "No, he doesn't. He used to, but not anymore. He can't abide the fact that I'm intelligent and have opinions of my own. He says I'm stupid and gullible."

"Because you disagree with his opinions?"

"Exactly. He used to be really proud of me. Said I was a beautiful marble chip off his old block. But as I've got older, I realise that I am nothing like him. And he now treats me with contempt. And I don't like him. In fact, at this moment I hate him." Ginny sobbed. "Oh God, that's a terrible thing to say. I'm sorry."

Kinz squeezed her shoulder. "Don't be. That's just how you're feeling at this moment in time. What about your mom?"

"We're very alike, but she defers to him. She never sticks up for me. I think she's muzzled her opinions as she hates conflict."

"Will you walk with me a while?" Kinz asked. "My legs get gyp if I sit too long."

"Of course, Uncle Randolph."

They walked slowly up the steps of the Memorial. Ginny put her arm through Kinz's. Kinz stopped half way to draw breath. "Do you know the story of the War of the Titans?"

"I think I've seen the movie. It's where Zeus gets to be king of the gods," Ginny said.

"Yes. But it's more than that. At its heart, it's about the conflict between father and child. Between one generation and the next. Uranus sees his children as a threat and he locks them up. But his son Cronus castrates and kills him. Cronus goes on to have children and is told a prophecy that they will overthrow him. So, he eats them. But Zeus survives by hiding and poisons his father forcing him to vomit up the swallowed babies. Zeus and his brothers and sisters then go to war against Cronus and the Titans, and after a 10-year struggle, are victorious."

Ginny feigned a look of horror." So, you want me to poison my dad, Uncle Randolph?"

Kinz chuckled. "No, maybe just recognise that conflict like you're experiencing has been happening since time immortal, and in time it gets resolved."

They reached the imposing statue of Lincoln. "Do you know from where Lincoln got his quote: "A house divided against itself cannot stand?" Kinz asked.

"No. But I'm sure you going to tell me."

"The Bible. Matthew 25. *And Jesus knew their thoughts and said into him. Every kingdom divided against itself is brought to destruction; and every city or house divided against itself shall not stand.*"

After saying goodbye to Kinz, Ginny was delighted to get a text from Clem saying he was in Washington and inviting her for coffee. Ginny suggested Starbucks. Clem said no way, too capitalist, and they met at Swings on G Street.

Ginny had gone to the same Washington high school as Clem and they had been friends. This had turned into a deeper attraction when they went to summer camp. But Clem had then moved to New York and got himself a girlfriend. But they still kept in touch through Facebook and met up occasionally.

"What's up Clem?" Ginny asked casually.

"I wanted to ask you about Senator Kinz. He invited me for a meeting. I need to know if I can trust him."

"That's weird. I've just had a meeting with him."

Clem narrowed his eyes but said nothing.

Ginny continued: "I trust him absolutely. What was your meeting about?"

"What was yours?"

"I can't say. It's confidential."

"Yeah, so was mine."

Ginny giggled. "I trust you absolutely Clem as well. You show me yours and I'll show you mine."

Clem laughed. "He wants me to take part in a secret project to make a video."

"Snap."

"Are you going to do it? It will mean losing thirty days of classes."

"Yes. It's a once in a lifetime opportunity. I might even be able to get through to my dad."

"Things bad?"

"Yep."

"Snap."

"Why's that? I think your dad is cool."

"It's all a show. He trades off being this great rebel lawyer. The tribune of the people. The conscience of the Democrat Party. But it's all a sham. He just wants money and power like the rest of them. He thinks I'm a dope-smoking slacker, wasting my time with fantasies of making films when I should be studying law. It all just sucks."

"But he plays a mean sax."

"So did Clinton."

"I like the Clintons. Who are you going to vote for in November?"

"It's a wasted vote. Republican or Democrat, two sides of the same coin. But at least Ralph Nader is taking a stand against capitalism and cares about the environment."

"Nader. Isn't he a bit kooky?"

"He's a man of principle and he's mobilising young people."

"But Hillary is doing that as well."

"Hillary Clinton is a good organiser. But she's not a radical. She'll be like every other president."

"But maybe our video can make a difference."

"Maybe. But Kinz is a Republican and I'm not sure he really wants to hear what some of us have got to say. "

"Kinz is different. I feel he genuinely wants to hear our voices and he has the power to get the message out. When you met him did you think he took your views seriously?"

"Yeah, I suppose. He didn't agree with me but he wanted to understand where I was coming from."

"Well then. Doesn't that say something?"

"Okay, I'm in."

Ginny squealed and reached out to squeeze Clem's hand. "I'm so excited!"

Clem squeezed back and smiled. "Yeah. So am I. But remember this is all Secret Squirrel."

Ginny made a zipping motion across her lips. Secret Squirrel.

Chapter 5

Quantock read carefully through the files he had compiled.
Two men fitted the job specification perfectly for delivering the
operations side of project Arizona Gambit: Martin Gonzalez and
Ralph Anderson.

Martin Gonzalez was the son of a Mexican illegal who had
managed to get naturalised and save enough money picking
oranges in California to put his eldest through college and into the
officer corps of the Marines. Martin had fought with distinction in
Operation Desert Storm and been selected for the Special Forces.
During the 1990s he had devilled in Bosnia, Somalia and West
Africa. After ten years' service, he had retired and joined Blackwater
as a CIA contractor. Sent to Afghanistan after 9/11, he worked
with the Northern Alliance in eliminating and rounding up Taliban
terrorists for interrogation and extraordinary rendition. In 2006
he had been transferred to Pakistan to help with the hunt for Bin
Laden. In Islamabad, while driving in the centre, he was intercepted
by two men on a motorbike who tried to hold him up at gunpoint.
Believing they were terrorist assassins, he had shot both of them
dead with his Glock. But his escape was impeded by traffic and he
was quickly surrounded by an angry mob. He was facing a choice
between being lynched or arrested, when a colleague arrived to
rescue him. The colleague was Ralph Anderson.

Ralph Anderson was a good old boy from Texas, the son of a rancher. After three years' service in the Air Cavalry, most notably in Somalia where he assisted in the rescue of the Black Hawk crew downed in Mogadishu, he joined the CIA. He spent most of the rest of the decade in South America, working with the Columbian government to eliminate the FARC terrorists. In 2002 he was transferred to the Middle East and was embedded in Kurdish northern Iraq. He helped prepare the ground for the successful uprising against Saddam which was synchronised with the US invasion of 2003. Ralph was then outsourced to Blackwater and joined Martin in Islamabad. Until the incident, the only black mark on Ralph's record had been a car crash while under the influence on a Thailand R&R break, in which two bar girls had been hospitalised. Quantock smiled. In Texan terms this record made the good old boy a choir boy.

Ralph had taken point in the drive through Islamabad, as he and Martin pursued a Bin Laden lead, and was stuck in traffic ahead, when Martin had radioed him over his predicament. Ralph had driven back recklessly along the crowded pavements in his Toyota Land Cruiser and rescued Martin. In the process, he killed a pregnant woman in a burka and her young daughter. He had also engaged in a brief firefight with the local police.

Ralph and Martin found sanctuary at the US embassy. But the Pakistan government, media and mosques went mental. A US flag was burnt by an angry mob. A serious diplomatic incident was avoided by diplomacy. The US ambassador presented evidence that the men on the motorbike were Pakistan secret service agents, either acting rogue or with official sanction. The US agreed to pay 'diywa', blood money compensation, to the victim's families and Martin and Ralph were spirited out of the country. But they lost their jobs with

Blackwater and now scraped a living doing close protection work for the rich and famous.

Quantock took a final look at their mug shots. Ralph's face was characterised by what looked like a permanent scowl, a high forehead caused by a receding hairline, arching bushy eyebrows and a small goatee beard. His eyes were as hard and black as obsidian. Martin's face looked like it was carved from sandstone. His black hair was pulled back into a ponytail revealing a slab of forehead, boxer's nose, square chin and cheeks chiselled with laughter lines. His eyes were green flecked with brown and he maintained a Zapata moustache. He smiled for the camera, revealing brilliant white teeth.

Quantock judged that both men were decent but flawed. But they had the physical presence, skills and professionalism to deliver the project. They were also suitably off the radar. He rang them and arranged a meeting at the Vietnam Veterans Memorial.

Ralph and Martin sat in a strip club just north of the White House watching two girls dressed only in thongs revolve around poles that reached from floor to ceiling. The official name was the Camelot Gentleman's Club but it was anything but. It was a cacophony of sound, light and female flesh. In the performance area floor-to-ceiling mirrors showed the pole dancing girl's images from several different angles. About twenty men sat around the circular stage at small tables and shouted enthusiastically at the girls. In darkened booths along the sides other men enjoyed the company of lap dancers.

Ralph and Martin's table was littered with glasses and bottles. Ralph turned his gaze from the pole dancers and looked at Martin through bleary eyes and said, "Who does the goddamned dirty work buddy? Tell me that man? Go on buddy just you tell me?"

Martin regarded his friend through less bleary eyes and said, "We do bro, we do. But don't you worry amigo we'll soon be on the up – we stick together don't we?"

Ralph slapped his friend on the shoulder and said, "Sure we do, sure thing!" Then he reached into his inside jacket pocket and pulled out an oblong shaped silver box. It was his coke kit. He opened it and took out a packet of white powder, sprinkled it on the glass table and then moved the powder into lines using a razor blade from the box. He rolled a ten-dollar bill into a tube and snorted the cocaine. When he had finished, he sat back and looked at the ceiling – he was in a different world. Euphoria.

Martin regarded him with amusement. "For Chris' sake bro, you'll have no nostrils left in a year. If our esteemed masters knew you were a coke addict there would certainly be no way back, sideways or forwards or whatever." He drained his beer bottle.

Ralph looked angry and said, "Aw, shit, slack off man. What kinda job have we gotten into this time anyway?" He sneezed. "That FBI guy, who wants to be called Mr No Name. Who does he think he is, fucking Clint Eastwood? More like Mr No Balls if you ask me." He then sat back in his chair and contemplated the ceiling again.

Strobe lights flashed in sync with hi-energy bass beats. They reminded Martin of the opening night of Desert Storm. Shock and awe. Shock and awe, man, he thought. Martin knew Ralph was as high as a kite and if he told him to go and tango with a tiger he would. It was becoming more difficult being his buddy, but he owed him. He pondered on what Ralph had said. They were both fed up of babysitting the pampered and this job was more of the same except the pampered were kids. Mr No Name was anal in the detail he insisted on for the prep work. He had, however, told him in confidence the name of the senator who owned the project:

Senator Randolph Kinz. That intrigued Martin a lot. It was really very odd indeed and somehow it didn't feel right. His previous jobs had rarely had any identified owner of a project, either as a person or a department. The fact that No Name had told him in confidence also implied that he thought Martin should be leader. Why else was he going to give him, not Ralph, the emergency cell phone. Line of command: Kinz, No Name, Martin and then Ralph. A spot-on judgement, but why not tell Ralph. Ralph would eventually cotton on and get ornery. And it would be down to him to manage that. But neither of them could ignore the money. His stake would be enough to set up the restaurant he had always dreamed of running. His own business. Doing something he was passionate about. That would also free him from Ralph.

Ralph swayed left and right then sat up straight staring at one of the pole dancers who had just finished wrapping herself around a pole. She was dressed only in a soft leather pink thong. He beckoned her over and took out his wallet. "Hey honey, you want some dough? Here look lots of dollars, c'mon, let's put it in your thongy thing eh?" and he smiled like an imbecile.

Unwisely, she proffered her hip for the money. Ralph lurched to his feet and slipped the note carefully inside the thong and blew her a kiss. "Want some more, honey?" he said, proffering his open wallet.

She stayed where she was and pouted at him. Then he took out another ten-dollar bill and put that in the front of her thong. Only this time he hooked his index finger tightly around the thong strap. She was trapped. "You can go honey, but leave this iddy biddy thing. With my dollar bills I damn near bought the factory that made it." He laughed out loud at her predicament.

"Please, sir, I have to go now. Let go please?" she said and pulled away from him. But his grip was secure and it only served to pull her costume away from her body. This delighted the other punters who urged Ralph on. The dancer looked for the bouncers, but to her horror they were at the far end of the bar talking to some troublemakers. Ralph began to pull harder and the thong became contorted as they both tugged at it. He fixed the girl with a glazed look.

"Honey, I just want my money's worth. Now what do you think twenty dollars is worth?"

"At least a peek!" shouted a man from a nearby table.

Martin laughed, but kept a close eye on his friend, uncertain as to his next move.

Ralph leered: "See now honey, these boys here are not stupid! I've been watchin' you intently. I wanna know – are you a natural blonde?"

Sensing what was coming the girl squirmed and pleaded again, "Sir, don't be silly, let me go please?"

"Aw, c'mon, give old Ralphy a peek, then I promise to go home like a good ole boy. Here kitty, kitty, here kitty, kitty!" He began to pull the thong away from her body. It was made of strong stuff and didn't break. She wriggled some more and before she knew it they were both engaged in a tug of war.

By now the audience was yelling support and Ralph was in his element. "Just a peek honey, just a little peek-a-poo?" Ralph said through gasps of laughter. Then, as the thong ripped away, he added to a cheering audience, "Hey boys, just what I thought, the dame's a red-head!"

The audience howled with laughter and hooted support for Ralph's efforts. The dancer screamed and at last the bouncers saw what was happening and rushed over. One them whipped out a sap and whacked Ralph on the back of his head. He collapsed.

The dancer, freed from Ralph, rushed to her dressing room crying. Martin put himself between the bouncers and Ralph.

"Whoa boys, just a misunderstanding and a little excitement. Here's a little something on account," Martin threw down a handful of dollar bills on the table. "My friend here has been under a lot of strain and he ain't so smart. I'll just take him home to sober up and he'll be back in the mornin' to apologise. We'll just go now eh?"

The bouncers picked up the money and signalled for him to leave. Martin had no doubt that to refuse would lead to a severe beating. He dragged the unconscious Ralph out of the bar. The fresh air hit them both like an express train. Ralph regained consciousness almost immediately and he shook his head.

Eventually a taxi stopped for them and they fell into the back.

Martin turned to Ralph and said seriously, "Hey bro, I can't decide if you're mad, bad or sad. You got to get your shit together. I'm always having to dig you outta situations! You and your damned cocaine and sexual perversion!"

Ralph looked at him through bleary eyes and just smiled. Then he said, "Yeah man, you're right," he started to giggle. "An y'know what? I lied man. I lied to my bestest buddy. She weren't no goddamned redhead man. Y'know that?"

Martin looked perplexed.

Ralph stopped giggling, and caught his breath. "She weren't no redhead at all. She shaved man – she shaved!"

They both burst into uncontrollable laughter.

PART TWO

ELECTION COUNTDOWN

"The duty of a patriot is to protect his country from its government." Thomas Paine

Chapter 6

E-Day minus 30

Dulles airport was bright and cloudless and the arrivals entrance rang with the whooping and yelling of six teenagers as they greeted each other. Jo Anne Dempster, blonde and bubbly, screeched and kissed everyone, including a surprised but nevertheless delighted bystander waiting for a taxi. Her ample figure was exaggerated by a tight fitting white blouse and denim shorts. Matt Dawson, tall and gangly in baggy clothes, wearing a baseball cap on back to front, was reserved and quiet, but he beamed at the sight of Clem, his old summer camp buddy. Jon Masters a ginger headed bright-faced young man kidded around and kept saying to everyone, "Hey, look at you!" when confronted by a friend some six to nine months older than when he had last seen them. He was a handsome young boy and knew it. Dressed like the Midnight Cowboy in jeans, hide jacket and a flamboyant cowboy hat, he had a way of sauntering rather than walking. Only Walt Danberry remained reserved and aloof. He had always been the bookish, philosophical type, given to smart remarks at someone else's expense; he knew everything, or at least that was what he believed. He was old for his age and his round face, short Afro hairstyle and dark rimmed spectacles set him apart from his friends.

Walt turned to the others and, with the kind of pomposity his friends were used to, said: "Hi guys. This is quite a group and quite a project. I'm real glad I was chosen, because I have such a great deal to offer."

Then he turned to Matt, smiled sarcastically and said, "Boy, you must have improved your political science grades a lot Matt."

Matt grinned. "No idea what you're talking about Walt. My grades were so good I had lots of time to spend in the out-field."

Walt smiled patronisingly and Clem stepped in just like he used to do at summer camp. "Where's Kevin Pollak? Where's the birthday boy?" He asked grinning. Walt and Matt chuckled. "Did your parents buy the story of going to Atlantic City to celebrate his twenty-first birthday?" Clem questionned.

"Hook, line and sinker," said Matt. "Hell, my Mom claims that she's met him."

"A simple text, sufficed for me. My parents don't need detailed explanations from me about my movements. That was so last year." Walt said.

"Who is Kevin Pollak?" Jo Anne asked. "Is there a real person out there with the name or is he totally makie-uppy?"

"Oh, he's real," said Clem. "He's an actor who was in the Usual Suspects but no-one can name him."

"Great movie," said Ginny.

"Hey guys," said Jon. Don't you think we should go and see the tour guides over there?"

He pointed to two men wearing leather drivers gloves and dressed in black sweat shirts and jeans leaning against the front of a white rental minibus. A black UPS mail van was parked behind. The men saw them coming around the side and came to meet them. The man with the pony tail and moustache smiled broadly.

"Hi there. My name is Martin and this is my partner Ralph." They exchanged names and fist-bumps with the teenagers and waited for them to calm down.

"Look guys, we need to talk before we set off," said Martin. "You need to stack your gear in the rear of the UPS van first of all. That will give us all more room in the minibus. Before you do that, and this is important, give me the letters you were instructed to write to your folks and I will make sure they get them. We don't want mom and pop getting worried about you! We are in for a long journey, about two or three days in all."

There was a low groan from the teenagers and he smiled and continued, "But it will be worth it. When you get to where we are going – top secret I'm afraid so don't ask – you will find good quarters and very good sound and vision equipment to make the video show. I know the equipment is good guys, I bought it myself!"

He showed some pictures on his cell phone to Clem who yelped with delight, as his friends clamoured to take a look. Martin continued: "One more thing guys, hand over your cell phones please." There was another low groan. "Yeah, I know, it's a pain, just like school huh? But it is essential that there are no mistakes or contact with the outside world. This way we remove all temptation. I'm sure you understand that the operation must not, repeat not be compromised. If that happens then, well, we may as well all just go home, end of story. Okay?"

The teenagers obediently did as they were told and dropped their phones in a cloth satchel Martin held open. Ralph then helped them stow their bags in the UPS van before returning to the minibus and climbing into the driving seat. The teenagers then all squeezed in. Only Walt tried to get more information out of Ralph and he was curtly reminded that he would be briefed fully a lot later, but until that happened he should not ask again. Walt just looked over his spectacles and smiled in his patronising way, which irked Ralph, who made his mind up not to like the snot-nosed academic.

Ralph drove the minibus smoothly out of the airport complex and navigated the mid-morning traffic with ease. He took Interstate Highway 81 heading southwest and drove on past Front Royal, Harrisonburg and Staunton, Virginia. Just after a junction where Highway 60 connects, Ralph took a left down a minor road.

After a four hour drive they stopped in the car park of the General Lee gas station and general store just to the east of the town of Lynchburg. Martin in the UPS mail van pulled in front of them, at an angle which obscured the minibus and the rear door of the UPS van from the gas station. The kids welcomed the break, but Ralph said they had to follow certain rules.

"Look guys, I know you could probably do with a proper break and we'll have one soon. This is a pit stop and we need to keep our route as secret as possible. I know it sounds kinda crazy. The idea is that no one should know where you are going, not even your parents, and we don't want anyone who might know you to spot you by chance and spill the beans. If the media get wind of Senator's Kinz project it's dead and we all go home. There's a little boy's and little girl's bathroom at the back of the station. If you do need to get a soda, please be quick, no dawdling. And if you're asked where you're going you say to a conference. Don't give any further details. Understand? Now I will warn you, the place ain't very pretty, but if you're bursting for a pee I guess that it's the best sight in the world!"

The teenagers laughed.

He continued, "So, please get out quick, jettison fuel and get back on board that there UPS van. We're switching vehicles to throw any media watchers off the scent. I'll answer any questions you have when we reach our destination. Not before. Now, let's go to work!"

They murmured their acceptance, one or two claiming to be bursting and beyond care. Walt added, "A secret pee station, well, what do you know!"

Ralph was beginning to seriously dislike him.

As Jo Anne squeezed out of the minibus, Ralph took her hand to help her out.

"Thank you!" Jo Anne simpered. Then she cried out, "Oww!"

She pulled her hand out of Ralph's and looked at her little finger. Blood was trickling down it. "You cut me?" she said, shocked.

"Oh, my Lord!" Ralph said. "I'm sorry Jo Anne. It must have been my ring. It's too big for my finger and keeps slipping." He looked at his finger and twisted the ring so that the rough-cut diamond stones in the skull of silver ring were once again pointing outwards.

"I'm bleeding," Jo Anne whimpered.

"Here, let me see?" Ralph held her hand and pulled some tissues out of his pocket. He pressed a wad of tissues around the cut to soak up the blood and then rolled a clean tissue round the finger like a bandage. "Keep it tightly rolled, honey" he advised, "and the bleeding will soon stop."

Jo Anne nodded and hurried after her friends to the rest room. Ralph took the used tissues and smeared them on the side window of the minibus.

Martin came up. "How far is the RV from here?"

"Ten minutes, max." Ralph said. "I've parked her in the car park of the Appomattox Court House museum. Wait till you see her, she's a doozy."

"How much?"

"$75,000 cash. A steal."

"Jeez, bro. That's some wedge."

"Money no object, right buddy? Plus, I figure we can keep her when this job is done. We could go see your folks in Mexico."

"Or yours in Texas."

"No offence, amigo. But they don't like Mexicans. They'd shoot you dead."

Vern Quayle watched the six teenagers walk across the carpark from his cashier's window. It was good to get some custom. Since they built the new highway, trade had collapsed at the General Lee. He glanced at his granddaughter Nancy. She was sitting behind the candy counter stuffing her face with potato chips and reading National Enquirer. "We got customers, girl."

She ignored him and carried on chomping. She had become a liability. Her wages and the stock she ate were getting to be more than the store's income. Maybe it was time to retire thought Vern. Find a buyer for the station. Some young thruster with imagination. More could be made of the location's Civil War links and Appomattox was just up the road. With a bit of capital something could be made of that.

The teenagers spilled into the store and bought soda and candy. They smiled but did not talk much, but were very polite to Nancy. Then they were gone. Six sodas and a few Hershey bars. That wasn't going to help pay Nancy wages.

A well-built man with a black moustache wearing a black and white patterned cotton scarf with tassels wrapped around his head and neck and a black satchel slung over this shoulder came loping towards the store. He looked like trouble. But Vern wasn't sure whether he had come from the white minibus or the black UPS van. Vern reached under the counter and checked that his Remington 870 pump-action, shortened-barrel shotgun was within easy reach.

It was and he felt reassured.

The man pushed open the door and came in. He ignored Vern and Nancy and went to the auto parts and tools shelves. He selected several rolls of duct tape and three packets of heavy duty bungee straps and piled them up on the counter. He said something in Arabic to Vern. Sounded like "Some need a licking." Vern said. "Say what?" The man spoke again. This time it sounded like "They all at the bar." Vern smiled nervously and rang up the items on the till. "That'll be thirty bucks." The man threw down a fifty-dollar bill and turned away with his purchases. "Mister, your change!" The man ignored him and left the store. Goddam A-rib, thought Vern. He watched as the man slipped around the side of the UPS van. He wondered if the white minibus was still there. He thought there's no harm checking it out. He said to Nancy, "Mind the store, girl. I'm just going yonder for a looksee."

As he walked across the car park, the UPS van belched smoke from its exhaust and reversed at speed. It then turned violently, wheels on one side lifting off the tarmac and headed for the road. Vern clearly heard screams and banging coming from inside the back. The white minibus stood there. All the doors open. Vern broke into a half run. The minibus was completely empty, except for a thick well-thumbed paperback book with a title in Arabic script and a pink cell phone. Blood was smeared on the window of the side door.

Vern was panting when he returned to the store. He looked frantically for his company cell phone and then heard it ring.

"Hello?" He gasped.

"Is this Vern Quayle owner of the General Lee general store?"

"Yes, it is. Who's asking?"

"Special Agent Ironside. FBI. We're on the tail of a suspect and think he's heading your way."

"Is he driving a black UPS van?"

"Yes sir. He is. What can you tell me?"

"He's just left the car park. There's been an in-ci-dent. An ab-duc-tion I reckon. Six kids from a minibus. They were locked up in the back of the van. I heard their screams. There was blood and an A-rib book left behind."

"I need to stop you sir. You've got to listen to me. You're in danger. Serious danger. But we're on our way. We're minutes away. In the meanwhile, lock all the doors and windows. Pull down the blinds and lie on the floor with your phone next to you. Is it charged?"

"Yes."

"This is really important. Do not call anyone until we arrive. Our suspect can monitor your calls. Understand?"

"Yes. But I've got a heart condition. I need to find my meds. And my granddaughter. She works here."

"Find your meds but do it quick. Get your granddaughter to lie on the floor as well. Tell her it will literally only be minutes. But do it. Do it now. I'm counting on you Vern."

The line went dead. Nancy was looking at Vern open-mouthed. "What's happening Grandpa?"

"Lock all the doors and windows and pull the blinds down and then lie on the floor with me. We need to wait a few minutes for the FBI to arrive."

"But I need to poop."

"No. You've got to hold it in. Just do as I say. Just freakin' do it!"

Martin closed his phone and laughed. "You know what Ralph, I feel sorry for the old man. I think Vern is a decent fella."

"What's the granddaughter like?"

"You'd love her. She's built like a pig. I bet you could make her squeal."

Ralph gave Martin the finger. "Do you think he'll call the local cops?"

"No. I think Vern is used to following orders."

The scene in the back of the UPS van was like a mass game of Twister. As the van reversed and sped away the teenagers were thrown around and entangled together. Luckily thick mattresses covered the floor and walls. After the initial screams, they began to laugh and the laughter became uncontrollable as they tried and failed to disentangle themselves.

Jo Anne was stuck under Matt. "Matt Dawson, could you kindly remove your hand!"

"That's not his hand, Jo Anne." Jon quipped. "Walt, what's your hand doing near my crown jewels?" There was more ribald laughter.

Ginny was glad that she was entangled with Clem and she could feel his chest pushing into her breasts and the thump of his heart beat. She wanted to kiss him. Only Walt wasn't laughing and he was getting more and more upset. "This is highly irregular," he kept saying.

The recreation vehicle in the Appomattox car park was a 36-foot, bronze Winnebago. Ralph pulled the UPS van alongside, and turned to Martin, smiling broadly.

"I bought it from a private buyer for cash. It's a mobile hotel buddy. Top of the range. Should get ten miles to a gallon of diesel. 100-gallon fuel capacity. Air con, huge fridge-freezer, CD, three TVs, BBQ grill. Seats eight. We'll get about thousand miles from each tank of diesel. That makes, let me see, about twenty hours motoring, meaning," and he reached into his top pocket for a piece of paper which he peered at, "meaning, about four stops over about two to three days, tops. I figure we split the driving into three hour shifts. Down south and out west these Winnies are everywhere.

We'll be invisible. It's gonna be a long trip but comfortable! But I really can't wait to get to the 'baby-sitting centre'."

The teenagers pretended to be grumpy when released from their cramped conditions, but their giggles betrayed them. Walt, however, was grumpy. "You treated us like animals. That was cruel and unusual treatment which is forbidden by the Constitution."

"Lighten up, Walt!" said Dan. "Some of us enjoyed it and we were only in there for fifteen minutes."

When they entered the RV they were amazed. "Oh wow, look at this!" said Clem pointing to the digital entertainment stack and large screen TV. "Satellite dish on the roof," Ralph said. "But I you won't be able to use it. Same way as we don't want the world knowing what you're up to, we don't want you getting distracted by the world. "

"Ah, man!" Clem said. "I need my TV."

"It will do you good to have a break from it," Ralph said.

"What about radio?" asked Walt.

Ralph shook his head. "No cell phones, no internet, no TV, no radio, no newspapers. That's the deal."

"A kitchen," trilled Ginny behind them. "A fridge packed with food. Worktops. Sink. Eye-level oven. I'm in Greek heaven."

"We've also got a gas-fired BBQ which flips out from the exterior side," Ralph said.

"OMG!" Ginny screamed.

"I'm bagging this bed!" Jon hollered from the back of the RV. "It sleeps two. Even got a hook for my hat. Walt, do you want to join me?" Walt stood speechless, gazing around but he could not stop a smile breaking out.

Dan flopped on the sofa and found a set of controls. A foot-rest extended from underneath and elevated. "Oh boy, slacker delight!"

Jo Anne came running from the back. "The bathroom is just so cute. I love it."

Ralph grinned. He visualised her in the shower, soaping her body. "We've also got an outside shower. So, no need to fight for washing space," he said, languidly, his thoughts racing.

After more joking and the stowing of bags and coats, the kids settled down. Clem and Ginny took the sofa and the other four sat around the diner-style table. Ralph and Martin strapped themselves into the driving seats. Ralph connected his iPhone to the media centre and selected the Best of Megarock Kicking Country from his iTunes collection. The name amused him; it was the kind of foot tapping music that made everyone feel energised – even if it wasn't quite their style. He yelled at the kids to look into a brown cardboard box on the table which contained cookies and doughnuts. They fell around laughing as they wrestled to get to the box. Ralph eased the RV forward. The drove west along the 460. There was no sign of any flashing blue lights. Vern must still be obeying orders. After skirting the Blue Ridge Mountains, he picked up Interstate 81 at Salem and headed south. They were entering the heart of Dixie. He smiled. It was a job well done.

Martin texted No Name using the agreed code. "Tenderfeet on their way to camp. All A-OK."

The teenagers settled down. Walt was using his laptop to type out something lengthy whilst at the same time trying to explain to Jo Anne that Lynchburg was named after a Quaker judge called Lynch. He delighted in explaining that Mr Lynch dispensed his own kind of justice, usually summary and usually at the end of a rope; hence the name given thereafter to lynching. By the time, he had explained that there had been over five thousand lynchings in the Deep South between 1898 and 1923, she had dozed off against Jon's shoulder.

Ginny also put her head onto Clem's shoulder and promptly fell into a deep sleep. Clem couldn't doze. This was no boondoggle for him. This was serious work and a chance to do something really important. He was going to lead this project and he was determined to do it well. His video skills were going to be tested to the full as well as those of producing and directing. Most important of all he knew he could encourage and lead the debate to bring out of his friends just what American youth really thought about the plight of the nation and its place in the world. In the quietness of his own thoughts his vision was already taking form; people would have to listen even if they didn't like what was being said. He just could not wait to get to the destination.

Clem watched the Virginia countryside whizz past. It was picturesque scenery with mountains rising and falling and patches of pine forest.

After a few hours, the girls reminded everyone that it was approaching dusk and they had only eaten breakfast and snacks. They demanded a stopover. In truth, everyone wanted a break and Ralph stopped the coach by a patch of woodland on top of a hill that sat between two mountains. It was a beautiful early fall evening and the orange sky was breath-taking. The kids stretched their legs, while Ralph pulled out an exterior slider from the RV and fired up the BBQ. Martin stayed in the RV making salads. Ginny came in.

"Can I help?" she said.

"Very kind. I'm making guacamole. Do you know how to make a salsa?"

"Sure do," Ginny replied, grabbing an onion, knife and chopping board.

As Martin scooped the flesh from the avocados and mashed it roughly in a bowl, he glanced at Ginny. Her knifework was good. The onion was diced real small. "Can I have some?" he asked.

"I'm honoured," Ginny said, offering the chopping board. Chillies, tomatoes and coriander were then rapidly chopped by Ginny's knife and shared. Next, Ginny squeezed some lemons and limes, added some seasoning and tossed her salsa.

As Ginny took the bowls outside. Martin slid a stack of tortillas into the microwave.

Outside Ralph cupped his hands. "As your assigned tour leader, ladies and gentlemen, I am here to inform you that it's chow-time!"

As the kids gathered around the picnic table, he brought over a plate heaving with strips of steak. The meat, salads, dips and tortillas were demolished in no time. Martin came down with a big jug of red liquid, swirling with fruit, and poured out six plastic glasses. "Sangria!" he said proudly.

After they had feasted they stretched their legs a bit more. The teenagers asked Martin and Ralph several times where they were going, but to no avail. They were all too tired to press the matter further and uncomplainingly got on the RV and just crashed where they had been sitting without making the beds. Martin smiled. The sleeping powder he had put in the sangria had done the job. It was going to be a very long journey and he wanted no complaints or problems. After five more hours and two driver changes, the RV stopped to refuel at a lonely three-pump gas station. A road sign informed them that they were on the outskirts of Nashville.

Martin got behind the wheel. "You look bushed buddy. Get some sleep, I'm okay until about four o'clock. Besides, I fancy listening to some real music. With that he reached down and searched iTunes until he found a soul collection. Ralph didn't need to be told twice and he curled up and covered himself with a blanket. Martin really didn't need any rest. He had a lot on his mind. It was really quite fun looking after the teenagers and he needed to get a lot of facts straight in his mind. He had made elaborate preparations for the project and wanted to use the four hours to go over the briefing that he would give the teenagers and run through a mental checklist of provisions and other things.

Ralph seemed to have a stabilised. The mission seemed to have rekindled his sense of responsibility and professionalism. There was no sign of coke or booze either. He took over the driving at four in the morning and although the teenagers stirred no one woke up. Martin commented that either they had wet themselves or they had bladders of steel.

Ginny lay across the sofa with her head in Clem's lap. The others lay in various positions and Ralph got a good view of Jo Anne's cleavage as he passed on the way to the bathroom. Walt sat upright with the blanket under his chin making him look like a rather comic child pretending to be asleep. Jon and Matt lounged awkwardly and snored loudly.

As the RV motored across a Texas countryside that was turning from large forest to rolling plains, the sun began to rise higher in the sky. The explosion of light was like an alarm clock and the teenagers reacted to the intrusion, waking and rubbing their eyes. Martin turned on the air conditioning. Clem yawned and his eyes widened, all too aware of the state of his body early in the morning. Ginny rolled on her back, with her head still in his lap and Clem looked uncomfortable and a little sheepish.

"Mornin' partner, it's a bit lumpy down here!" she said.

Clem blushed bright red.

Ginny laughed and smiled at his discomfort. She kept looking at him. He must be the only guy in the world who was good looking and sexy, and yet so alarmingly innocent. That had a kind of cute appeal to her.

At the gas station, Ginny beat Martin to the kitchen and prepared breakfast and set the table. There was a choice of cornflakes or Cheerios, yoghurt, orange juice, a big pot of steaming coffee and scrambled eggs with bacon, pancakes and maple syrup. It was all wolfed down. The kids then worked as a team to clean up. Soon they were back on the road again and a political discussion started. It quickly became a passionate argument. Clem brought out his camcorder and started filming. The video wouldn't be the same quality as Martin's high end bit of kit, but it would do for what he wanted. Raw action shots and talking heads intercut with more glossy footage. It would add pace and drama to the narrative.

"Do not misrepresent what I'm saying," Walt demanded. "Read my lips. I did not say I want all Mexicans deported. If illegals are here and working and acting as good citizens I say give them a Green Card. But if they are unemployed and into crime and drugs, deport them. And we've got to stop more criminals coming in. It's not just Mexicans. Every gang banger, coke dealer and rapist in South and Central America wants a piece of the American pie."

"But that's exactly the language which was used to demonise my grandparents in the 1920s." Ginny snapped. "It was said that the Greeks, the Turks and the Italians were all thieves and rapists. It's racist Walt, can't you see?"

"Don't talk to me about racism," said Walt. "It's African Americans who suffer the most from illegal immigration and the Latino drugs trade."

"So how are you going to stop the illegals entering, Walt?" Matt asked.

"We need to invest in better border security. Make the fence higher. Use drones. More border guards. You know we could learn from the Israelis."

"Build a wall?" said Jon.

"Yes. We need to stop the flow of sewage by any means necessary."

"Pardon my Greek, Walt, but you're full of shit!" Ginny spat.

Martin ambled up. "Okay guys. Time out. We've got a little treat for you."

Ralph slowed the RV, pulled off the road and followed a track that led through a small copse of trees to a small creek. He stopped by the edge of the slow running water and worked with Martin to set up the BBQ and chairs and table. The teenagers stretched their legs. "Chow will be ready in thirty minutes. The creek is good for swimming if anyone wants to."

"Oh yes!" screamed Jo Anne and rapidly stripped down to her bra and panties before running giggling to the water. Ralph's eyes almost popped out of his head. Ginny followed suit but kept her t-shirt on. Jon and Clem ran in wearing boxers and Matt with Calvin Klein's. Walt did not undress. But he took off his shoes and socks and paddled at the water's edge.

After a change of clothes, the teenagers tucked into chicken, burgers and corn on the cob. They then relaxed beside the creek in the afternoon sunshine and all was well with the world.

Clem walked over to Martin, who was whittling a stick with a Bowie knife.

"How much farther, Martin?"

"It's another overnight ride I'm afraid," Martin replied.

"Overnight? Jeez, man o' man, we'll be on the West Coast at this rate," spluttered Clem.

Chapter 7

E-Day minus 27

As dawn broke, the RV topped a large ridge and they looked down onto the sub-tropical Sonoran Desert, lit by the glow of a yellow-gold sun that now rose over the horizon. They descended the hill and made their way along a badly made-up road dotted with potholes and littered with boulders, surrounded by small shrubs, trees and Ocotillo and Saquero cacti. Before them lay a sprawling range of hills that rose gradually on their left before levelling out, taking on the appearance of a light blue-purple brush stroke between sky and ground.

After ten more minutes driving, during which they endured a boneshaking ride along a narrow pot-holed paved road running between two ridges, they bumped over a low gauge railroad track leading into the entrance of an abandoned mine, which had been dug into the side of the ridge. A wooden sign proclaimed: "Danger! Keep out." A rusty wagon sat on the track. The RV had to negotiate a chicane of old tyres before the road opened out in an empty expanse of gravel, where the foundations of long-demolished sheds could be seen. Now it was only home to the brown skeleton of a pick-up truck and some tumbleweed. To the right, wind bent, on a knoll in the hillside were a few lonely Palo Verde trees that could only mean that water was nearby. Ahead was a collection of single story timber buildings. A peeling sign in front of the main building read: "San Quiller Tin Mine, Site Office. All visitors report to reception." The RV stopped and parked next to a four-by-four Nissan Prairie.

Although overjoyed to arrive at last, the teenagers were a little apprehensive and Martin and Ralph shepherded them into the main building. Their eyes widened. The building may have been bleak on the outside, but inside it was quite different. It was well decorated with new wooden floors, whitewashed walls and modern leather and stainless steel furniture in the main seating area. To the right was the kitchen and dining area with up-to-date equipment and two long oblong tables with bench seats. To the left, beyond the main lounge was a large room with a conference table, the door of which was open wide allowing a glimpse of the sound, video recording and lighting equipment that Martin had told Clem about. The internal wood cladding was new enough to still smell of pine. The teenagers stood and stared – it was very impressive.

There were two toilets and Martin explained that the main sleeping and bathroom block was next door. Girls were to be located at the far end and boys at the opposite end of the building close to the mess hall and breakout area. He was to be the chaperone sleeping in the middle. The teenagers hooted at this. Walt made a comment about being here to work and no one responded. He maintained his gloomy mood during the walk around the accommodation block, complaining about the creaking floors and water flow until Martin sharply reminded him that he was after all in the Arizona desert. Martin made the comment that it was better than the old tin miners had to endure.

Walt retorted dryly, "Well I'm not a tin miner!"

As the group moved on, Ralph went over to Walt and backed him into a corner pushing his knuckles into Walt's flabby chest, staring into his face. "Well, ain't you the lucky one. Chunky boy like you would've gone down a real treat in the mining community." He patted Walt's face and the boy winced with pain and surprise. Then Ralph laughed cruelly and walked on. No one noticed a thing.

The girls had spacious quarters and single beds, whereas the boys had bunk beds. They all started to unpack and then take showers.

Martin was singing in the kitchen and the smell of his cooking pervaded the air, making everyone's mouth water. Every now and then he banged a pot on the kitchen range and started a new song. Ralph was not so relaxed. His mood had changed since the drive. The kids were beginning to annoy him and he now wanted the whole exercise done and over with. He hadn't had a drink or a line of coke for five days and his body was crying out for a little stimulus. He had done well by being abstinent for so long. Now he needed a little reward. He went to his room and grabbed a small rucksack and then left the building. There was a nice spot by the rocks back down the road where he could smoke and drink some Jim Beam bourbon in peace. He would eat later, on his own.

After the meal of chilli, rice, salad and nachos, Martin was voted 'Chef of the Desert' by the girls. Walt made some comment about the rice being overcooked and Martin tossed a bread roll at him. It bounced off his head and the girls squealed with laughter. Walt stomped off in a sulk.

Martin stood up and addressed them.

"Well now guys, that's the end of chow time. Let's have a little break and then I'll answer some of the questions you've been burning to ask. But talking about burning, we need to make sure we're warm. Although it's still kinda mild in the evenings, it gets real cool late at night. So, let's get some logs in and light a fire in that enormous grate over there, what do you say?" The boys whooped.

Matt, Walt and Dan went for some logs. But Clem, Ginny and Jo Anne wanted some fresh air and to investigate the area. They asked Martin for permission to do so. Martin felt strange at his new role as 'Daddy'. He wasn't used to it and yet controlling them came easy; he even enjoyed it. He didn't want to dissuade them, but explained that the desert can be an unforgiving place if they strayed and got lost and that they should keep within sight of buildings and be back in twenty minutes.

The three teenagers walked towards the mine. It felt good to stretch their legs. The ridges were bathed in a soft violet light and a full moon made the boulders shine white. The shadow of a huge lizard scuttled across their path and both Ginny and Jo Anne squealed and grabbed Clem. Clem laughed but he became more watchful as they gingerly approached the entrance to the mine. In the twilight, it looked like a large gaping mouth ready to snap shut on any unsuspecting living creature that went anywhere near it. He could just about make out the content of a sign warning of rock falls. Blocking the entrance were some rusty metal crash barriers and another sign, warning, "Trespassers will be prosecuted". The three approached the crash barriers and Ginny rattled one of them. It was loosely tied to its neighbour and she was easily able to move it away.

"I want a peek inside," she said, squeezing through the gap.

Jo Anne looked wary. "It's too dark," she said. But Clem made as if to follow. From somewhere out in the desert came a long drawn out howl. Jo Anne screamed. Ginny and Clem froze. There was a second howl.

"Time to go back, I think," said Clem. "Whatever that is, it sounds hungry." All three of them turned and ran back towards the lights of the buildings.

Matt Dawson prodded the roaring log fire with a poker. The teenagers sat and reclined on the leather sofas in the lounge in front of the fireplace. "There's only so much excitement you can get from watching a burning log," he said.

"You need to really focus in the flames," Clem said. "I can see people and animals. It's like a movie."

"I see Gone with the Wind," said Jo Anne, wistfully.

"Frankly my dear, I don't give a damn," said Jon. "I'm bored. No TV, no computer, no internet, no text, no Facebook, no YouTube. This sucks"

Martin and Ralph came through and stood in the centre of the sofas. "Q and A time folks," said Ralph. "Everything you wanted to know about this project but were afraid to ask."

"Where are we?" asked Walt.

"Good question Mr Danberry," Martin said. "We're at the San Quiller tin mine, midway between Tucson, Arizona and the Mexican border. We're in injun territory. Apache, Navaho and some other tribes. Ulysses S Grant put all the tribes on reservations after the Civil War and the San Quiller was opened about the same time and was a working tin mine until 20 years ago. The main entrance tunnel runs for half a mile under the hill. At mid-point there is a shaft with winding gear which gives access to the galleries deeper down. Rumour has it that the last owner of the mine was so upset that it was closing he hanged himself on the winding gear. And even today some people say you can hear his dying moans on dark nights."

"OMG!", said Jo Anne. "Is that what we heard when we were out there?" Her eyes were wide with terror.

"Heard what?" Martin asked.

"It was a howl. In the dark. Like a werewolf," said Ginny.

The teenagers exchanged nervous glances.

Clem laughed. "There's no such thing as werewolves. Could it have been a coyote?"

"Did it sound like this?" Ralph asked and imitated the yip, yip, howl of a coyote.

"Stop!" Jo Anne screamed. "You're scaring me!"

Ralph grinned. "Or this?" he emitted a more constant drawn out howl.

"That's it," said Ginny. "What is it?"

"It's a Mexican Grey Wolf. But that would be very strange, very strange." Ralph said.

"Why?" asked Clem.

"Because they've been extinct hereabouts for fifty years," and he laughed at their innocence.

"Whatever it is," Martin cut in. "I would advise you all not to be poking around the mine at night. Wolves, coyotes. They're both dangerous. There's also snakes. Rattlers. You get bitten, chances are you die."

"Have you got guns?" Walt queried.

"Don't worry boy, we'll look after you. We ain't afraid of the big bad wolf or a sly snake." Ralph sneered.

Quantock put the phone down. Senator Randolph Kinz was pleased with the progress and more so with the excellent arrangements made for the teenagers. Quantock had used illegal Mexican labour and materials to fit out the San Quiller tin mine and Martin had bought the very best recording equipment. The teenagers had arrived safely and had not been spotted en route.

As agreed, the teenagers' letters had indeed been collected and Martin had put them in a single large A4 envelope, which he posted to a box number supplied by Quantock. Quantock had collected the envelope from the postal service and the letters sat on his desk in front of him. He thought of destroying them, but instead put them in the safe in his office; he might need them again one day; he wasn't sure how all this would turn out. He was leaving nothing to providence.

Quantock began to type up his report, referring occasionally to various papers and files in his trays. For once, this was actually quite enjoyable work. He paused for a moment to gather his thoughts; he couldn't wait to see the President's face and his immediate reaction when he read the report. It was quite a unique experience: writing a report about a situation based on incoming reports, but all along knowing the answers. How easy it was for positions to be taken on the slimmest of information and all kinds of explanations given to provide an answer as to why the teenagers were missing and who was to blame. Human nature hates a void and needs it to be filled.

Clem lay in his bunk running through the plans for the video. He knew that to achieve the goal set by Kinz he had to get the team to form together first of all, to work all the rough edges off each other's personalities before they would start work properly. Then he would outline the time scales and set an achievable objective. No sense in wanting to put together something as big as War and Peace when they had limited time. A tight objective was crucial. They must do this before they even touched the equipment. If they didn't then they would lose their focus. He knew his friends well.

He thought back to his business management classes – what had he learned? There was a quotation that went something like, "If I had to chop down a big tree in two hours I would spend at least one hour sharpening the axe." Who the hell said that? Whoever it was, they were right and he would prepare the group well before work was to begin.

Clem was energised and he knew that he had to divide up the skills and then set tasks for the team so that together they would have a final product. The youth of America speaks. He lay there with his arms behind his head. Then he thought about Ginny.

Ginny had no such luck sleeping. She wanted to think about Clem and his cheeky boyish face and firm young body. But images of her father's angry face kept intruding. She turned and buried her head in the pillow. The next few weeks would be different. Dad couldn't butt in now; when she finished her part of the video he would have to listen. All America would have to listen. The youth of America would have its say. No sham rallies, bright lights, pizazz or spinning of the facts to suit the politics of the moment or the good ole boys. Just the bald facts would be presented and discussed, as seen by young people who care.

Chapter 8

E-Day minus 26

Alarm bells had only rung for the parents of the teenagers, when they failed to attend their classes. The parents had not seemed to worry when they were out of touch for twenty-four hours. They had seen it all before. No contact for days then the inevitable call for spending money or a quick visit home with an enormous bag of dirty washing that needed seeing to. But there had now been no contact for four days. And none of their friends knew where they were or who they were with. One by one, they began to get seriously worried. Mrs Grivas found one of Ginny's address books and, as well as ringing all the friends listed, also spoke to the parents. Slowly the identities of the other teenagers were discovered and a network established with the parents. The Atlantic City police were phoned but they had no record of the teenagers. Then Quantock's office was contacted.

Quantock did a final check on the report of the interview with Vern Quayle. The shaky facts blended together into a compelling narrative.

- A man of Arab features had entered a general store shortly after a party of six teenagers had been there. He spoke mainly Arabic, with a smattering of American words.

- He bought duct tape and bungee straps. For what purpose?
- He substantially overpaid for the items, indicating a possible lack of understanding of US currency.
- An abandoned rental minibus coach was found and contained a discarded copy of the Koran, maps of several US cities and some blood stains on the window. (The DNA was being checked). The minibus had been rented at Dulles Airport that morning in the name of Yusuf Islam and paid for by Amex.
- Witness statements indicate that a black UPS mail van was seen driving away from the drug store at high speed. The witness heard the screams of frightened teenagers.
- Finally, all the teenagers reported missing were children of US senators.

The report was supplemented with details of supposed last sightings of the teenagers and various assumptions, detailed but fanciful notes on the possible routes of entry to the US for terrorists or criminal groups. It's not so much that the facts were important, more that they were woven together in such a way that the conclusion was all too obvious; precisely what was intended.

Quantock sat back and read the report several times to ensure that he delivered the evidence in such a way that it left the reader in no doubt at all that evil was afoot without actually saying that.

There was a knock at his office door and a young administrator popped her head inside. "Mr Quantock, sir, it's the DNA you asked for. We got samples from all the parents and a match has been found for Senator Dempster's daughter."

Quantock looked at her and took the envelope. "Thank you, Miriam. Please keep this to yourself. If it gets out, I'll know whom to blame. Right?"

"Right, sir, no problem." She turned away and frowned, thinking to herself, "Asshole! Why do men in power think that young women are likely to always give away secrets?" She stomped up the corridor.

Quantock smiled and added a late note to his report about the DNA. Good work had been done by the agents; so far so good. Kinz's plan was working well. He sat back in his chair and put his arms behind his head. There was a knock at the door again.

"C'min," he said, "what is it, Miriam?"

Miriam half-smiled. "Mr Quantock, it seems as though the management of information on this, er, situation, is getting out of control, sir. One of the witnesses in the Lynchburg incident has been selling his story to various local newspapers. It won't be long before it gets to the big guys!"

Quantock feigned dismay and shock and hit the table with his fist. "For God's sake. Get me the press corps, we need a news blackout and get me an appointment to see the President himself. Here," he wrote a name on a piece of paper and gave it to her, "call this woman and tell her it's of national importance!"

Newly inspired because of Quantock's obvious discomfort and pleased that secrets can get shed from sources other than young female administrators, Miriam trotted up the corridor to enter the world of national security. Typical man – fancy not trusting her?

She couldn't wait to get home to tell Mom and Dad!

Within two hours Dan Quantock was summoned to the White House and was sitting outside the Oval Office on a long leather bench seat. Various high-ranking government officials passed him by without giving him a second glance. He recognised the Chief of Staff, Fred Spiker, the Chief of the Armed Forces, General Kilgore and his own boss, Troy Hammond, Head of the FBI; there was also someone who looked suspiciously like a CIA man, as well as several other familiar faces. His boss walked past him with no acknowledgement, his face stern and without expression. Then he was quite alone in the corridor. He remained calm, rehearsed his lines and breathed deeply.

After about twenty minutes he was summoned by a young man who leaned forward whispering in a strangely high voice, "The President will see you now, sir."

Quantock smiled and followed the man into the Oval Office.

Brannigan was in shirtsleeves, perched on the edge of his desk, hands grasping the edge, legs apart. He was a big man with a square head that matched his bulky square shoulders. He was built like a defensive tackle. His dark rimmed spectacles gave his countenance a frightening appearance. In front of him, squeezed into two large sofas were his top brass, with their aides sitting on chairs behind. The President's voice was like a bark.

"Come on in Quantock. I've read your report and frankly I find it reads like a Hollywood script. Give me the facts as you see them. And keep it brief."

Quantock saw that he was expected to deliver his report standing. He cleared his throat and, without a sign of nervousness, carefully outlined the information he had. He cleverly used the intonation in his voice and the odd expression in his face to convey how much of an insult it was to the American people. He also gently suggested that it could be part of a conspiracy to reduce US global influence at a time of growing military and economic tension in the world, especially the Middle East. He knew what this inferred. Since ancient times any nation that lost the respect of its neighbours, lost its influence and became an easy target for its enemies. That did it. Brannigan scowled and clenched his fists.

Quantock wasn't fooled by this show of indignation. This was precisely what Brannigan needed to divert attention from the nation's economic woes and his failing grip on the presidency. It was the oldest trick in the book and Kinz had read his man perfectly and the situation was eagerly grasped.

Brannigan railed against the enemies of the US who would do such a dastardly thing to innocent children. He refused to let the country be held to ransom and pledged revenge. Brannigan went on for another five minutes before exhausting himself. He then asked for the views of the others in the room, but it was patently obvious that he was not ready to listen.

You son of a bitch, thought Quantock, if you could press the red button for the slightest reason and nuke your enemies and get away with it, you damned well would!

It never ceased to amaze and amuse him how politicians, in the western world at least, created their own political spin and propaganda, then had the temerity to actually believe it themselves. The art of selling, he thought idly.

The President turned to Spiker. "Fred, what do you make of this?"

Spiker decided to play a defence game and appeal to Brannigan's common sense. "Mr President. We need perhaps a little more time. We are as yet unclear as to the perpetrators of this evil act and it may be precipitous to react too quickly. I believe that…"

Brannigan interjected, "What more evidence do we need. This is an Al Qaeda plot if ever there was one. We have six missing high profile young Americans and an Arab jihadi at the scene of the crime. What do you want, personal introductions? All this happens at a time when our fortunes in the Middle East are being usurped by terrorists and unstable governments run by crazy Ayatollahs. What's wrong with you? Why shouldn't we at least show the goat fuckers how big our dick really is?"

General Kilgore got the President's attention. "Sir, I believe that Fred's correct, sir, we should wait and see. Our forces are at readiness sir, and once we have verified the facts we can discuss the next move."

Brannigan seethed openly. Then he exploded and banged his fists on the table.

"Wait, wait, wait? Is this what Americans are made of? When Democrats did that in the past we ended up looking like pussies."

Quantock clasped his hands and watched the ideological ping pong with interest, realising that this President was writing his memoirs before the conflict, whatever that was supposed to be, had even begun.

Brannigan got to his feet and stood there like a prize fighter waiting to start a bout. "General, put the forces on alert. I want a naval battlegroup with carriers moved into the Gulf of Arabia. Fred, get the son-of-a-bitch Saudi king on the phone and tell him to invite a US infantry and a tank division into the country for joint military exercises. Get some airpower to Riyadh airbase. Get me patched through to the Israeli prime minster so I can give him the heads up. Do the same with the Turks. Finally, I want a goddamn Mediterranean battlegroup with cruise missiles moved to the Syrian coastline.

General Kilgore paled. "But Mr President, I…"

Brannigan broke in, "I am in no mood to wait or be patient. Do it!" He rammed the command home with a pointed finger.

The room was deathly silent. General Kilgore was already seething at other military initiatives that were being enacted, 'below the line'. This was almost the last straw. Getting up slowly, he put on his hat, saluted and left the room. He would do as ordered, because he was a good soldier. He would do it, even if he was not sure who the hell they were waving the sabre at.

Brannigan turned to Quantock. "Well, what do you think?"

Quantock deliberately waited a few seconds then answered. "Sir. You have decided to get our enemies worried and I think that is the correct decision. Someone is behind this incident and it's better to deal with it right now, and hard. I can only guess at the next move. Before long we will end up on the wrong end of a ransom note or ghastly video and if you react then it will seem as though you have been pushed into taking action. You are choosing to go straight for the throat without delay."

There were several grunts of approval from the Secretary of State for Defence who had remained silent so far and one or two acolytes seated at the table. Brannigan smiled and nodded.

Quantock was pleased with his quick response. It was merely a sycophantic summing up of Brannigan's ranting, together with a little encouragement. No one would ever be able to say that it was he who rattled the President's sabre.

Then the President, much calmer now, turned to his aides and said, "Okay guys, contact the Washington Post, CNN and all the other major press players. But nothing goes out until it has been cleared by the Press Office." He turned to the only woman present, "I want every piece of text on this matter cleared by you and me, Sadie. Do you understand?"

Sadie Burrows his communications chief smirked. She was a tall, elegant, African American lady with glossy bobbed hair and her whole demeanour screamed confidence. Although in her early fifties, she looked years younger. She dressed in a chic manner, and wore clothes that flattered and accentuated her voluptuous figure and substantial cleavage. Today she was wearing a red bolero jacket and tight black skirt, slashed at the thigh. Quantock looked at her and she brought to mind the kind of moth that sports a vivid red colour to frighten off predators – it said, you can eat me, but if you do you'll die.

Brannigan smiled broadly straight back at her, "I also want a nationwide campaign started, you know the kind of thing Sadie, hearts and minds and all that stuff. Yellow ribbons on trees, set up some young friends of the kids to brief on their relationships, likes and dislikes, what they did at high school and so on. I want all the American people behind our action on these bastards. I don't need whining from pinko liberals, so I need tears to fall all over the US – do you think you can do that?"

Sadie Burrows stood up holding a file to her ample bosom. She raised her head and said, "Mr President, by midday tomorrow the US will be drowning in lakes of tears!"

The President's eyes stayed on her as she walked out of the Oval Office, he seemed transfixed; Quantock thought that the man might actually dribble at any moment.

Quantock reflected on the rumours that abounded about the pair of them. It was said that the President had bedded her in almost every room and on all the furniture in the White House, but had never ever been caught out. Some said that he had even had her on the coffee table in the Oval Office; Quantock grimaced, looked at the shiny surface and instinctively moved his soft leather briefcase onto the floor beside him.

The President turned to him, and said, "Dan, this is a mighty fine piece of FBI work," he patted the report folder with the back of his left hand. "Isn't it Troy?"

Troy Hammond, mumbled something inaudible and nodded.

Quantock replied, "Thank you, Mr President."

Brannigan continued, "Anyway, I have a mind to let you run the operation to track down these bastards. What do you say to that?"

"Well, sir, I ..."

Brannigan wasn't listening: "Quantock, the job's yours. I want your assessment of the staff requirement and your operational plan by the end of the week."

Quantock kept a straight face, even put on a slightly strained look, enjoying Hammond's impotence. He wasn't usually into Schadenfreude, he actually quite liked the man, except that his boss had gone along with earlier directives to keep Quantock out of the front line.

"Mr President, I will do my best," Quantock said with a half smile.

Brannigan's face changed hue slightly and his eyes narrowed. "You'd better Quantock, or I'll fry your ass!"

Quantock left the office and walked slowly down the corridor past the guard on duty. He was amused at the irony. Here he was having put into action someone else's plan to deal with a conundrum, effectively having to bring himself to justice, earning money to boot. Now he had the unenviable job of uncovering his own deeds. This effectively meant that he should organise a nationwide search for six missing teenagers when he already knew exactly where they were. At the same time, he had to make his efforts look good, even when it was obvious to him that they would be unsuccessful. For the finale, he had to co-ordinate an operation that would see them apprehended at some point but without compromising the release of the video to a despairing and hyped-up nation. The question was how to work the two tasks together? He pursed his lips – this could be fun!

Troy Hammond played with the rocking chrome balls of his desktop Newton's Cradle toy and reflected on the situation. Undeniably, Quantock had done a good job. He had been fortunate to follow up on various clues so quickly and his report was very clear and concise. Now he was running the investigation, answering directly to the President. This troubled Hammond, it was not a good idea at all. He was effectively unsupervised and on such high profile work this was dangerous. If he made errors or took the wrong course of action that left the President horribly exposed. All security investigations had to be checked, verified and discussed in a team environment; this work was effectively now in one man's hands.

The balls on the toy had run out of momentum and come to a halt. Hammond swung an end ball against its neighbour to get them rocking and clacking again. He had long since given up being astonished at how this POTUS circumvented normal protocols and common sense. Instead he used patronage to cut across the workings of the administration in all directions and to divide his enemies. He was an astute man who knew just who he needed to groom for maximum effect and the tightest control. It was the oldest strategy known to leaders throughout history, and most of the time, it worked – until of course all the acolytes deserted or screwed up big time. Personality driven adventures are fine in business, but not when running the most powerful country in the world.

Things were looking bleak. How long would it take for public support to wane completely? Importantly, did he, Troy Hammond care? He knew the President was running out of friends. It was pretty dumb to take such a chance.

Chapter 9

E-Day minus 25

A small group of senators from safe Southern states gathered as they always did on a Tuesday morning in one of the many common rooms in Congress, getting coffee and gossiping. This was a particularly important group, all of whom held key positions in the Republican Party. They liked to meet and talk about events of the day and make predictions on short-term political outcomes. Two of them broke away from the main group and made their way to some leather chairs nearby, settled in the seats and noisily sipped their hot coffee.

"So, Carl, how's your week looking? Are you going to the Thursday Prayer Breakfast?" asked Georgia's Senator John Radcliffe.

"No John, I won't and neither will you," replied Carl Rigby, an elderly and experienced senator from North Carolina. "So it's a black mark for you too my friend."

Another senator, Jeb Beardsley from Louisiana, joined the group, laughed out loud and said, "Prayer breakfasts are good for the Baptists and Catholics as well as the rest of us with souls that need redeeming. Hallelujah!"

From the coffee point a small wiry man with sharp features, Senator Eugene Caldwell, from Alabama, shouted across to them, "Now that's not good at all gentlemen," he poured his coffee and walked across to them, "that kind of talk is…"

"Treason?" someone added.

"No," he continued irritably, "not treason, but vile talk. We are all of us, God fearing Americans, so why not pray in Congress?"

John Radcliffe, the senator who had started the debate looked annoyed and put his cup down on the saucer, so loud that his colleagues thought it would crack.

He stared at Eugene Caldwell and said, "Look, I know you to be a good man, Eugene, but you know as well as I do that this prayer stuff has been going on for about three years now and has nothing to do with religion," he paused and glared at the group, "no, let me finish. The last president claimed to have been guided by God, so what did he do when he stood down half way through his second term, hand the telephone number to Brannigan?"

Some laughed; some did not. Senator Radcliffe continued. "Have we learned nothing at all from history? The whole process of 'independence' introduced into our politics a couple of hundred years or so ago, meant cutting ties with the mother country, England, and becoming truly independent. It was about separating the people from the King and, don't you know, religion, focusing on the needs of the people, Eugene, the people."

Randolph Kinz cut in. "Now, now, John. No need to give Eugene a history lesson. We have to focus our firepower on the Democrats. How are your numbers looking?"

"My numbers are fine so long as no one mentions Brannigan. But I hear Eugene's in trouble," Radcliffe said waspishly.

Caldwell harrumphed. "Brannigan needs to up the game on the economy. We're being bled by the Chinese and other blood suckers are gathering. My constituents are hurting."

"I'll pray for them," Radcliffe said sardonically.

Caldwell ignored him and continued. "This subprime market

business is worrying me. Brannigan needs to say no Federal bailouts. In Alabama, folk don't go borrowing money to buy houses they can't afford. They build their own."

Kinz turned towards the door and said quietly, "Talking of God, here's one of his key disciples."

They looked up and saw Sadie Burrows walking towards them.

"Hello boys," she said, knowing the older men hated that label. "Why are you still in Washington and not on the campaign stump. Not plotting insurrection, are we?"

Carl Rigby smiled sardonically. "Well hello Miss Burrows. May I offer you a coffee? Kind of you to ask how we are. Well we're having one last conclave before we go to battle. We're like gladiators limbering up. Feel free to give us all a massage. We've heard you're good at massaging facts and figures."

Sadie Burrows had the thickest skin in the political jungle and continued with a smile. Tilting her head to one side like a motherly schoolteacher she said, "I'll pass on that kind offer, Mr Rigby. Anyway, here we go, today's summary of our news agenda, all done for you. Aren't I kind?"

Nonplussed, the senators reached for the eight-page leaflet as they were handed out. They read it in a stunned silence.

Eugene Caldwell, ever the Republican apologist, looked shell-shocked. He broke the silence and spluttered, "What is this Sadie, I would never say that about abortion, I am pro-life, but I would never say that. And look at this, I would never insult an opponent like that." He held the leaflet in front of him with his left hand and hit it with the fingers of his right hand with a loud smack.

Sadie Burrows regarded him as one would a child in a man's world. She knew only too well that the American people had a rather contrary attitude to negative campaigning – a kind of a love-hate relationship. Whilst most voters, when asked directly about this style of campaigning, claimed to despise it, they found the rough and tumble of politics irresistible, with its salacious trysts, corruption and skeletons in cupboards. Such were the similarities – two horses in the same dirty stable. The current administration had taken mudslinging to even greater heights, as it ramped up campaign spending. Overfed by dollar hungry and unregulated television advertisers, they surfed the societal waves driven by greed, selfishness and decreased civility in public life. Politics had always been dirty, it's the nature of the game; but nobody played that game better than Sadie Burrows.

She gave him a patronising look and said, "Well, sorry about that Eugene, but let's see, that is what you said, er," she looked at her watch, "back in Florida about two hours ago. At least that's what was reported in the Florida State newspapers."

Caldwell was left open-mouthed.

Jeb Beardsley was equally perplexed. "Sadie, why do you do this? My press release is simply not expressed in the way I would articulate these issues here in the senate. This doesn't do justice to me or the debate on education."

Sadie Burrows drew herself up to her full five foot ten inches in height, and glared at them all. She was a formidable street fighter who took no prisoners. She exuded arrogance and aggression. Her mission was to create power and win elections. News media was her business and she knew what 'popped their toast', and she fed their voracious appetite for copy that was sensational or ladled with innuendo; her sources would often accept anything that they were given without bothering to check the veracity. She practised pure political kung fu, without mercy on any opponent.

"Look guys, I bust my ass getting the press and television messages right to make an impact so that our party can stay in power and you can keep your positions. That's my job, okay? What I wrote is better than what you would've written. It's on message, right? If you disagree with the message, then you aren't loyal Republicans. You either want us to win this election or you don't?"

The senators were lost for words. Except Kinz. He said: "*Princes who try to buy loyalty by threat and fear often become the threatened.*"

Sadie looked at him with the narrowed eyes of a rattlesnake poised to strike.

"Machiavelli. Have you read him, Sadie?" Kinz asked.

She smiled and walked away, saying, "I gotta go now."

It was a beautiful morning in Arizona. The colours of the desert, reds, oranges, ochres, browns, gold and silver were highlighted by a crystal-clear azure sky. After breakfast, the teenagers got down to creative business. They sat around a long table in the work area. Clem stood in front of a flip chart.

"Okay you guys, before we even touch any of the equipment and position our video filming, we have to sort out a script. That means we need to be sure what we want to achieve. So, what is our objective?"

Walt was the first to speak. His pomposity gone, he was a different person when focussed.

"Firstly, Clem, I think we should regard you as the team leader not just the director of our video shoot."

The others agreed, with shouts of "Yeah, skip!" and other jocular remarks. Clem smiled. The first hurdle was over with, thanks to Walt.

Walt continued. "Next I think it is safe to say that we all have preferences in our view of what is important for the America of tomorrow. I think we should focus our 'State of the Nation' message on the mistakes of the last five years or so, but end up with a list of recommendations for the future."

Jon looked at Matt and they nodded.

Clem said, "That's a good start, Walt. If we take that as our mission objective, we then need to sort out who feels strongly about what topic. We can maybe break into two groups to do that. But first can we have some volunteers for the key roles in the team. I need a second camera person. Someone for sound and someone for lighting. We also need someone looking after continuity and timing.

"I'd like to do that," Jo Anne said. "Can I have a clapperboard?" Clem nodded. "And I'd also like to look after makeup and dance choreography."

"I can't remember wanting to include dancing in the video," Clem said with a smile.

"No, you didn't but I have a brilliant idea which will work."

"Okay. Let's take that idea offline. What about other volunteers?"

"Can I be second camera?" asked Ginny, knowing that would keep her physically close to Clem.

"I'm happy to do sound and lighting," said Matt.

"I think it's important to have a producer," said Walt, "and I'm happy to be of service."

"Can I be best boy?" joked Jon. And everyone laughed.

Ginny started the ball rolling in her group. "I major on social justice and race relations. Fairness, respect and equality of opportunity is what I stand for." She playfully turned to Walt and said, "And if you ever tell me to check my privilege again Danberry you're dead!"

Walt smiled weakly and looked at his papers. He was not one for humour at the best of times, and said, "I want to focus on the US style of politics that the American people are coming so close to despising, but that isn't gonna be easy to change. There's too much money. The lobbies are too powerful. The media colludes. We need to get back to the Constitution. Government of the people, for the people, by the people."

There was an uncomfortable silence and everyone new that boring old Walt was right; he might be the odd one out – but he was right.

Matt looked up, "Well, I'm for the environment. I 'er, well, I guess I am kinda supportive to wildlife and conservation. But heck, it's about our environment that I feel strongest – y'know, global warming and all that jazz."

Clem selected himself as chair of the group and immediately took charge. "Jon, do you want to kick off?"

Jon coughed. "Okay. I want to look at something I don't understand but which I need to understand. The economy. We seem to be getting into one old major mess and there must be a better way of doing things. I want to tackle the subject from the perspective of the guy in the street."

"Very good," said Clem. "What about you Jo Anne?"

She responded by bubbling. "Well, hey, there's something neither of you know about me. I came out last year as bisexual."

Jon leaned across and took her hands. "Oh, Jo Anne, that's wonderful. You're such a wonderful person."

"Yes, you are," said Clem. "And this is a safe inclusive space."

"Thank you," Jo Anne continued. "I want to look at LGBT and women's issues."

Clem smiled. "That's a great theme that we can develop over the next day or so. I'm going to take foreign policy."

Jon and Jo Anne nodded enthusiastically. "Good call," said Jon.

Chapter 10

E-Day minus 24

President Brannigan puffed on a cigar in the Oval Office contemplating his future. His father had once said: "Son, when people have full bellies, good jobs and money in their pockets they will trust the State to look after them and will avoid politics like the plague. When any one or all of those things are missing, they will seek a strong leader."

The family tailoring business had been building slowly and its garments were respected by many that valued a good bespoke suit. But this did not make really big money. It was President Roosevelt's Four Freedoms speech on 6 January 1941 to Congress where he pledged to give material support to Great Britain and Europe that provided Brannigan senior with the chance he needed. Spotting an opportunity, he obtained large pieces of equipment for cutting cloth and stitching. Then he applied for government contracts to make protective clothing and uniforms. To his enormous surprise, he was awarded his first contract in the same year and others came long shortly afterwards – his financial success was assured.

By the time the US entered the war Brannigan senior's factories were well geared up for production and expanded even further to provide for US Department of Defence contracts, which he was able to bid for and get with ease. He had been able to diversify and built up a solid stake in the oil business.

Brannigan junior grew up in a privileged home and he did not have to struggle for whatever he wanted. He was a good sportsman and a tolerable student. But his key skills lay in his sense of vision and a wily disposition that ensured he was always one step ahead of his peers. He saw college friends leave for Vietnam and never come back. So, his father ensured, by giving a few dollars here and there to key political campaigns, that his son never went anywhere near a battle. Brannigan junior began to appreciate the power of money.

He was excited by the intrigue of high office and determined to enter politics. After a successful career in the oil industry, during which time he built a reputation for being a bully who, ironically or perhaps craftily, paid the people he bullied very well so, oddly, they stuck with him. He was particularly skilful in his dealings with people; he delegated difficult decisions to others and perfected the successful use of fall guys in situations where he needed clean hands to make a name for himself. His reason for running for Congress was also partly based on the influence he would be able to bring to bear on his various business interests.

His great wealth purchased enough PR and votes to ensure an easy victory to state governor. The rest was history. He used the same influence and techniques to become George W Bush's vice-president and stepped up to the plate when Bush retired as a result of utter "exhaustion" and went back to Texas to spend more time with his family. Brannigan believed that fortune favours the brave and luck comes to those who deserve it. He revelled in being POTUS and the patronage that came with it.

The evangelical lay preacher Senator Alan Murray from Mississippi was appointed his vice president. Murray was widely loved by white protestants of all denominations because of his deep religious beliefs and his outstanding ability to preach the best sermons in the US. Brannigan quickly grew to despise him. He also had copious files on Murray's nocturnal missions to certain seedy areas of New York over the years and Murray had accepted that he would not be vice president if Brannigan won the election.

Brannigan lit a Cuban cigar. It always annoyed his staff, many of whom were non-smokers. A nicer man might have agreed to withdraw to a smoking area.

There was a light knock at the door.

"C'min?" he said.

It was Sadie Burrows.

"Mr President, I thought that I might come and update you on the progress of the press and PR on the missing teenagers since our meeting the other day?"

She slowly closed the door with her rear, wiggling as she did so.

"Sure, Sadie, come on in, why not?" His grin almost separated one half of his face from the other.

She crossed the room to Brannigan and casually sat up on the front of desk. Smiling as she watched his eyes following her rising hemline.

It wasn't only her long and shapely legs that fired Brannigan's libido. Sadie simply had something very sexual about her; a kind of magnetism that was difficult to escape from once she locked onto a man. The way she looked at him, cocked her eyebrow or said something in a way that set the senses on fire. She had seduced him more by what she didn't say than what she did say.

Their relationship was charged with electricity but unconsummated. Republican America was not ready for adulterous sexual relations between a white president and a black subordinate.

He also needed her forensic skills as a media manipulator.

Brannigan's wife Christine was pleasant, plain and homely. She had given him two fine sons and he adored her without question. Christine put up with his absences and although there were the odd rumours of affairs nothing was ever proven and he never seemed to display the same traits as men who frequently play around. He also made plenty of time for his home life. Christine worked hard for his political career and was a tireless fundraiser for charity and the Republican Party.

Nevertheless, although Brannigan's libido was not as insatiable as one or two of his presidential predecessors, a sink of unsatisfied sexual energy had built up. At times Sadie only had to breathe on Brannigan and he would nearly explode into a thousand pieces. But he had to find release elsewhere.

Sadie put her files down, grasped the edge of the desk and leaned forward, revealing her cleavage, to look into his eyes.

"Before I update you on the kids, there is another urgent matter I have to clarify."

"Go on."

"The National Enquirer are running a story saying you are having an affair with Governor Palin."

"Goddamn!"

"They say they have two witnesses who can swear that you had sex with her in the Oval Office."

Brannigan smiled. "You don't say."

"Sir, why are you smiling? This could be as serious as the Monica Lewinsky Affair. It could cost you the vote of the Bible Belt. It could cost you the election."

"What do you want me to say? Did I or have I ever had sexual relations with that woman? Depends what you mean by sexual relations but in my book, no. I never did." He chuckled.

"It's not funny sir."

"Yes, yes, it is. Tell the Enquirer no comment and let them run the story. Then sandbag all the other media editors with threats of waterboarding and kill the lie. Because that's what it is. A big fat lie. But it's in my interest that some people believe it. Did I ever have sexual relations with you Sadie?"

"No. But you want to."

"Jimmy Carter said that just thinking about it was as bad as adultery. Do you believe that? But damn right. You're a beautiful sexy lady. Fortunately, I can restrain myself. But I know you would enjoy it if we did. I know how to please a woman."

Sadie smiled. "I bet you do."

Brannigan stretched the fingers in his right hand out, smiling: "Have I told you before that many experts believe you can tell the size of a man's Johnson by the size of his hands?"

Sadie laughed. "Yes, you have. Many times."

"It's true, you know."

"Yes sir. Now getting back to the kids," she said diplomatically.

Brannigan balled his fingers into a fist. "Do we have a nation drowning in its own tears yet?"

"Not quite, but almost. I can run through the details but it's all here in the resume. Yellow ribbons are sprouting like spring daffodils. Jeez, wish I had shares in the yellow ribbon business! All the channels are running the story as headline news. Calls to radio stations are coming in thick and fast. They range from, 'Nuke the Muslims', to, 'Round up the Arabs' Nice to know the American people care, huh?"

Brannigan unballed his fist and and used his left hand to pull and crack the knuckles of each digit. Popular demand and a president with the balls to give the people vengeance; this was what the nation needed. In his mind's eye, he could see the battle map and a picture of him cigar in hand directing action against the regimes supporting the terrorists. All Arabs were untrustworthy two-faced bastards and he had some scores to settle in the Middle East. He only needed the slightest excuse; he was certain he knew who the perpetrators of this horrendous crime were even if the incompetent CIA did not.

It was pleasing to hear that some of his military staff, initially reluctant to sabre rattle, were now supporting his calls for more direct action. It would be a major coup when Quantock caught the kidnappers.

Sadie saw his mind wandering and brought him back down to earth, "I've got all the media engagements outlined here. CNN interview in one hour. Do you want me to run through them all?

"Hell no, Sadie. That sounds good enough for me. How about a glass of the finest Tennessee whisky?"

Sadie smiled and put on a southern accent, "Well, Mr President, sir, you know how vulnerable a woman can be after working twelve hours straight on very little food if whisky is administered?"

Brannigan returned her smile and opened the drawer in his desk where he kept drinks.

Sadie looked sad. "Sorry Mr President, but I must decline. I've still got work to do." She turned abruptly and as she sauntered away, smiled coyly over her left shoulder.

Chapter 11

E-Day minus 23

Quantock paced the study of his apartment. Sadie Burrows had done a great job. Vern Quayle and his granddaughter from the General Lee general store made excellent unreliable witnesses and every detail was pulled out of them. Their views were sought, no matter how wacky they were and conveyed to a concerned and interested nation, by now hyped up to bursting point by newspaper articles, television chat shows and every kind of conjecture on the fate of the teenagers. News of the presidential election was relegated.

Almost all of the teenagers' parents and relations shunned publicity, but one grandmother was encouraged to be interviewed and she had no doubts whatsoever that it was an Arab plot to spread fear throughout America and bring down the democratic system of government. She expected her grandson to be ransomed and steadfastly demanded of the parents that they refuse – in the interest of the Free World of course.

Within twenty-four hours the nation became hysterical. A pipe bomb was hurled at a mosque in South Carolina, a member of the Saudi royal family was badly beaten up by a mob in New York and a Sikh restaurant was burned out in Wisconsin. Callers to talk radio stations angrily demanded that all Muslims be interned or deported. Copies of the Koran were publicly burnt in a number of places. Yellow ribbons were tied to anything that didn't move and sometimes to things that did.

Quantock had been in the FBI all his life; he had known nothing else since leaving university. He was a natural and treated each mission like a football game. It was a game of tactics to be enjoyed and played to the full. Once or twice his colleagues commented on his cold-hearted approach to dealing with criminals who crossed the line and failed to surrender. He would dispatch them without flinching. This behaviour contrasted with his off-duty open friendly style. He was dubbed, JH, "Jekyll and Hyde". He was good – invincible in fact. That is until the accident.

His wife Alison was driving their Chevrolet home with their young son in the back seat after attending a school parent and teachers' meeting. A local rich kid called Brett Ellis, high on champagne and crack cocaine, shot traffic lights and ploughed into the side of their car. Qauntock's wife and boy were killed instantly. Ellis was arrested by local cops but then released on bail following the intervention of his father. Instead of taking his chances in the court room, Ellis skipped town and Quantock assigned his team to the manhunt. When he got information that Ellis was holed up in a Palm Springs hotel, Quantock drove across the state on his own. Without waiting for backup, he kicked in Ellis' hotel room door. Witnesses later reported that they heard multiple gunshots.

Ellis' body was riddled with bullets and a 9mm Walther P99 was found at the scene, with one bullet fired.

Everyone felt enormous sympathy for Quantock, but there was strong suspicion that he had faked the crime scene. Ellis' father demanded an investigation and Quantock was suspended. Although subsequently cleared of the charge of unlawful killing and perverting the course of justice, Quantock was admonished for unprofessional behaviour and misconduct. Senator Kinz helped ensure that he kept his badge, but Quantock's route to the top of the FBI was blocked. He was shunted into a department that provided low level security passes for journalists and other non-government personnel.

Quantock never remarried and he was successfully rehabilitated after a nervous breakdown fuelled by heavy drinking. Now he never touched a drop.

Then came 9/11 and the horror of the Twin Towers in New York. This enraged him and he applied several times to be put back on security duties. Many of his old bosses had moved on. Eventually, his harassed department head agreed to consider a move and he was interviewed by doctors and other specialists and passed with flying colours. He was drafted back to homeland security. The work was not that much more exciting than his last job, but at least he was a departmental head again. This time he was responsible for organising security for US senators and their families, working with the White House staff. All he could do was to wait for a chance to shine. But after a while, he settled back into even more routine work and was sure that his chance would never ever come.

However, his job did help build a friendship with Kinz. Especially after one chance meeting in a Washington coffee house where Kinz had explained about the loss of his dear wife Clara and Quantock duly responded with the story about his own loss. Kinz was clever and prised all the other information out of him as well. He had said supportively to Quantock, "I'd have done the same son, believe me I would!"

They shared political views over a few months in different locations around Washington. Quantock found himself being unusually candid and open with Kinz who was easy to talk to. The Senator nodded sagely throughout their conversations and they enjoyed each other's intelligent and open company. Kinz told him that he would treat Quantock's comments with the confidentiality that they deserved, because they had now become firm acquaintances and thanked him for sharing his views with him.

It was with strange relief that Quantock got so much off his chest in just a few casual meetings with such an eminent man. Perhaps it was the open discussion with Kinz that acted like a form of counselling that made him feel so much better in himself – better than he had felt for many a year.

Quantock reflected on his past and the situation now presenting itself. Defining moments in life are often no more than casual encounters and these brief meetings were followed up by the surprise telephone call some months later from Kinz who wished to speak to him again, this time at his private residence in Washington.

Chapter 12

E-Day minus 22

Senator Kinz gazed out of his Phoenix mansion's French windows onto his rose garden. It had been stunningly beautiful this year; a masterpiece of well-tended lawns structured with formal beds growing a vast array of scented, heritage roses. If you knew what to do, roses thrived in the Arizona desert climate. His wife Clara had been a particularly good gardener; that was up until her cancer diagnosis. When she died, he had been inconsolable for a long time. During this period of mourning the garden had suffered and he had to hire a team of landscapers to come in and give it a makeover. It was amazing how many men it took to do the work that Clara had done steadily and lovingly, day in day out.

Now it was back to its prime and all summer the scent had wafted into the sitting room. He looked at the tidy pruned bushes in the late October sunlight and they seemed to give him some confidence that pruning is what is required of every system, horticultural or even those devised by human beings. It was for the best. That's what he wanted to achieve; a political pruning.

Kinz filled a crystal glass with a large Scotch whisky, drained the contents and tried to recall the scent of the roses in summer.

Then after another swallow he thought he saw Clara coming towards him through the doors and he stared in disbelief. Her laugh and smile filled him with joy. It was sweetness itself. He instinctively opened his arms to embrace her as she glided towards him smiling and laughing as she used to.

But as she came closer, her smile turned to a twisted frown and the skin in her face shrivelled, turned brown and shrank to the contours of her skull. Kinz's stomach went cold with shock and his heart beat faster, pounding his rib cage like a hammer.

Clara was hissing at him and waving a bony finger in front of her. He was shocked and could not move his feet. Then he became dizzy and everything seemed covered in a red mist. Almost at once he felt a searing pain in his left arm and tightness in his chest. He dropped his glass and gasped for breath. The room seemed to be spinning around. He blacked out and fell heavily to the thickly carpeted floor.

Martin walked away from the house and dialled No Name on his cell phone. It rang, but was not answered. This was strange, very strange. The agreement had been to stay in daily contact and the 2pm check-in time had passed four hours ago. Martin cursed. He would need to keep trying.

Clem felt good as he tidied his notes away at the end of the day. The scriptwriting sessions were going great guns. He felt a hand touch him lightly on his shoulder. It was Ginny.

"Hi, Captain. That was a good session. I got so noisy I feel exhausted. You want some fun?" she said.

He looked at her sheepishly and before he could answer she went on. "I noticed that there was a large rock pool, right by the trees. Let's take a dip."

"Ginny, you're forgetting the werewolf. Martin told us not to go out at night. Plus, the evening temperatures in the desert at this time of year are about forty degrees, is it wise?" said Clem in a playful tone.

Ginny smiled, "Aw c'mon, Clem. Martin said don't go near the mine. He didn't say don't go out. It was quite moderate last night, a bit chilly later on I grant you, but if we catch it early enough it should be all right. Hey, the Swedish do it all the time. Let's do it after chow?"

Clem looked at his watch. "Damn your hide, Ginny. Okay. We eat at six thirty, let's sneak away about seven thirty – we gotta let our food go down!"

She smiled at her success, tapped him playfully on the head and went to the accommodation block.

Chow-time came and Martin was in good form, despite convincing himself earlier in the day that he should avoid all emotional or friendly attachments. However, the lack of contact with No Name was eating away at him. He did well not to let his anxiety show. Everyone responded to his cheery attitude and his burgers and fries were given a high five. Ralph ate in silence in the corner of the room and Martin smelled the whisky fumes from where he was sitting.

After the meal, Clem and Ginny, with a blanket under her arm, left quietly and unnoticed.

Martin beckoned Ralph to the kitchen. He closed the door.

"Ralph, what gives man? Are you still sore at being on this mission or what?"

Ralph looked irritated. "Yeah, I guess I'm just plain bored. The kids just remind me of all those jackasses I hated at school. Taking the piss. Privileged kids who thought they were better than anyone else. No worries about money or parents who beat you when they got back from drinkin'. 'N what's funny is that we picked up this job so damned easy. Outta the blue. Kinda strange ain't it? Damn good money, no danger; why did we get such a plum job and not some others who are the golden boys of the CIA? It just doesn't make sense. I smell a rat."

Ralph's assertion made Martin uneasy. Had his desperation for the money disabled his bullshit detector? Why hadn't No Name responded to his calls and texts? He went outside and unlocked the driver's door of the RV. After the blinds were lowered, he turned on a TV. Photographs of the six teenagers filled the screen. They were national news. He was hit by a wave of conflicting emotions. Panic. Fear. Exhilaration. Hysteria. Shock and awe. He breathed deeply and then out slowly. He focussed on the story. But why hadn't No Name given him a heads-up that the news was out?

When the ad break came, Martin went to the kitchenette and took a bottle of tequilla and a glass out of a cupboard. He poured himself a large measure and lit a cigar. As he got the full picture of the story, he began to relax. The plan had worked, to the detail. He smiled and poured another drink. Then his eye caught the ticker tape banner along the bottom of the screen and panic rose as he took in the words. Breaking News…War hero Arizona Senator in critical condition after heart attack…

Kinz – heart attack? Who owns this project whilst he is ill? How did he get so ill so suddenly, he has always been an icon of fitness for a man of his age? Was this suspicious? Where does that put him and Ralph? Why hasn't he been able to contact No Name?

They had lived in a conspiratorial world for so long that anything out of the ordinary could have a devious or duplicitous meaning to it; it was the price to be paid for the kind of work that he did.

He reached for the bottle of tequilla and took a large swig, then another. After a few more drinks, he had convinced himself that something was seriously amiss. Maybe Ralph had it right after all. Then he dialled No Name again.

Ralph sat in a rocky outcrop overlooking the accommodation quarters just as the evening began to close in. He pulled out his special silver box and was soon cutting a line of cocaine on the mirrored inner surface with a fancy razor blade, ready for snorting through a dollar bill tube. As he drew the white powder deep into his nasal passages, he looked up at the now deeply reddening sky. Colours became brighter and the silence of the desert evening filled with electric shocks and lights all around him. He closed his eyes and great waves of pleasure rushed through his body. He was on fire and raring to go. After a while, he focussed again and started to laugh uncontrollably. Cocaine always had this effect on him. If Mike Tyson had challenged him to ten rounds he would have accepted, or he would have offered to stop a bullet with his teeth. He was invincible. He was horny.

The presidential campaign was slowly starting to reclaim the news agenda. On Fox News, Martin watched Brannigan deliver a speech at a packed rally in a Miami sports arena. He was masterful.

"And let me promise you friends. The net is closing in on the perpetrators of this heinous crime against our young people. The biggest manhunt in US history is afoot and no resources will be spared until the Lynchburg Six have been rescued and the terrorists brought to justice. Dead or alive."

There was a massive cheer. Placards with Brannigan for President bobbed up and down. A chant of "U, S, USA!" was taken up. Brannigan flapped his hands downwards to silence the crowd.

"Some pinko liberals in the media say it's too early to say that this crime was committed by Muslim jihadis and I should sit back and wait until the facts are known. Well I tell them this: if it talks like a terrorist duck, and walks like a terrorist duck, it goddamn is a terrorist duck. The Arab terrorists came here in 1993 and bombed the World Trade Centre. They came again on 9/11 and flew planes into the Twin Towers killing three thousand Americans. Our security services have prevented dozens of attempted atrocities since then. This attack has Muslim, Arab, Al Qaeda written all over it. These people hate our democracy. They hate our freedoms. That's why they choose to do this during our presidential election. But I promise you and I promise them: they are going down. There is no place for them to hide. No place to run."

The crowd again erupted into chants of U, S, USA!

"I'll say one more thing. Our friends in Israel have a saying. It takes a village to grow a terrorist. They never, ever do it on their own without the support of others. And just as we will catch the terrorists in our country, I will also identify their backers and supporters in the Middle East. And I swear to you, we are going to bomb the shit out of them."

The crowd went mad. A chant went up: "Kill, kill, kill, the A-ribs, Bomb the goat-fuckers now!" Everyone took it up. Fists pumping in the air. Respectable looking elderly white women. Small children. Glamorous blondes. Fat men with baseball caps.

Ginny led Clem up the ridge to where the Palo Verde trees grew. The lime-green foliage was luminescent in the moonlight. The trees obviously grew there because of a plentiful supply of water and as they rounded a rocky edge there was a large pool. It was just as Ginny had described it. It was small with a gravel edge and the water was as still as could be, giving the impression of a large round glass mirror. It reflected the darkening red evening sky and the rising moon and made it look like an eerie fiery pit; half beautiful and yet a little frightening.

Clem stood on the water's edge, bent down and put his hand into the mirror-like surface.

"Wow. It's still warm as bath water." he said.

"Come on! Get in quick. It's cold as an ice box out here." she said and started to remove her clothes.

Clem was a little slower, shyly matching her garment for garment. When they were both naked, she laughed at his embarrassment and turned and walked into the cold water. He nervously followed suit. As he entered the water, he dove forward and down into the depths of the pool.

Ginny swam on her back, slowly, mesmerised by the huge, starry sky. Clem surfaced and came to join her.

"It's beautiful," he gasped.

"Isn't it just," Ginny said.

The cold hit them as they emerged dripping from the pool. Shivering, they dried themselves quickly and dressed. Then they settled into a cleft in the rocks, sheltered by the spreading roots of a tree, on a blanket that Ginny had the good sense to bring.

When she looked up at his face her eyes sparkled and she smiled enticingly. Then they kissed. It was a wonderfully delicate kiss; he slowly warmed her cold lips with his lips and then probed the moist softness of her mouth and tongue with his tongue. Clem enjoyed holding her tight and felt the warmth of her body as she nestled into him. It was the nicest feeling in the world and he wished it could go on forever.

Ralph had nodded off. But he awoke to see that a light had been switched on in the end room of the accommodation block. Struggling with the counter-effects of too much whisky and the cocaine, he fumbled for his binoculars. It had been a good show last night, perhaps tonight it would be better? He sang some country music to himself whilst he waited. After a while Jo Anne came into view. She was dressed in the briefest of underwear and happily swung her wash bag around, unconcerned at the open curtains, expecting no prying eyes from the desert. Ralph focussed in on her and he began to laugh.

"Go on honey, give me a good show, that's it gal!" he said, as she removed her bra and began to apply body cream to her arms and breasts, arching her neck as she did so.

Ralph couldn't contain himself anymore and he took several swigs of Jim Beam and slithered down the slight rocky incline towards the block. He had had enough. This gal needed a man, a real man. He, Ralph Adams was just that man.

He slowly and quietly opened the main door, made his way down the corridor slowly past half open doors to the boys' rooms. He needed no directions, the smell of female perfume was enough to guide him to his prey.

Martin's head was spinning and he was hopping mad. The kidnapping was on every news programme and he still couldn't contact No Name. His nerves were jagged and raw, and he prowled around the RV swigging more and more tequilla. Grabbing his jacket, he put it on against the cool evening air and went to look for Ralph. They had to talk and think about this situation. It had to get sorted out; it damned well had to. He walked into the rocky area in front of the buildings with a flashlight in his hand moving it slowly over the ground in front of him, shouting Ralph's name in a low voice. He scoured the rocky outcrops and at first saw nothing, and then something flashed. When he reached it he saw that it was an empty bottle of Jim Beam. He took stock of the situation and stood and surveyed the area. Then he caught sight of a light in the female part of the accommodation block.

"Oh no!" he muttered to himself and he ran towards the building.

Martin entered the accommodation block and crept quietly past the boys' rooms. He looked into Ginny's room her light was on, but she wasn't there. Then he stood outside Jo Anne's room.

There was no sound. He opened the door slowly. As he did so, he saw Ralph sitting at the foot of the bed. Ralph turned slowly and when he saw Martin he gave a crooked smile and shrugged.

"It was an accident man, we were sorta, er, rompin' an' she kinda fell and, well..." His voice tailed off as he waved an unsteady arm at the bed.

Martin opened the door wider and saw Jo Anne's body lying face up, naked, on the bed. Her head lolled to one side and her neck appeared to be broken. There were purple bruises on her breasts and thighs. He entered and closed the door, snarling at Ralph.

"Jeez, Ralph, you've been drinkin' 'n snortin' that stuff again, haven't you? How did this happen?"

As Ralph began to mumble an explanation of sorts, the door burst open and Matt burst in.

"Hi, Jo Anne, can I borrow…" his words fell short.

Out of basic instinct, Martin turned, grabbed him by the collar and smacked him across the head with the heavy flashlight. Matt fell heavily to the floor.

Martin looked down at the body as he quietly closed the door. He bent closer and lifted Matt's head, and then put his fingers on the boy's neck to feel a pulse. There wasn't one.

Ralph turned to Martin and half smiled, "We got one each man!"

"Madre de Dios!" Martin replied, "As if things weren't bad enough already."

Ralph looked perplexed. "Whadya mean buddy?"

Martin explained about Kinz's heart attack, the frenzy on the news and not being able to get through to No Name. Ralph's face changed from 'dumb-don't-care-druggie' to a snarling angry animal. He jumped up and prowled around.

"I damned well told you. Didn't I?" and he glared at Martin, "There's a plot here that we don't know about and we are the patsies. We're the guys who failed in Pakistan. We're gonna be set up. Duped. Dumped. I bet our faces will be spread all over the place soon, newspapers, TV, and then we'll be surrounded and taken out. Damn. No Kinz and no Mr No Name, just us playin' baby sitters."

Ralph's eyes were red with rage and he paced the room scratching his scalp hard with his fingers like a mangy dog, repeating: "I just knew it."

Martin was getting wound up now. He sat, as Ralph paced, clenching and unclenching his fists. Both of them groped mentally for an exit strategy. Then the germ of an idea began to form and be articulated and they both became calmer and more coherent. The plan was cold, clinical and comprehensive. When they planned like this they were formidable and very, very dangerous.

"So Kinz and No Name wanted a pretend terrorist outrage and we're the patsies," Martin said grimly. "Well my amigo, seems to me like we need to give them a real terrorist atrocity. Let's see how they will explain that."

"I'm with you bro. What's the play?" Ralph said.

"Time to terminate, with extreme prejudice, all the assets. Burn this shithole down and head to Mexico in the RV. I've got amigos in the Juarez Cartel. They'll look after us."

"Roger that!" Ralph said.

The silence of the moonlit night was broken by a scream. Clem sat up and Ginny pulled away from his warm body and gave him a lazy gaze.

"What was that?" she said.

"Someone screamed." said Clem.

"The wolf?" asked Ginny.

"No, it was different, sounded human. We'd better find out what's going on."

"I'm scared Clem."

"Here, take my hand. I'll protect you. Probably just Jo Anne getting spooked."

Together they carefully walked down the slope towards the lights of the buildings. Clem stopped in his tracks, putting his hand across Ginny's mouth.

They couldn't believe their eyes. Under the glare of the entrance light, Martin and Ralph were standing over the bodies of Jon and Walt. Ralph held a gun. Martin his Bowie knife. Martin bent down and seized Jon's hair and pulled his head up. He stabbed the knife into Jon's neck and vigorously sawed through the flesh and bone. Blood, black in the moonlight spilled out of the gaping cut. With a final slash, Martin severed Jon's head and tossed it aside. He passed the knife to Ralph who used a similar level of butchery skill to hack off Walt's head. He wiped the knife on Walt's shirt front and passed it back to Martin, who in return gave him back his gun.

Ginny's eyes were bulging with terror and Clem was having trouble suppressing her scream with his hand. He felt sick and feared he was going to pass out. His hand slipped from Ginny's mouth and she howled.

Martin and Ralph turned instantly towards the sound and Martin shone his flashlight in their direction. Clem pulled Ginny to the ground and covered her mouth again. He whispered. "You've got to be quiet, Ginny. If you scream we're dead. Can you keep silent. Secret Squirrel? Ginny nodded.

Ralph called out. "It's okay, Ginny and Clem. There's been a bit of an accident that's all. C'mon over here, 'sokay, c'mon now?"

Clem put his arm around Ginny and got her to crawl alongside him back the way they had come. Ralph lost his temper, swore, raised his gun and fired; the shot missed Clem's feet by inches spraying stone splinters everywhere. Clem's adrenaline was flowing like electricity through his veins and he grabbed Ginny's hand and shouted, "Run!"

They crouched and ran down the slope to the road and on towards the mine. They had the initial advantage of running towards the lighter side of the ridge and ran as fast as they could, their legs wobbly like jelly and hearts beating like steam engines. Soon the entrance to the mine came into sight and, without changing step or slowing, Clem bundled Ginny through the crash barriers.

After a few yards, feeling their way quickly in the pitch dark, their steps faltered as they came across rocks and debris. Clem fell and cracked his shin against a barrier and he yelled in pain. He rubbed it furiously and prepared to move on.

Ginny had by now regained her wits.

"Do you remember that map Martin showed us. There was a safety barrier marked on it. He said it was too dangerous to go any farther into the mine," she said.

Then they heard Martin and Ralph arrive at the entrance about fifty yards behind them. They had no choice, they would have to go on and quickly.

Ginny said: "Can you feel the railway tracks with your feet? If we follow them they will take us all the way to the winding room."

"Let's go!" whispered Clem. And they both hurried through the blackness

Ralph and Martin's progress was slow because they were carefully checking the walls of the tunnel with torches looking for hiding places. Ralph was getting angry.

"Damn. They could be anywhere. I can't see a damned thing outside this damned torch beam."

Martin put his hand on Ralph's shoulder and squeezed it; they both listened carefully for a few minutes, but there were no sounds. Then he said quietly still squeezing Ralph's shoulder, "Let's go back to the main entrance. This is the only way in and the only way out. Slowly, slowly, catchee monkey."

Ralph shouted: "Okay, let's get outta here, I've had enough."

They made their way back to the entrance and Martin told Ralph to bring up the Nissan so that they could stake out the entrance. It would get cold tonight and they had to think hard about how to locate the teenagers.

Clem and Ginny saw the light of their pursuers torches recede.

"Do you really think they are going?" said Ginny.

"No, I don't, but let's rest here a while," he whispered, and they sat and held each other tightly.

"What the hell is going on?" said Clem, putting his hands to his head. "I just can't believe it. One minute we are all friends and everything is going so well, and the next, two of us are dead and we are running for our lives. This is just crazy. We've got to find Matt and Jo Anne."

Ginny held him tighter. "We've got to look after ourselves first."

After a few moments, Clem said, "Ginny, you remembered the layout of the mine. How did you do that?"

She replied, "I developed a good memory technique at high school to get the grades I needed."

Clem was beginning to feel his muscles contract. "Ginny," he said, "we'd better move. If they come back, we will be too cold and numb to find our way to the winding room."

Ginny agreed and they stood up. After rubbing each other hard to get their circulation flowing, Ginny led the way along the tunnel.

What was it that Martin had said? The old mine owner had hanged himself in the winding room. The winding room was deep under the hill. It would need ventilation. The air from this tunnel wouldn't be enough. That was it!

"Clem. There's got to be an airshaft in the winding room. It could be a way out," she said.

"Yeah, could be," said Clem. His voice sounded tired and dispirited and she realised that he was now in a state of shock having been so positive earlier. It was now her turn to be strong and she had to encourage him.

They made their way gingerly down the tunnel, tripping over small boulders and then after about fifty yards blundered into a wall of rocks and sand. Ginny gripped Clem's hand in fright.

"Oh, God it's blocked," she said.

Groping along the base of the rubble from one side of the tunnel to the other, they fruitlessly sought a gap. Then they felt upwards towards the roof of the tunnel. After a few moments, Clem stopped.

"It's no good, we can't get through," he said dejectedly.

"No, we must keep on. Stop a minute," said Ginny and they both stopped still in the darkness, so total it was intimidating.

"What?" Clem said.

"I can feel air. A waft of air, coming through the rocks. Help me pull this boulder away."

Together they prised the boulder away and Clem put his arm into the gap. "Yep. It's a definite breeze and there seems to be lots of space back here. Let's clear some more of this rubble away."

They worked furiously, ignoring the pain of torn fingernails and scratches. Soon they had created a hole through the wall the size of a TV.

Ginny's heart sank. They were going to have to crawl through the hole. "I can't do it," she said, "I can't stand small enclosed spaces."

Clem knew that he had to pull himself together. Ginny had to cope with the ordeal that was surely their only possible way out. "I know how you feel, I am claustrophobic too. But we have to do this if we are to survive." He held her hand tightly, "It's different when you are with someone else. I'll go first, and you follow but only when it's safe. What do you say?"

Ginny took a deep breath. After about a minute she said, "Okay. I'll do it. But promise you'll keep talking to me."

"Promise," said Clem, holding her hand tightly.

Clem snaked his way into the hole and Ginny felt his shoes disappear. Then she heard his voice. "It's okay. There's room enough to crawl. Just follow me."

Ginny clambered into the hole. She winced as her elbows grazed sharp rocks but crawled forward. "Clem?" she whimpered.

"Attagirl! It's a bit more of a squeeze ahead but the breeze is getting stronger," Clem said.

Ginny crawled on. Her heart was racing and her mouth was dry with fear, then to her horror she felt the roof of the tunnel close in on her buttocks. As she lowered her hips, her head went up and banged against rock. She began hyperventilating.

I gotta get out of here Clem, I gotta get out!" she said hysterically, and began to lose control.

"Wait, Ginny, I can see something," Clem said. "It's a bit of grey, but I'm sure it's light," he paused for a second trying to adjust his eyes, "Ginny, it is light, it really is, I'm not joking."

Ginny slowed her breathing. Then she felt Clem's hand on hers. "We're through," he said. "Just another few feet. Take my hand." She made herself as small as she could and crawled forward. Then suddenly there was light and Clem's dirty but smiling face.

She emerged from the tunnel into a large chamber in which stood a rusty steel winding frame and wheel. The cause of the light was a bright silver beam that looked as though it came from a large search light, shining down from the roof of the chamber onto the ground, spreading out as though it was liquid. Looking closer she could see that the light was funnelled down a shaft. A ventilation shaft, that could be reached by a metal ladder, was suspended above the winding frame.

"We did it," said Clem, "we did it," and he held Ginny in his arms

For the first time since they left the pool, Ginny felt safe. She held him tightly and said, "We did too."

Clem looked up and assessed the route out. "How's your head for heights, Ginny?"

"Fine, but I'm gonna need a rest first."

Clem saw a pile of sacking on the floor and took Ginny over to it. The sacking was bone dry and smelly, but it would do for a bed. He made Ginny as comfortable has he could and rested her head on his lap. She closed her eyes and was soon asleep.

Her face looked beautiful in the dim light and he realised then and there, that he was falling in love with her. He wanted to protect and keep her safe. He brushed her left cheek gently with his fingers and slowly caressed her neck. He then glided his hand ever so softly down over her breasts and let it rest to feel her heartbeat. She half opened her eyes and smiled: "You're not gonna take advantage of a girl in distress now are you Clem Johnson?"

Clem grinned. "If I thought for one moment that I had the energy ma'am, I would do just that."

Chapter 13

E-Day minus 21

Quantock had not had a good day. He had mislaid the cell phone he used to call Martin, and was now hurrying back to his apartment to search for it there. He did not lose important items like phones, guns or wallets. What the hell was going on? To make matters worse, Hammond was putting obstacles in the way of his attempts to build an effective team to co-ordinate the manhunt for the missing teenagers. His boss seemed determined to ignore the President's wish for Quantock to direct the operation as he saw fit and was trying to regain control of it. He was trying to stuff Quantock's team with stooges who would report every move back to him. Then came news of Kinz's heart attack and Quantock felt genuinely upset and worried for his friend.

When he got home he searched the jackets and coats in his closet. The cell phone was in the coat he had worn the day before. And the battery was flat. He cursed. Then he remembered he hadn't taken his meds today or yesterday or the day before and could be suffering withdrawal side effects. After plugging his phone in to charge, he went to the bathroom and found the packet for his pills and swallowed one, then another and finally a third for luck. Then he checked the cell phone. There were a dozen missed calls and several messages and texts. The texts got increasingly frantic. As he listened to the first few messages he could sense Martin's anxiety clearly building. Then his heart sank as he listened to the last one. Martin's voice was slurred and he sounded almost hysterical.

"Okay, man. So, this is fucking it. If Kinz is dead, who did it I wonder, eh? You ain't answerin' calls. This is it then. It doesn't matter anyway. It's all gone wrong Mr No Name and it ain't my fault. See you in hell, man, see you in hell!" Then the call abruptly ended.

Quantock's stomach turned to ice. He quickly called the airport and booked a flight to Tucson and a taxi to the airport. Then he changed into a lumberjack shirt and blue jeans and laced up a pair of sturdy walking boots. His gun holster went over the shirt. A leather jacket completed the ensemble. He checked that the magazine of his Glock was full and slipped the gun into the holster under his armpit. Extra ammo and a silencer went into a small leather rucksack, alongside a map, cell phone charger, some toiletries and his medication. He then did a final check on cell phones, credit cards and cash and left the apartment.

After showing his FBI badge to airport security and getting the okay to carry his gun onto the plane, he was in the air to Tucson. He wondered what the hell he would find.

As dawn broke, Martin was snoring loudly in the back of the Nissan, parked about ten yards from the entrance to the tin mine. Ralph was hung-over, edgy and angry and hadn't slept at all. He wasn't prepared to wait any longer. The teenagers were in that mine and he was gonna get them out – smoke 'em out in fact. He had seen a stack of timber and brushwood nearby and got out of the vehicle and began to pile it inside the entrance to the mine. After about forty-five minutes he had a substantial amount of combustible debris such as wooden pallets and boxes in place and he took a can of petrol and sprinkled the contents onto it. Minutes later he threw in a match and it burst into flames.

Martin woke up with a start. "What the hell are you doing?"

"Smokin' 'em out buddy, and if they ain't smoked out then they'll end their days chokin' to death."

Martin didn't disagree. He had nothing else to offer as a suggestion. If it didn't work, then perhaps the fire would bring down rocks at the entrance and this would trap the teenagers and give them a head start to get away undetected. They didn't just need to get across the border and into Mexico, but had to go deep into the country, avoiding the police so as to hole up with his cartel contact.

Ralph watched the flames and realising what could be achieved he quickly grabbed a couple of old tyres lying alongside the road and threw them on too. Then he got some more and added them to the flames. They burned fiercely then gave off thick black smoke that swirled and disappeared into the mine – surprisingly quickly he thought.

Clem and Ginny climbed up a sequence of ladders on the winding frame. They reached a narrow platform above the winding wheel. A suspended ladder led up into the ventilation shaft. Clem tested it for stability. "Ladies first," he said. Ginny smiled. She grasped a rung of the ladder and began to climb, fluidly and surely.

Clem was about to follow when he realised that his nostrils were itching. Then he saw flecks of black material floating up the airshaft. Looking down he saw smoke billowing through the tunnel they had escaped through. He hurried up the ladder.

Ginny had reached the top of the shaft which was enclosed inside a square wooden frame. The sky was above. The problem was the ladder did not extend the five feet needed to reach the top of the frame. She looked for handholds. The frame was made of old planks and there were gaps between them. She put her fingers in a gap and pulled. The wood disintegrated in her hand. Then she smelled smoke and heard Clem coughing underneath her. He shouted: "They're trying to smoke us out. You've got to get up and over."

"I can't," Ginny said. "There's no way up."

"God, it's getting thicker, quick Ginny, quick!"

Ginny felt tears pricking her eyes and panic rising. They were trapped. She screamed.

Two faces suddenly appeared above her. The light was behind them so she couldn't make out the identities. She felt herself fainting. Then she found herself held by a strong male arm and being hoisted out of the shaft and wanted to scream with fear. But the arm did not belong to Ralph or Martin. At the top, her rescuer released her and she crumpled to the ground. She saw a second younger man in a red bandanna descend by rope into the shaft and he was soon assisted by his companion. In appearance, they looked like Native Americans. What tribe she did not know; but despite their western dress of jeans, boots and denim shirts, they were Indians for sure.

The young man with the red bandanna popped out of the shaft. And then Clem's head appeared. His older friend helped him pull him out.

Ginny scrambled to her feet and ran over to hug Clem. The two Native Americans let them have some space and coiled their climbing ropes. The young man with the bandanna then produced a bottle of mineral water and offered it to Ginny and Clem. They took it gratefully and between them drained the contents.

"I am Ira and this is Frankie. We are Tohono O'odham. That means desert people." He smiled warmly and added, "Before you ask, we both have degrees from US universities and help to run business ventures in our community, namely casinos and tourist goods. We don't carry tomahawks or wear feathered head-dresses, unless it's a party and then it's obligatory! Oh, and we regularly climb up and down these kinds of shafts for fun, we abseil our way around these ridges, so we are quite good at ropes."

"This early in the morning?" Clem asked.

"It's the best time to catch snakes," Frankie said. He opened a tote bag hanging from his waist. "Want to see?"

Clem jumped back in fright. "Nooo. I'm shit scared of snakes."

"Can I see?" said Ginny, too enthusiastically for Clem's liking.

Frankie pulled a Diamond Back rattlesnake out of the bag and dangled it. "We use the skin and the rattle to make and sell craftwork for the tourists. The mine is full of them, so there is plenty to go around."

Clem looked back in horror at the mineshaft, from which a plume of smoke was now emerging. "Can we get outta here?" he pleaded.

Ginny said: "Excuse my friend's rudeness. He's Clem Johnson and I'm Ginny Grivas and we're in big trouble. Can you help us?"

She quickly and briefly outlined their predicament, as Clem nervously scoured the surrounding desert.

Ira and Frankie nodded gravely, then Ira said: "Okay. Come with us. We'll get you somewhere safe." They set off at a brisk pace, down the ridge away from the mine. Frankie took point. Ira carefully covered their backs.

As they scrambled down the slope, dawn gave way to day and golden rays of light seemed to flash up into the sky like fingers of gold. The dim light gave way to increasing sunshine and the long shadows cast by the cacti gave them the appearance of soldiers marching to war across the craggy and barren desert. The light also picked out lonely patches of Joshua trees that seemed to huddle together as if discussing the plight of the two young people. It was beautiful and yet eerie.

Walking through a patch of tall cacti, they emerged onto a track on which was parked a Toyota pickup truck. Frankie jumped into the driving seat while Ira helped Clem and Ginny into the back of the vehicle.

"We will now go to San Xavier, our reservation. We can settle down and smoke a peace pipe before having a pow-wow!" said Ira, clumsily trying to lighten the mood, but Clem and Ginny were now in each other's arms and too tired for humour – or anything else for that matter.

Martin and Ralph stood mesmerised watching the fire, drinking bottled water to quench their thirst.

"That ought to do it," Martin said. "Let's go back to the hacienda and clean up."

They gathered the teenagers' belongings together and stored them with the expensive video equipment in the RV – they would sell what they could in Mexico. Ralph drove the RV a distance from the buildings, then joined Martin inside the accommodation hut. They dragged the bodies of Matt and Jo Anne outside and dumped them alongside Walt and John. Martin took his Bowie knife and carefully cut through Matt's scalp to remove his hair. He dropped the bloody scalp on Jo Anne's naked body.

Martin went through the buildings with a can of gasoline, sloshing its contents on the most flammable items of furniture. He poured a trail of gas behind him until he reached the outside. Then he struck a match, lit the fuse trail and walked backwards to where Ralph was standing. There was a crump as the gas ignited and the windows filled with the orange of flame. Then a huge roar as the fire took hold. As they both walked towards the RV, Martin let out a curse. "Manda huevos! Ralph, look there!" he said and pointed up the ridge. "I'll be damned if that ain't the smoke we're making?"

A thin plume of black smoke rose into the dawn sky. They looked at each other and their thoughts were as one. There had to be an airshaft and, if it was easy to climb, then it was a way out. They ran to the Nissan.

The Toyota bumped north through the desert for an hour. Finally, a settlement came into view, comprising a large number of low adobe style buildings, some with large roofs as if to drain off the rain, and others without. In the middle of the settlement, Clem could make out a large white painted basilica-style church with twin towers with rounded edges, and a mixed white and terracotta brickwork centre.

Frankie saw him looking, leaned out of the window and shouted to him, "The White Dove of the Desert, the mission of San Xavier del Bac. You will love it."

Clem settled back. He was sure that they would, but what next?

Martin and Ralph drove the Nissan towards the plume of smoke. Their problem was that to reach the top of the ridge they had use a winding track that was narrow, fissured with large cracks and potholes and strewn with large boulders.

Eventually, they reached an area close to the now thinning smoke. Ralph and Martin ran up the hill. When they reached the top of the ridge they looked at the entrance to the airshaft. There were footprints all around it. It didn't take much deduction to see that the teenagers had been helped. Martin walked calmly to the edge of the shaft and saw deep fresh rope marks indented into the end of the wooden surround.

Ralph spoke first. "They got help, but from whom?"

Martin looked at the map. "My guess is that this wasn't hikers or tourists. They wouldn't be around so early in the morning. Must be locals. And the only locals around here are Indians or folk living in homesteads. He raised his binoculars to his eyes and scanned the landscape. There was nothing in sight. Then he looked back at the map. "Okay, buddy, then my guess is that it's Indians from a reservation. And the nearest is San Xavier, right here," and he stabbed the map.

Ralph trusted Martin's instinct. When they worked together, they worked in harmony and played hunches; they were good at that. It usually meant that someone would suffer in the end.

Martin continued: "There's a beauty spot here close to San Xavier and the highway. I think you should take the RV and park it up. Make it look like someone's camping. I'll drive the Nissan and pick you up. We then go to San Xavier and get the kids."

Ralph smiled. "Sounds like a plan."

Quantock landed at Tucson airport and got himself a hire car. The flight had been uneventful, but he was filled with foreboding. He drove quickly out into the desert.

As he approached the San Quiller tin mine he saw a big, black column of smoke, shaped like a twister, reaching high into the sky. He accelerated. On his left, he spotted a pile of smoking debris outside the entrance to the mine and a smaller column of smoke rising slowly from the ridge. Rounding the bend, he came to the site of the buildings. But there were no longer any buildings. Just a mass of throbbing-red, blackened wood and ash and twisted metal. The place had been incinerated. He got out of the hire car and felt the raw residual heat of the fire. It was like stepping into a furnace.

Through a haze of smoke, he saw bodies on the ground in front of the ruins. He moved forward as far as he could go and counted four bodies and two severed heads. He stumbled back towards the car and vomited violently.

He sat for a while sipping mineral water and tried to think. He listened again to Martin's slurred message on his cell phone. It became clearer. He had been stupid not to have the cell phone at the ready to answer any queries that Martin and his side-kick might have. Then Kinz's heart attack happened. The operatives panicked, got drunk and convinced themselves that they had been abandoned, perhaps set up as the fall guys. But why kill the kids and in such a brutal fashion? There had been nothing on their records to suggest this level of barbarism. There were four bodies. So, where and who were the other two? He needed help. And he needed it fast. He thought some more then dialled a number.

"This is Arab Blue. I need a deep cleaning team sent to the San Quiller tin mine south of Tucson immediately. You are going to need to chopper them in."

He then gave the map reference.

Quantock was a careful and thoughtful man. He drove to the mine entrance and inspected the smoking debris. He then drove up to the ridge and found the highest vantage point so that he could get a 360-degree view of the terrain. Then he took out his binoculars and searched the horizon.

Martin and Ralph must have had at least a two-hour lead on him, perhaps more. Nogales on the Mexican border was only fifty miles away. If they were in Mexico, he was stuffed. Martin was a goddamn wetback with Lord knows how many criminal contacts in Mexico. But what would they do with the two kids? Keep them hostage until they were across the border and then kill then? Keep them hostage in Mexico for a ransom? That would be his worst nightmare. The Mexican press would have a field day if the truth came out. But why was he so sure that they had the kids? Where was the evidence?

The fire at the entrance to the mine shaft looked like an attempt to smoke someone inside the mine out. So perhaps the kids had run there to hide. And what about the other smoke? He strode over the ridge until he came to the shaft entrance hole. Only wisps of smoke were emerging now. He surveyed the ground around the hole and saw footprints and fresh rope marks on the wood surround. Goddamn! Had Martin and Ralph got to them? Or had the kids got help from someone else to get them out of the mine? Martin and Ralph needed the kids. Dead or alive.

"This is Arab Blue. I need a dragnet put around a section of the Arizona Sonoran Desert and the highway to the Mexican border. Take these details. Suspects. Two males. One Caucasian. Six feet tall. Two hundred and forty pounds. Age thirty-five. Texas accent..."

Frankie drove the Toyota truck to within half a mile of the San Xavier mission and stopped by the side of the road. He got out, went to the back and said, "Okay you guys. If you are in a lot of trouble, then I guess the fewer people who know you are in the reservation the better. Get under this tarpaulin, just for a short while, okay?"

Clem and Ginny obeyed without question and the vehicle then continued on its way into the reservation. Curiosity got the better of Clem and he peeked out from underneath the cover. The Mission church was magnificent, like a fairy tale Moorish palace. It had two towers over one hundred feet, each was bleached white like the main body of the building. The middle portion was, however, made out of a kind of clay or terracotta material on which there was considerable design work. Each of the towers and the central portion had a black balcony. In front of the Mission was a large wall enclosing a paved area. The hard sand and clay surface around the Mission, dotted with coarse leafed bushes and trees of a small or medium height gave the building superiority over the landscape. There were many other whitewashed buildings as well as a large number of adobe dwellings, some with large roof structures that would provide shelter from the sun or allow heavy rain to flow off easily, whilst others were simple square or oblong structures. It was fascinating –- and not a tepee in sight.

Frankie drove on past the Mission for about fifty yards and turned into a large secluded courtyard behind what seemed to be a modern public building. He and Ira jumped out and went to the back of the vehicle.

Clem pulled the tarpaulin to one side and was surprised to see that Ginny was fast asleep. He shook her awake slowly and gently. She awoke and gazed up at him, then took his hand and smiled.

Frankie helped them down and into the rear entrance of the building. "This is the tourist information centre and gift shop," he said. "Open every day of the year except Christmas Day and Easter. We get some two hundred thousand pilgrims and visitors a year."

Ira disappeared through a beaded curtain behind the sales counter.

The store was a treasure trove of handicraft. There was a variety of pottery: plates, shallow bowls and square glazed tiles as well as large pots of different designs. Some of the patterns were of butterflies or star shapes, but most of the objects had a circular maze design, with a small wedge shape inserted from top to middle with a human shape in it. Ginny was fascinated by it and wondered about its significance. Most of the pottery and ceramic colours were of a blue tinge. Artefacts made of snakeskin, purses, wallets and rattles sat next to elaborate beadwork belts. There were some robes and feathered hats, but it was obvious that these were simply tourist items. Not so the blankets and rugs that were obviously handmade and looked as though they were made of heavy woollen material.

An old lady dressed in a simple fawn coloured shift with a face like a pickled walnut swished through the bead curtains behind the counter. Frankie spoke to her in their language and she gave a toothless grin. He talked some more and she looked concerned, very concerned. Then she went over to Ginny and put an arm on her shoulder.

Frankie smiled and said, "This is my grandmother and she will look after Ginny, I promise you. Clem, come with me and we can sort out somewhere for you to hide and make an escape plan."

Clem walked with Frankie toward a nearby adobe. Suddenly, Frankie stopped and grabbed Clem, pushing him roughly behind a wall just as a four-by-four rounded the corner. It cruised past with two men in it who were looking left and right. Then it stopped by the tourist centre.

Martin and Ralph got out of the vehicle and Ralph marched straight into the tourist shop without pausing. Thankfully, the old lady had been looking out of the window and saw Frankie give her a quick wave and worried gaze, which was enough for her to realise that the two men were after Ginny and Clem. Without thinking twice, she turned to Ginny and made her lie down by the rugs which she piled over the top of her; then she sat on top of them.

Ralph burst into the centre. "Hi there old squaw," he said with a sickly grin, "I'm looking for two good friends a boy and a girl, you understand me. Huh?"

The old lady beamed at him and showed several gaps in her teeth, but said nothing.

"You understand what I'm sayin'?" Ralph repeated menacingly and he walked towards her.

She just smiled at him, beaming toothlessly. Then without ceremony she raised the left side of her bottom and broke wind noisily. Ralph recoiled.

"Ugh, you miserable old hag. Jeez man, I bet you're a beauty in bed!" He turned and quickly made for the door, exiting without shutting it. The old lady heard his footsteps walk back to his vehicle and then saw him stand by the front of it, obviously waiting for his companion.

Martin came around from behind the tourist centre and joined Ralph. "The vehicle in the compound at the rear is a Toyota pickup truck. Cream coloured," Martin said softly, and he passed Ralph the registration that he had written on a piece of paper. "The engine is warm and it's covered in desert dust. They are here somewhere buddy, but where I do not know."

Frankie walked up to Martin and Ralph. "Hi there, can I be of any assistance?"

Martin took the lead. "Why yes, young sir, thank you very much. We need to find the whereabouts of two young people. You see, they've run away from their parents who are now very worried about them both. They are causing a lot of distress, but hey buddy, you know what kids are like, eh? Anyway, me and my friend have been taken on to look for them. The last sighting we had was up at the San Quiller tin mine. Have you seen them? The boy is called Clem and he is medium height, a hundred and fifty pounds, fair hair and is dressed in a denim blue shirt and jeans. The girl is called Ginny, she is about five foot six, slim build, with auburn hair and dressed in a white blouse and blue jeans."

"Are you police?" Frankie asked.

"No, we're private detectives. Look, if you do get to hear anything call this number eh? We're staying locally." Martin looked left and right. "There's a very good reward for information, you know what I mean. The parents are very wealthy and keen to make sure that their children are safe and sound. You would too if they were your kids, wouldn't you?"

As they were speaking, a coach pulled up outside the tourist centre and a party of elderly tourists descended, cameras at the ready.

Frankie took the piece of paper with the cell phone number on it. "We'll get some of our folk to look for them sir, and if we find them we will call you straight away, you betcha. But as you can see we get a lot of visitors."

Martin and Ralph returned to the Nissan and drove away past the Mission building and onto the main road back to the desert. A mile down the road Martin stopped the vehicle and turned to Ralph.

"We're gonna have to watch the reservation from here. There is only one large road out of here. If they're confident that we have gone on our way, then they may be stupid enough to use the same vehicle. Let's hunker down and do what we are good at. If we get no joy in twenty-four hours we take our chances and run for the border come what may. What do you say?"

Ralph grimaced. "Can't we just tour around the reservation making offers of hard bucks for information?" he said.

Martin shrugged: "We could, but my guess is that these people are highly suspicious of authority and any outsiders and more likely to take sides with those being chased. We've sown the seeds of financial reward, maybe we will get a call maybe we won't. But I reckon our best bet is to be patient."

"Okay," Ralph said. "Let's find a good observation point."

Ginny hugged the old lady and they both laughed at her last-minute tactics to avoid Ralph's attentions. Ira came out from the back to serve the customers from the tourist coach. The old lady took Ginny's hand and took her through into a back office, which had desks, computers and filing cabinets. Boxes of stock and piles of rugs occupied most of the free space. The old lady sat down with Ginny on the pile of rugs. By dint of sign language and some English words they chatted. Ginny took off a silver ring that her mother had given her for her sixteenth birthday. She gave it to the old lady, who smiled. The old lady got up and retrieved a large carpetbag from under a desk, which she brought back and opened. She indicated that Ginny should select something. The contents were a mixture of soaps, necklaces, old coins and small carved models. But Ginny's eyes immediately fell on a small Nokia cell phone. Without hesitating she pointed to it and the old lady readily reached for it and then passed it to her with a broad smile.

Ginny pressed the keys to access the past calls and found that only one number had ever been called on this cell phone, it had Francis as the contact. It could have been a present from the boy so that they could keep in touch. It had a low charge. She kissed the old lady. She would call home – she simply had to. Her mother would be worried sick when the news of the massacre was discovered, as indeed it would be soon. Ginny punched in the numbers and got a connection. She wondered what she would say if it was her father. But it was her mother who answered. For a moment, she could say nothing and a big lump formed in her throat.

"Mom, it's me," she said almost gasping the words out.

Her mother choked back a scream. "Oh, honey, my little girl. Oh God. What's happening, we are so worried Ginny. Where are you?" She started crying.

"Mom, I can't talk for long. Listen. We started out on a mission to make a political video, like I said in the letter I wrote you. And…."

Her mother broke in, "What letter, I got no letter."

Ginny's heart sank. "But we all wrote letters to our parents it was a secret mission. Oh God, what a mess. Mom, the important thing is that we are safe and being looked after. Look, there is something terribly wrong with all this and I want you to promise me that you will not, repeat, not tell anyone outside the family of my call. I will call again, I promise Mom. I love you."

Her mother sobbed words that were barely audible, but sounded like 'I understand'. She started to talk again, but the signal started to crackle and then the phone went dead. The battery was out of power. Ginny bit her lip and tears welled in her eyes. The old lady looked at her with concern. Ginny waved the cell phone at her and said, "Please, cable, er, wire, charging," then she shook it as if it were empty, "please, I need to call my mom…"

Then she burst into tears.

The old lady jumped up. She took Ginny in her arms and cuddled her whilst Ginny cried like a baby. Then she went and retrieved a box of junk from under a desk. With a big broad smile on her face she brought out a cell phone cable and plug. Ginny squealed with delight and hugged her again. Soon the cell phone was being charged. Ginny would be able to use it again.

Ginny resolved not to tell Clem just yet about the phone call or the missing letter. He would be angry and anxious, unnecessarily so. For the moment, she would keep the information to herself. Something was terribly wrong. Why was the letter not delivered? Senator Randolph Kinz was such an honourable man, what was he up to? Why were their friends killed? But the most important question was: who could they trust?

Frankie came into the office. "Come, we go," he said. Ginny took the phone and charger and followed him outside. He led her to a small adobe building, through a narrow doorway into a room that was furnished with a pine sideboard, an Indian-style stool with three legs and a large brass bedstead with a massive mattress. Clem was fast asleep on the bed and snoring. Frankie left and Ginny joined Clem, snuggling up to his body and cuddling him.

They slept until early evening and were woken by a knock at the door. Ira came in. "Hi guys. We reckon that you ought to get out of here pronto. I want you to meet a very interesting guy, he's called Hobo Joe, he's an Apache would you believe? In the past we would be enemies. But today we are friends and if one man can get you to safety, it is Joe."

Ira beckoned behind him and a squat, stocky man entered the room. He was about sixty or seventy years old – it was hard to tell, his skin, wrinkled by the continuous attention of the desert sun and wind, an old shrivelled appple. He wore his long salt and peppper hair in a ponytail tied with a leather cord. His eyes sparkled and his smile was broad and encouraged even more wrinkles to appear in his face. He was dressed in a leather waistcoat and jeans, and wore cowboy boots. Around his neck, he had a leather and silver necklace studded with blue stones that shimmered in the light. It seemed to be quite special to him because he kept touching and stroking it throughout his conversations.

Ira introduced Hobo Joe as a man who travelled the railroads, but without paying. He would show them the way out of the desert.

Although his accent was thick and his language was peppered with a lot of slang and Apache expressions, there were no problems communicating with Joe, the only problem they had was stopping him from talking. He talked for some time about his antics on and off the Union Pacific and BNSF freight trains that travelled west to east from well beyond San Diego through to San Antonio and on to New Orleans. He described the many trains he had hopped on.

His eyes sparkled as he mentioned the locomotives, almost like long lost girlfriends.

When he finally paused, Clem looked at Ginny and smiled.

Hobo Joe noticed this and smiled back. "The way outta here for you two is to let me show ya how to get onto a slow-moving freight train, s'easier than you think. Then you only need to hang on until Benson town. It's a very large junction and the loco' will slow down. Once you know how to hop on, hopping off s'easy. Do it just before the loco reaches the station and you'll be able to walk into town without being seen. Benson 'tain't that big, has a population of p'raps, four thousand folks. Best of all though, it's smack on Interstate 10. Get yourself a hire car and you're goin' places pard." He smiled as though he had planned escapes all his life.

Clem turned to Ginny, but said nothing. She turned to him and raised an eyebrow. "Jeez, Clem. I got you to skinny dip and you get your own back by getting me to crawl through a hole in the ground, then up a steep shaft. Now you want to make me to jump on a train."

Clem laughed and turned to Hobo Joe. "I guess that means yes!"

Ira was good to them and gave them a hundred dollars in cash. They should pay it back when they could. Clem shook his hand and thanked him profusely and Ginny gave him a big hug. Luckily Clem still had his wallet with his driver's licence and other documents. Once away from San Xavier, they would hole up for a few days then head home. He hadn't really thought of a plan – he just wanted to get away from the desert and the murderers on their tail.

As it got darker Hobo Joe explained in detail what would happen. He showed them a map that highlighted a sharp curve in the rail track, which was at a beginning of a short incline and explained that they would jump on a the end of a freight car at that point.

Frankie brought Clem and Ginny two San Xavier waterproof hiking tops with fold away hoods and lined with wool, from the tourist shop. Each had a small motif on the top right side of the waterproof, of a man with a broad brimmed hat. Frankie explained that it was the priest who had founded mission in 1783, Father Eusebio Kino.

Hobo Joe went outside for a smoke. Clem sipped some hot tea and said, "Frankie, I really appreciate what you guys are doing for us. It's a far cry from what people think about Indians, you know, I mean, well, sorry but I know my friends would know nothing about you guys. Yet you are the indigenous people of America. You are a key part of our history."

Frankie smiled and tapped his mug with a spoon. "Yes, the Sonoran Desert has been our home since before Christopher Columbus. Despite what has been done to us, we have kept a strong sense of personal and cultural identity." He paused and drew a breath before continuing. "I brought my new learning and skills home from college, as other Native Americans have done, but nothing shakes my belief in my background and sense of being Tohono O'odham. We are Catholics. But our faith is flavoured with a lot of our ancient spiritual customs. You know something, our tribal view of wellbeing revolves around the spiritual harmony between individuals, family, the community and the land. The individual has never been the main focus. We reach decisions by consensus. The needs of the many outweigh the needs of the few."

Clem laughed. He held a palm out and split his fingers into a V sign. Frankie tried hard to suppress a smile. "Live long and prosper," Clem said dead pan.

Frankie laughed. "Oh okay, you got me. But Spock's Vulcan spirituality was based on Tohona O'odham."

"I believe you," Clem said with a broad grin. "Thousands wouldn't!"

Chapter 14

E-Day minus 20

It was approaching four in the morning and Martin was wide awake. Ralph was snoring. He wondered whether or not his plan would work. If it didn't they would have to run for it. But he couldn't be sure that they wouldn't be caught before they made it to their contacts in Mexico. The Mexican and US governments had an edgy relationship because of the lack of security on their borders, but when they got their act together, fleeing criminals were easily caught. On the plus side the Winnebago gave them perfect cover and they would be joining hundreds of snowbirds looking to spend the winter south of the Rio Grande. Nobody else, including No Name, knew about the RV. They might need to change their appearance, but scissors, clippers and hair dye could work wonders. Some window dressing provided by a pretty female hitchhiker or two could also help. All they had to do was to catch the kids, dispose of them and head south. And yet, Martin thought. The kids were worth money.

As he mused on his new insight, he noticed vehicle lights coming out of the reservation. He sat bolt upright, shaking Ralph with his right hand. Ralph snorted and woke up. "Wha's up?"

"Lights. Aha, as I hoped buddy," he said, as the cream coloured Toyota drove past them and down the road.

Martin turned on the engine, but not the lights and followed the Toyota. It was a moonlit night and he had to keep well behind the vehicle so as not to be noticed. They had taken the precaution of wetting the Nissan with a bottle of mineral water and covering it with dirt to cut down the reflection of their vehicle. A couple of miles on the Toyota stopped and after a while it turned around and headed back up the road at speed. Martin only just managed to reverse off the track and get out of sight before it passed them on its way back to the reservation.

Martin was confused. This was crazy – what were they up to? But as he looked closely he could only see one person in the Toyota: the driver. He was sure there were other passengers when it passed before. Clem and Ginny must have been in the back and they were now getting help from the passenger at the point the Toyota had stopped.

Martin started the engine again and set off slowly down the road to where he thought that the teenagers had been dropped off. He stopped the Nissan in a small lay by as close to the spot. They both got out and listened carefully. The Sonoran Desert was so quiet they could easily hear the faint sound of voices ahead and set off in pursuit.

Ahead of them, Hobo Joe was guiding Clem and Ginny between the cacti and brushwood. Luckily it made them hard to spot, as the landscape appeared speckled in the moonlight. In the distance, they heard the unmistakable sound of an approaching locomotive. Martin looked at Ralph and they instinctively knew what was being planned. They hurried through the rough terrain and made more noise than they should. Ralph grazed his hand on a nearby cactus and yelped.

Hobo Joe stopped dead in his tracks. He put his fingers to his mouth. "People come," he whispered.

"Where?" said Clem.

They waited, but the sound wasn't repeated. The Union Pacific locomotive came around the steep bend to their right, its headlights casting a harsh white light across the desert. It came slowly as it negotiated the bend and the gradient. Hobo Joe stood by the track and motioned them to watch him and follow his lead.

As the train came past he loped alongside, then as a gap appeared between two freight cars he pointed to a ladder with a step at the bottom of one of the trucks, he let this pass, and then he pointed to the next one. He was telling them that each one had such a ladder and foothold. Clem gave him the thumbs up and told Ginny.

Then Hobo Joe waited for the next truck and deftly hopped on, grabbing a rail with one hand and putting his foot on the step. It was easy to haul himself upright.

The train carried on at a slow steady pace.

Clem got Ginny to go first and to do the same as Joe had done following behind her as she ran alongside the trucks. He needn't have worried. She was fit and negotiated the manoeuvre with ease, although the soreness of her scratched hands proved excruciating. She looked back and he gave her a thumbs-up. Then he did the same.

When they were both safely on the train, holding on as hard as they could, Hobo Joe waved and yelled, and then he hopped off. The train took a few minutes to pass him completely and he watched as it disappeared into the distance. Then he sighed and turned around to go home.

Facing him were Martin and Ralph.

Clem and Ginny hung on tightly to the cold metal ladders as the train gathered speed towards Benson. They wished that they had gloves, but managed to console themselves that they were putting miles between them and Martin and Ralph. The journey only took thirty minutes, but it seemed like a lifetime. They were overjoyed to see the lights of the Benson rail junction come into view. Just as Hobo Joe had predicted the train slowed to walking pace and Clem shouted ahead to Ginny to get down.

They jumped from the train and despite falling a little awkwardly, Ginny got up and ran to Clem. "Another triumph, Clem. Aren't we the best?"

She kissed him passionately, a kiss which turned into a smouldering snog, and, as her and Clem's breathing quickened, she drew his hips to her pelvis.

The nearby Dragoon Mountains looked black against the dim light of the sun trying to crawl up into the morning sky. But Clem and Ginny had no time to take in the scenery as they made their way into Benson. It was six in the morning, lights were on in some of the houses and folks were just beginning to rise and take breakfast, but all Clem and Ginny wanted to do was to find a bed. Benson wasn't a large town. It was well known for its location near to the famous western town of Tombstone and being located on the rail intersection that acted as distribution hub for the metal ores of the local mines.

At the approach to Main Street, Clem and Ginny found a small and badly decorated budget motel with a neon sign flashing "We have vacancies". They entered the small and sad foyer and saw a tired looking reception clerk, a man in his late forties with unkempt hair that concealed a large bald patch. He was wearing wire spectacles that hung loosely on his small nose and dressed in an open necked beach shirt and appeared to be reading a travel brochure. Somehow coconut trees and surfers on the shirt seemed out of place in this

Western town. The clerk looked up indifferently, as if preferring not to see to them.

"Can I he'p you, son?" he said with a southern drawl.

"Yes sir, we'd like a room," said Clem.

The clerk leaned over the counter and looked around them. "Travellin' light?" he sneered, as he turned to Ginny looking longer at her body than was absolutely necessary.

Clem was angry and said in a strong voice, "Just a room and can we make it quick, buddy, we're mighty tired. Like, now, please?"

The clerk shrugged. He pushed the register towards Clem and slapped a cheap biro on top of the blank page.

Clem signed the register and thanked his lucky stars he still had his wallet with Ira's dollars, his credit cards and driver's license. After signing the register, Clem took the room key and walked Ginny to their room.

The room was shabby and smelled of stale cigarette smoke. There were ancient yellow nicotine-sweat stains on the pillow case. But to Clem and Ginny it was luxury. Ginny immediately shed her clothes and sat in the bath while it filled. She then sank back in the warm water. The feeling was out of this world, relaxing, sensuous and dreamily smooth – even if it had taken all the hotel sachets to get even a minimal level of suds in the water. The scratches and cuts on her hands and body hurt at first, but the irritation soon subsided. She heard Clem yell that he was going out for a while and didn't complain. It meant she could make another call to her mom. She lurched out of the bath, wrapped herself in a towel and fumbled in her jacket pocket for the cell phone. It took a while to ring and her mother answered.

"Mom?" she said.

"Ginny, oh Ginny, my God, are you all right?"

"Mom, yes of course, look I'm sorry that I got cut off yesterday. Clem and I are safe, okay?"

"But, honey, the man from the FBI said they found six bodies in a tin mine in Arizona and they were afraid you and Clem might have been…" She started sobbing and continued with difficulty. "Ginny, what's going on? Your father is confused at not being able to shout about your safety and wants to get to the bottom of things. You know pop? He's so happy you called and yet so upset, it means his depression is returning. Oh, God this is so stupid, me worrying about depression, what am I saying?"

The sound of her mom crying again made Ginny's heart ache.

"Mom, I'm just as confused as you are. We just need a little more time. Look Mom, this is getting so confusing and difficult. I don't know who to trust. Just believe that we are both okay. I promise I will call you when I can. I love you Mom."

Ginny was crying and didn't want to press the red disconnect button, but she had to and knew it.

Her mother was distressed, but agreed to end the call and await the next one. Ginny felt the goose bumps on her body and quickly hopped back into the hot tub of soapy water. She felt sad but knew that she had to be strong.

Clem walked the length of Main Street. The town was coming to life and he smelled the fresh coffee and fast food being prepared. As he passed a shop selling newspapers he saw the headlines for the San Pedro Valley News-Sun. "Missing teenagers sought by the FBI – still no news."

At the end of the strip of shops and cafés, he spotted a car hire office, which was just opening for business. It took him about thirty minutes to hire a Volvo station wagon giving his driver's licence and credit card details and a deposit for two day's hire. After checking the vehicle over, he drove it back to the motel and parked outside.

Hobo Joe held out for as long as he could, but Ralph and Martin were accustomed to meting out punishment that got results. Hobo Joe's head swam with pain and at its height, he saw the orange sun lighting the desrt all around him. His ancestors were standing some way off shouting encouragement to him, but he couldn't hear what they were saying. Then he could stand the piercing pain no longer. With tears in his eyes he muttered the word Benson. The light dimmed all of a sudden and there was a swirling feeling in his head as the pain stopped. The people in his vision stopped waving and encouraging him. They stood deathly still and slowly lowered their heads. Then they turned their backs on him and began walking away. Joe cried out to them to come back, wanted desperately to explain how agonizing it was, but they didn't listen. He felt the pain of humiliation and sorrow.

As he sobbed, Martin silenced him with a single deep cut to the throat with the Bowie knife. He wiped the knife on Hobo Joe's hat and walked with Ralph back to the Nissan. As they got in, Ralph held Hobo Joe's blue gemstone necklace up to the light. The moonbeams seemed to be attracted to its centre. Then he casually put it into his pants pocket, started the vehicle and headed for Benson. With luck on their side this should now not take that long to finish the job. Then they would be Mexico bound. He smiled to himself, perhaps his luck was changing after all?

Pure guesswork, good luck and a pliant hotel clerk made the job of locating Clem and Ginny an easy one for Martin and Ralph. Clem answered a quiet knock at the door and, before he could understand what was happening he was quickly overpowered by Martin. Ginny stood transfixed, wearing only her panties, holding a hair dryer. She looked in shock at Clem's face, reddening and swelling under the pressure of Martin's iron headlock.

"Now, honey. I'm not going to hurt you. Just sit back on the bed." Ralph said.

Ginny looked down and saw the Bowie knife in his hand. She dropped the air dryer and stumbled back, falling on the bed, with her legs splayed out. She scrabbled for a pillow to cover herself.

"Now, now, there's no need to hide your pretty body," Ralph said dropping onto the bed next to her. "I just want some fun."

Ginny felt an odd mixture of humiliation, embarrassment, vulnerability and fear. She was powerless. Her stomach was full of a thousand butterflies as the adrenaline drained out. She wanted to speak, but her throat was paralysed with fright and she felt her heartbeat hard against her chest.

Clem tried to object, but Martin only tightened his grip causing him great pain and no words came.

Ralph came closer, smiling and ran the blade of his knife up Ginny's thigh. "Ain't you the prettiest thing, lovely soft fair skin and you smell so good?"

He inched the point of the blade under the side of her panties and flicked upwards. The flimsy cotton sheared and he unbuckled his belt with one hand. "Now see, here's the deal. If you're nice to me, I'll be nice to you. You and your boyfriend will live. Then, you just need to come with me and Martin here on a little road trip. If you are not nice to me or if your boyfriend does anything stupid, you both will die. Understand?" Ralph brought the point of the knife up to Ginny's throat. Ginny nodded.

"Good. Now brace yourself, honey."

Ginny lay back, closed her eyes tight and opened her legs. Ralph put the knife on the bed and dropped his jeans and boxer shorts.

As he crawled on top of Ginny, the door was kicked open with a loud crash and a man in jeans and a lumberjack shirt stood there, gun with silencer in hand.

Martin released Clem and scrabbled in his waistband for his gun. The man shot him three times in the face and he toppled to the floor. Ralph grabbed his knife from the bed and tried to struggle to his feet, but his jeans were tangled around his ankles. As the man aimed his gun he flipped the knife so that he held the point and attempted to throw it.

His head dissolved in a hail of bullets showering the cowering Ginny with gore.

Then there was complete silence and no one moved an inch.

The man closed the door quietly and grabbed a bathrobe.

"Here kid, put this on," he said, throwing it to Ginny, then he unclipped the silencer from his Glock.

Ginny grabbed the dressing bathrobe gratefully with one hand, covering herself with the other and rushed to the bathroom crying. Clem got up slowly stroking his neck.

"By golly sir, am I glad to see you?"

"It's okay Clem. FBI. You're safe now. Relax. My name's Dan Quantock." He reached into his shirt and pulled out his badge. "These boys are real bad, but they won't be hurting anybody any more. I'll explain a lot more to you later, but not right now."

Ginny came into the room, her eyes red with tears and the bathrobe wrapped firmly around her. Quantock explained they needed to wait until the crime scene investigators arrived before he could take them to a place of safety, but in the meantime, he would book another room for Clem and Ginny, so they could relax while they waited.

Ginny was pleased to be able to get away from the bodies, but her relief was short-lived.

"Can I phone my mom please sir?" she asked.

Quantock looked awkward and quickly, too quickly, replied, "Oh, Ginny, don't do that yet. Your, er mom, well she knows that you are safe and well, and she will not have known about these guys chasing you. I'm just worried that they may have a tap on your home and there may be more bad guys around, you know what I mean? Besides, no sense in worrying her. You can call her a little later when I have you both in a real safe place. Let's just get you out of here first, eh?" With that, he disappeared to make arrangements for the extra room.

Ginny turned to Clem, put her fingers on his lips and said in a low voice. "Clem, I didn't tell you, and don't be angry, but I phoned Mom on the cell phone I got from Frankie's grandmother. I know you didn't want me to do it. It was a short call I promise. She said that she had been told by a FBI man that six bodies had been found at the tin mine, every one of them dead. I actually had to try hard to persuade her it was me calling her. He's lying Clem."

Clem held her tight and they didn't say anything for a while.

"But why is he lying? What does that mean?" she questioned.

Clem's face hardened. "It means we are still not safe and we both don't know what all this is about. You must not contact your mom again Ginny, the line will be tapped and if we cannot trust Senator Kinz or the FBI, then who the hell can we trust? We need to run again."

He went to the window and could see where the rental car was parked. He pulled Ginny close and whispered. "Ginny, see there, it's the car I hired earlier, the blue Volvo. We need to get to the car."

Quantock returned. Clem's whisper turned into a hurried kiss and then they parted as if embarrassed.

"Oh, gee, sorry. Er, the room is just down the hall, number eight. Let's get you outta here?" said Quantock.

Ginny went to dress and Clem moved across the bed avoiding the bodies. Together they went to room eight.

Quantock opened and closed the door for them but remained in the corridor. He made a call. "This is Arab Blue. Code Red. I have an extra job for the cleaners in Benson. Send them to The Budget Motel on North San Pedro Street, just before you get to Main Street. Two pieces of rubbish to be disposed. Also, I have two items to be brought back to the San Quiller Mine and disposed of without delay."

The cleaners were good. They were professional and absolutely discrete. Every department could use them, but only through selected contacts; Quantock had kept his old codes and numbers. The feral Blackwater boys had to be eliminated, but he was not going to sully his hands with the deaths of the two remaining teenagers. He felt bad about that, but what had to be done, had to be done. If they got to talk to the authorities or the media, then the whole story would come out and he risked being implicated. He turned to the door of number eight and knocked before he entered, then opened the door and smiled.

"Don't want to catch you two a kissin' now," he said and laughed almost apologetically. "The crime scene investigators are on their way and we should be able to get you home very soon."

Ginny looked up and smiled. "Oh, thank goodness for that, sir. Listen, I wanna thank you so much for saving our lives. I was real scared I can tell you."

Quantock noticed that Clem looked more cheerful and relieved. He was sad that things would have to pan out the way they would. But at least they were cheerful and he knew that professionals would do the job quickly and cleanly. If killing could be called clean that is. They would not see it coming and there would be no distress.

"That's okay now. It's all in a day's work," he said. "Why don't you guys get some rest now?"

Ginny jumped up. "No sir, no. I am really hungry. I could murder a burger and fries and four quarts of Coke!" she said adding: "Oh don't say no. I need to get out of this motel if only for just an hour or so and I'm starving. You do understand, don't you? Please, please can we go, sir?"

Quantock hesitated for a moment then, as expected, said, "No. That's too dangerous at the moment until I get back up. Tell you what, you stay here and I'll go out to Micky Dees."

Clem and Ginny looked at each other. Clem nodded.

Quantock locked the door of the motel room on his way out. Clem immediately ran to the window on the other side of the room and wrenched it open. He helped Ginny through and followed. They crept around the back of the motel and checked the front car park. There was no one about. Clem indicated to Ginny to stay where she was and ran to the rental car. He got in and reversed, holding the passenger door open for Ginny. She clambered in and he drove slowly out onto the street. Soon they were on Interstate Highway 10 and driving out of Benson. Clem kept his speed within limits, not wanting to attract attention or get arrested for speeding, but it was a strain. All the time his feet itched to floor the gas pedal but he kept his composure. They were soon heading east along the highway, which was bordered by arid and dusty land on either side with the skyline broken only by the small blue-brown frames of the

Dragoon mountain range to the northeast.

"Why are we heading east?" Ginny asked.

Clem smiled. "Because anyone sensible would head west to Tucson and go to the airport. I used my credit card at the car hire place and Quantock is bound to get details of the car. He'll put out an APB and if I were him I'd concentrate resources around Tucson."

"But why east?"

"I'm not heading east," Clem said. "We're going north and then west. We're going to visit dear old Uncle Kinz in his hacienda in Phoenix to ask him some questions. Highway 191 coming up soon should take us there."

"What makes you think he'll be there?"

"Look at the signs in the fields and the billboards with his name on them. He's in an election. Of course he'll be home."

Quantock was sore as hell. The teenagers had outsmarted him and that didn't happen often. He was messing up left right and centre. All the instincts and sharp sense of judgement which had made him a good G-Man had deserted him. He had been so confident about the capture that he had greenlighted the press release on the murder of all six kids. Soon the news would be all over America and the world.

The deep clean team arrived and Quantock shared out the burgers, fries and sodas he had bought earlier. He explained that one part of the job had already been sorted and there were just two items of rubbish to deal with. The team did the job rapidly and methodically. The hotel receptionist deferred to them, giving up the hotel register without demur and Quantock took out a penknife, opened it slowly and then cut out the page with Clem's name on it. He would also arrange a cancellation of the bank card payment so that there was no trace of it having been used. Luckily the hotel clerk was so lacklustre that he couldn't remember the name the room was booked under. Quantock explained that two kids had been part of a minor drugs ring and that they had been apprehended earlier and arrested. The two men who had come and gone the previous day were small town crooks looking to exact revenge for non-payment for the last drug consignment. They too had been arrested. He passed the clerk an envelope containing fifty-dollar bills.

"Now, sir, this is for your co-operation. The FBI is generous to people who help us sort out the bad guys in our country," he smiled broadly and the greasy-haired clerk's eyes widened at the sight of the cash. "But, sir, I need to be straight with you now."

His eyes narrowed and he leaned forward and looked directly into the clerk's face.

"If another soul, anyone, should get to hear of what went on here, then we can get very, very angry. You understand what I'm sayin'?"

The clerk paled and nodded.

Quantock reached out and patted his cheek. Then he turned and left the hotel, walking to his car. Once inside his vehicle he dialled his phone. "Ah, hello, this is Dan Quantock FBI, can I speak to John Spielman, yes that's it, Spielman. He's an old buddy of mine. Thank you, yes, I'll wait."

Spielman was the Director of US Security Services in New Mexico. He and Quantock had gone through the FBI academy together and in their young days had described each other as Hoover's young Turks. They had been good friends but drifted apart as each pursued a different career, got married and moved around the country.

Spielman came on the line and greeted his old buddy. "Dan, you old gunslinger, great to hear you buddy. Jeez just how long has it been? Just so sorry to hear about your family tragedy. Marge and I wanted to call, but hell, what do you say?"

Quantock still grimaced when he was reminded of the past.

"John, it's okay. It was terrible, but life goes on, I'm more or less over it now – well as much as you can be!" he said.

"Sure, buddy, sure. Anyway, what can I do for you?"

"I need a trace on credit cards belonging to murder victims in a case I'm handling. The murders were done in Arizona and we think the cards might be used either in Arizona or in New Mexico."

"Go on."

"That's all I can tell you at this stage, apart from I am reporting directly to the President on this case."

"Okay, Dan, it's irregular, but I'll do it for you. What are the credit card details?"

Quantock gave these. After exchanging idle chat and each agreeing that they really must catch up with each other, he hung up. If the teenagers were caught, then he knew he would be called. He calculated his next move. Maybe he should visit Kinz in Phoenix to update him. But he didn't like the thought of bringing bad news to someone recuperating from a heart attack. No, he might as well go back to Washington.

It was getting dark as he headed out of town towards Tucson airport some forty miles away. The local Benson radio station KAVV-FM played popular music and interrupted to outline details of the teenage murders at the nearby San Quiller tin mine. The information was brief and exactly as Quantock wanted it to be. A little premature perhaps. All he had to do now was to apprehend Clem Johnson and Ginny Grivas –- and quickly.

He had to start second-guessing exactly what they were going to do next.

That wouldn't be easy.

Chapter 15

E-Day minus 18

Kinz spent two days in hospital and to the surprise of the doctors was soon on the mend. He was advised to cease drinking whisky and stop eating so much red meat. He resolved to do just that. It had been an uncomfortable experience.

Despite entreaties for him to stay in hospital, he discharged himself and agreed to employ a nurse on his staff. He couldn't wait to get home.

His housekeeper warmly greeted him and fussed him so much that he had to retreat to his study. He glanced at his whisky Tantalus, the crystal decanters nestling neatly in their cherry wood casing, and smiled, wagging a finger at it. Then he made his way to his chair. He sat and thought about the image of his lovely wife Clara and the effect that it had had on him.

He idly turned on the radio beside his chair and settled down to listen to his favourite radio station. As his eyes were beginning to close an announcement came on air. The words tumbled from the radio and he felt the blood drain from his already weak body; his jaw dropped.

"News has just been received that the bodies of the six missing teenagers, the sons and daughters of US senators have been found at a derelict tin mine near Tucson. They were discovered by a tourist who was hiking. There was no sign of the perpetrators of the crime. We will bring you more news as the story unfolds."

The music resumed, but Kinz wasn't listening. He stood up shakily and put his hands to his face, which was now wet with tears tumbling from his eyes. He now knew the reason for Clara's visitation. He had been an irresponsible fool.

After a while, during which he was rooted to his chair, unable to move or think clearly, he gathered his wits, stood up unsteadily and walked slowly to his desk.

Kinz sat for a while looking out the window at his beloved rose garden. On the oak desk in front of him was a pad of good quality, vellum writing paper and a Montblanc fountain pen.

His eyes welled with tears. It was not meant to happen like this. The deaths were a catastrophe and now he had to own up to his part in it all. He felt ashamed and sick to the stomach as most decent men feel, when they are tempted to act on impulse or against their better judgement and things go terribly wrong. Only this time his actions had cost lives.

He wiped his forehead and slowly unscrewed the top of his fountain pen. His eyes ran over its sleek black shape, edged with gold plate. The pen was perfectly weighted and balanced and he wrote steadily in elegant handwriting.

Kinz looked over his shoulder towards the TV in the corner of his study. CNN News was reporting that Brannigan was ahead in the polls. Brannigan was shown waving to a cheering crowd in California and making victory signs with his forefingers. Kinz shut the TV down with the remote.

After about twenty minutes writing he signed the last page of three, wrote neatly on the envelope before sealing it and propping it up against his crystal ink well. He then sat back in his chair and carefully put the top back on his fountain pen. It was a nice office, full of memories, pictures and his extensive library of books on American political and cultural history. He got up and removed a classical music CD from its cover and put it on the player; the sound of Mozart wafted around the office. Then he poured himself a large single-malt whisky, his favourite, Glenlivet. He sipped it slowly. The smoky flavour of the spirit filled his senses and the warmth of alcohol flowed into his veins. He sat down and reached for the revolver.

If he had lived in ancient Greece, he would have added hemlock to the whisky. Ancient Rome and he would have taken the whisky while lying in a hot bath before reaching for the knife with which to release the blood from his wrists. But ex-Marine Colonel Kinz chose the American officer's way.

The gun was a shiny-silver 1873 single action Colt 45 with mother of pearl inlays in the handle. It had belonged to General Patton and Kinz had paid a fortune for it at auction. While it was not a very practical firearm, it felt good in his hands. It was only when he was loading the sixth bullet in the chamber that he realised what he was doing and laughed out loud. He poured some more whisky and gulped it down in one before putting the empty glass next to the envelope that was marked: Private and confidential. For the personal attention of President Jake Brannigan.

Then he laughed out loud again at his idiocy in loading six bullets when he only needed one.

Kinz was still chuckling when he stuck the revolver in his mouth and pulled the trigger.

Clem's heart pounded when he saw a highway patrol car parked at the side of the road. But it did not react to his presence. The weather was closing in. The sky had turned a dirty grey and heavy rain clouds billowed up on the horizon. "We've got to ditch this car," he said.

"How?" Ginny said sharply. They were heading for their first fight, Clem thought. First fight and they hadn't even consummated their love affair.

He tried humour. "I don't suppose you know how to hot-wire a car?" Ginny shook her head. "Or there's always the old hitch-hikers trick. Get a pretty lady like you to show your legs and boobs by the side of the road. The horny redneck pulls over. Pow! I knock him out and we take the pickup."

This time Ginny cracked a smile. "How do you know the redneck is not gay?"

Ahead of them in the distance a large family saloon with a bulging roof rack, turned out of a private road onto the highway. Clem slowed the car instinctively so as to maintain some distance between them.

"This is not quite how I imagined we would ever, well, we would ever enjoy each other's company!"

Ginny smiled, "Well, it certainly isn't your fault," and she touched his arm, pinching it for good measure.

Clem huffed, and then said playfully in a mock southern accent, "I thought it would be you and me, and two kids, huh honey-bunch, my little Ginny-Bell?"

"Two kids," she said, playfully holding her hands to her heart.

"Two kids, two jobs and two bank loans," he continued.

"Two kids, two jobs, two bank loans, two automobiles and two vacations a year," she grimaced.

Then they laughed and looked ahead at the laden family vehicle that they were now slowly catching up with. There was a dull second or so as their brains both synchronised and they suddenly looked at each other. Clem braked and the vehicle skidded to a halt.

"Two of everything, yeah, that's it. Two automobiles! Yeah two of 'em! That family is going on vacation and in their garage, I bet there is another auto!" yelled Clem and he quickly turned around on the broad country road and headed for the turning that the family ahead of them had come out of. It was a rough track that was lined with large pine trees for about fifty yards and when they rounded a bend a modern ranch-style house with a big lawn came into view.

"What if it's alarmed?" said Ginny.

"What if it isn't?" Clem replied, too excited to be put off by anything so sensible. "Besides, this is a long way from other houses by the looks of things, so who will respond?"

They parked the car and walked up to the front door, past two large election signs reading "Brannigan for President" and "Re-elect Kinz. A man to trust". A more permanent sign warned in English and Spanish "Trespassers will be shot."

Clem called out: "Hello anyone there? We need some help. Anyone there?" He went up to the front door and rang the bell and for good measure pounded the door knocker a couple of times. Ginny walked along the side of the house trying to look through curtain windows. Clem turned around to check the road. He listened for the sound of a car. Nothing. Then Ginny called out.

"Clem, you were right, they've got a Chevy in the garage. It looks in good condition, definitely a second family car. Clever boy!"

It didn't take long for Clem to break the garage lock. The keys to the car were helpfully hanging from a hook. The Chevrolet was a standard family saloon with half a tank of fuel. Then they quickly switched cars, putting the hire car in the garage and leaving the Chevy in front.

Ginny tried a door inside the garage. It opened. "Do you want to have a look see?" she asked mischievously.

"Ginny, we shouldn't."

"Chicken," Ginny scoffed and walked through the door. Clem followed. The door led into a utility room which opened into a large open plan kitchen. Ginny snooped around and opened a huge stainless steel fridge freezer. The fridge was empty and spotless. The kitchen was soulless. Everything had a place and was in its place. A split-level lounge led off the kitchen. Hunting trophies snarled from the walls. A bear's head. A wolf. A doe with big soppy eyes. "This is giving me the creeps," Ginny said. "I'm going upstairs, wanna come see?"

In the master bedroom Ginny looked at herself in a full-length mirror. "OMG, what a state I look." Clem came up behind her and put his arms around her waist. "I think you look beautiful. Like a Greek bandit." He kissed her neck.

"Have you seen the film Bonnie and Clyde?" Ginny asked.

"Have I? It's one of my favourites."

"Well now, you know how Bonnie gets turned on by crime?"

Clem nuzzled deeper into her neck. "Mmmmm."

"Well so do I! Let's see what you're packing Clyde." She turned and pointed her fingers in the shape of a gun and prodded Clem in the chest. Clem put his hands up and moved backwards towards the king-size double bed. Ginny prodded him again and Clem fell back his arms spread out. Ginny jumped on him and kissed him. First softly and then voraciously. He responded equally so. She unbuttoned his shirt, pushed his t-shirt up and kissed his chest. Her hand caressed his flat stomach and was soon working at undoing his jeans. Clem moaned. "Wait, wait!" he whispered, "I don't have any protection."

"I don't care," said Ginny, and straddled him.

Their love-making was fast and furious, fuelled by pent-up lust, the previous day's fear and elation and the sudden return to comfortable reality. Despite some fumbling and awkwardness on Clem's part, the sex was deeply passionate and climatic. Afterwards they lay in the warmth of the duvet staring deep into each other's eyes and exploring the contours of each other's faces with their finger tips before falling asleep.

In the morning, they went to the kitchen and found a tin of sausage and beans and some crackers. They ate it cold straight from the tin washed down with some tap water. Ginny took care to rinse the can and put it into the recycling bin. They then went back to bed and spent the day having slow, sensual sex.

Chapter 16

E-Day minus 17

Quantock regarded his chess pieces and contemplated his next move. What a mess! The cleaners had taken care of Ralph and Martin and disposed of their bodies. Clem and Ginny had proved to be clever at evading Quantock, so they had one less task to do, and all he could do was to return to Washington. On the flight back, he read a copy of the Arizona Daily Star. The headline read: "Slaughter at the tin mine – bodies of missing senators' children found."

With the news out and Clem and Ginny on the run, his next challenge was managing Clem and Ginny's parents, especially when they were contacted, as they would be, by the runaways. He went through various scenarios trying to assess whether his defence was sound.

It was then he noticed that the cleaner, or his cheeky young administrator, had moved a single chess piece out of sequence on his board. Far from being upset, he enjoyed this interference and saw it as the kind of challenge, one that came from outside the rules of the game. That kind of thing happens in life – a plan is made then a random event derails it. He reached for a black bishop and moved it to the centre of the board in a threatening position to the white king. This was the way to deal with such random events: intervention of the pious kind!

Then he turned to another real-time random and unexpected event. He leaned back in his chair and looked at the envelope lying on the table beside his chair. It had been hand-delivered to the office by a FedEx courier and had Kinz's unmistakable handwriting in black ink on it.

Kinz's suicide had shocked everyone, but none more than Quantock. He felt his loss keenly.

He opened the envelope and read the letter slowly taking in every word. When he had finished, he put it to one side, ran his fingers through his hair and closed his eyes. Kinz's conscience was understandable and he should have foreseen it after the mission went horribly wrong. Sadly, in the short time available to him, he had not been able to get to Kinz to persuade him that although terrible things had happened, the end game could and should still be played out for the good of the US people. He cursed. He should not have returned to Washington. He should have gone to see Kinz in Phoenix. Kinz's death was down to him.

Kinz, meanwhile, true to his word, heaped all the blame on himself and he did not implicate Quantock in any way whatsoever. He made it clear in a covering note that he had mailed Quantock because they were friends and he respected Quantock enough to trust him implicitly. He wished to ensure that the enclosed letter to President Brannigan was delivered personally and without being seen by anyone else.

Kinz's story to the President was exactly as it was and left out nothing. Except that he said that he had worked alone and had made all the necessary arrangements. Things had obviously gone badly wrong and he deeply regretted it. He explained why he did it and pulled no punches, adding that the President's actions had been precisely as he had predicted. Nevertheless, the tragic death of the teenagers meant that he should take full responsibility and nothing would ease the guilt and pain he felt. He was therefore going to take his own life and ensure that the President was fully apprised of the situation so that he could explain it to the media in any way that he wanted. Kinz wished the President well and ended his letter with the words: God bless America.

Quantock felt a wave of pity for the old senator and instinctively reached to his chess pieces, the white pieces this time, and castled the king in an effort to protect his position.

He went out to the photocopier and copied the letter, putting the copy into his office safe and the original back into an envelope, which he sealed and addressed to the president. He poured himself a glass of mineral water and sat down again in his armchair. Contemplating the board again he reached to make another move. Life was like a game of chess. It was always the first moves that dictated the game, and then later came the 'events' that turned a winning situation into a losing one and vice versa. But chess was all about planning ahead and Quantock was a good player.

Quantock considered the options open to him and, as if to illustrate the fact, he moved black king pawn to king pawn three in order to open a route for the queen.

He could advise the President that the two remaining teenagers, Clem and Ginny, should be encouraged to see him and the situation be explained to them with full television coverage. This would ensure openness and may just get the President off the hook. Then he turned the board around and moved a white knight into a well-protected position in front of the white king and thought for a while.

On the other hand, this would make America and Brannigan look stupid in the eyes of the world, given Brannigan's war rhetoric against Iran and Syria. Brannigan could not bear to be made to look stupid. No, he would want something spun so that he could continue to try and take the minds of the American people away from the country's current economic problems.

There was another option. He then moved the black queen out to black knight seven, aggressive and ready to attack anything in sight. The two teenagers should be apprehended and moved out of sight – there were ways of doing this. The Kinz letter would then never be made known to anyone else other than the President and Quantock. The heightened state of alert would be maintained and who knows where the game would go from there. With luck, another event would, by sheer chance, as is the way with history, come along and muddy the waters. He would keep his new job, or better, be moved to a more powerful position. He dispassionately considered the two options and chose the more attractive and less risky second; less risky, because he was in control.

All he had to do was to convince the President that it was the best and only thing to do to achieve the optimum result for all concerned. Minutes later he put the telephone down after talking to the President's personal assistant and made his way across town to the White House. Eventually, he negotiated the various security stations and as he passed the pictures in the hallway on his way to the Oval office he saw his reflection in the glass, paused, adjusted his tie and straightened his shoulders.

President Brannigan was in a foul mood. The Washington diner riot had been followed by an escalating tide of violence across the country. More and more identifiable Muslims were being attacked on the streets, as were Sikhs, Hare Krishnas and anyone with a bushy black beard. Several mosques had been firebombed by the

Aryan Brotherhood. The Black Muslim Brotherhood said it was mobilising armed volunteers to defend their neighbourhoods by any means necessary. The KKK called on White Americans to stockpile ammunition and emergency supplies as the Race War had started. Gun and survivalist shops were mobbed by desperate customers. Shares in gun manufacturers soared. The liberal press was blaming Brannigan for stoking the flames with his intemperate language. Extra security had to be brought into his campaign rallies to stop left wing activists disrupting his speeches. Things were getting out of control and Sadie Burrows was failing in her job.

Quantock was announced by the President's personal assistant.

Brannigan barked, "C'min, Quantock. You want to see me urgently. It had better be fucking good. Tell me you've caught the son of a bitch jihadi killers of the kids."

"I can quite understand if you decide to shoot me as the messenger, Mr President, as I bring bad news. Very bad news. I have to give you this letter from the late Senator Randolph Kinz. I got it this morning. It was in an open envelope so I read it and resealed it immediately; it explains everything. You will need a few moments to read and digest it, sir."

The President took the letter glaring at Quantock as if insulted by his insistence that he read it. As he read it his forehead furrowed and his fists balled. Then he put the letter down, took off his spectacles and began to clean them without saying a word. He thought for a moment then with some reluctance passed the letter back to Quantock. After a pause the President spoke.

"Well whadya know? Who would've thought it of fuddy duddy old Kinz?" Quantock felt he detected a gleaning of sorrow in the President's voice. But it was quickly obliterated by his familiar bark. "Give me a full verbal, now!"

Quantock weighed his words carefully and then explained how he had received a lead about teenagers being seen at a deserted tin mine and had gone down to the Tucson area only to find four dead bodies."

"Four?" exploded the President.

"Yes sir, four. I tracked the remaining two through a local Indian reservation called San Xavier. Two men were chasing them. These were the men that killed the four teenagers at the mine. Eventually, a stroke of luck really, I was directed to Benson by the Indians who had hidden the two remaining kids. I decided to check the motels in the town and found one that had a four-by-four similar to the killer's parked outside. I arrived just as the murderers were about to kill the kids. I had to shoot both of them in self-defence. We've since identified them as two rogue ex-Blackwater operatives – a really weird couple of whackjobs. Lord knows why Kinz recruited them. I wondered what their involvement was and now Senator Kinz's letter explains it all. The teenagers escaped before I could question them, I guessed at the time they must've been shit scared. And I suppose I didn't look like a federal agent. Casual clothes, no suit. They're still on the run. But looking back, I think there is another reason why they flew."

Quantock feigned a worried look and squeezed his hands together for good effect. "Mr President, I believe that despite their terrible plight they were, well, I hate to say it, about to make a subversive video rather than the gentle and innocuous mission that Kinz had given them. That's why they ran out on me. I think, for what it's worth, that they are politically motivated, anarchists at best, communists at worst. We've done background checks and it's scary what we've found. I guess they knew that their political views could put them in a position to be arrested. Precisely what for I don't know, only they do. Poor Senator Kinz had unleashed more than he bargained for. Anyway, it's my guess that they are intent on making a fuss before the election, sir, to prevent your attaining the next presidency, or worse to bring about revolution or instability. Heaven knows who else is involved. We think the two fugitives may have the incendiary video in their possession which they will broadcast."

Brannigan sat quite still looking at Quantock. After about half a minute, which felt like an age, he spoke.

"So, what do we do about it, Dan?" he said.

Quantock paused and prepared himself for his delivery.

"Sir, we could try and call the kids in and assure them that they are safe and all is well. They can air the video and allow viewers to make up their own mind. But this means we would need to release the Kinz letter."

"Answer my question Quantock," barked the President, "what the fuck are we gonna do about this?"

Quantock stiffened and answered without delay.

"Catch the kids and put them into a secure hospital under sedation – like it or not sir, other administrations have condoned this action to protect America. It's standard practice. The kids will be safe and well looked after. Then we spin the story that the kids were killed by jihadi terrorists. The original brief remains and, right up to Election Day, you establish the fact that whosoever kills American teenagers will one day pay the price. We find four Arabs, arrest them and then put them firmly into the frame. Put simply sir, the American people will always give support to a sitting president in a crisis, all we need to do is to tie up the loose ends and show how your administration cleaned up this mess."

Brannigan's composure changed perceptibly. He didn't speak and he sat up straight in his chair. He offered a cigar to Quantock who declined and he went through the lengthy protocol of clipping it, rolling it in his fingers and smelling its quality. Then he lit it and blew the smoke out slowly after letting the taste roll around the inside of his mouth.

"I was so busy thinking about this smoke, that I didn't catch a word of what you've just said. And I don't want to hear it repeated. The Cubans may be son-of-bitch communists, but they still make one hell of a cigar! I want you to know Quantock that I like you. I think you are a shrewd cookie and you know your business. I take it that only you and I know of the content of this letter?"

"Yes sir," Quantock replied earnestly.

"Then, in the interests of the American people, I suggest that it is of no value whatsoever that political agitators be given the slightest pretext to make mischief. The country has enough problems to deal with. I therefore intend that you should be solely responsible for leading America out of this morass."

Brannigan then lit a match and held it underneath Kinz's letter. It soon caught light and burned quickly. He put the glowing blackened embers into his large ashtray and he fanned away the smoke. The fire alarms had long since been turned off to cater for his cigar smoking.

The President turned to Quantock, "Dan, I will give you full authority to set up a search for the two remaining teenagers. You have your own department already so you need no more resources I'm sure. The mission is to be top secret. When you catch them you are to ensure their safety. Their absolute safety and of course security. Do you understand that?"

Quantock said, "Yes, Mr President, I understand."

President Brannigan wrote a short note to Fred Spiker to ensure Quantock was given special security clearances and a budget for the mission. Then he buzzed his intercom. A bright young female intern answered and the President said, somewhat dismissively, "Get me Sadie Burrows, tell her it's urgent," and in his customary manner he put off the switch without waiting for a reply. That marked the end of Quantock's audience with the President and without exchanging any further words Quantock left the office and walked down the corridor to the main entrance. This was getting to be quite a game.

PART THREE

COUNTERATTACK

"When you see a rattlesnake poised to strike, you do not wait until he has struck to crush him."

Franklin D Roosevelt

Chapter 17

E-Day minus 16

Passing Mount Graham on the left, Clem approached the interchange at Stafford. He saw a line of patrol cars with flashing blue lights on the approach road to highway 70, the route he planned to take to Phoenix, and instead changed to highway 191.

"What are you doing?" said Ginny.

"They could be there waiting for us. I'll try to get around them."

"Do you know where you're going?"

"Not exactly. But trust me. Try the radio again. There might be some news."

Ginny tried. Only to get more static.

They were heading into driving rain. Several trucks overtook them and splashed dirty spray on the windscreen and this made visibility worse. Clem cursed. After about fifteen minutes Ginny shouted.

"Clem, you missed it, you missed the turning," she said.

"They'll be another one further along. We need to stop at the next services and buy a map."

Ginny cut Clem some slack and peered through the rain-swept windscreen. They were in a desert devoid of human habitation. Far ahead, appearing sporadically through the black clouds were the snow caps of the mountains. The only sign that they weren't on

Mars were the red tail lights of the cars in front and the headlights of those approaching.

Finally, they reached a little outpost called Three Ways with a general store standing opposite a Jehovah's Witness Temple. They filled up with gas, used the facilities, bought coffee and doughnuts and a map. As they came back to the Chevy, Ginny said. "Clem, you need a break. I'm taking over the driving. You can navigate."

Clem nodded dumbly.

In the car Ginny pored over the map. Clem thumped the radio and turned it on. A human voice. A newsreader's voice. "News just in. Arizona Senator Randolph Kinz has died at the age of seventy-two…"

Clem and Ginny listened open mouthed as brief details of the circumstance of his death were given. The word suicide was not mentioned, only that Phoenix police were not treating the death as suspicious.

"Guess that means no point in going to Phoenix," said Clem.

"We were not going to get to Phoenix anyway on this route," said Ginny. "We'd be better heading for Albuquerque. Poor Randolph. No matter what his role was in our situation, I can't believe he was an evil man."

"I can't believe anything, anymore," Clem said morosely.

The radio newsreader gave an update on the manhunt for the killers of the six murdered teenage children of senators. There was nothing to report.

"We've got to keep on keeping on," said Ginny. "Albuquerque here we come."

They headed north, overtaking monstrous yellow tipper trucks on their way to the Morenci open cast mine. The countryside was rolling hills with pine and oak trees, empty of human habitation except for the occasional holiday park, with ranks of log cabins. Signposts everywhere branded the highway the Colorado Trail.

Weather conditions were worsening. The rain battered the Chevy's windscreen. Flurries of autumn leaves and twigs flew across the road in crazy billows. Visibility was down to a few metres. A gust of wind slammed into the car and almost wrenched the steering wheel out of Ginny's hands.

They passed through the pretty hamlet of Alpine where the houses looked like Swiss chalets. After twenty minutes or so and with the rain easing off, Ginny took a tight bend strewn with small stones and the steering wheel locked. She slammed on the brakes and the Chevy skidded across the road. She saw to her horror they were headed towards a woman standing in front of a 1980s Plymouth station wagon that was up on a car-jack. The woman saw them and jumped to one side, just in time, as the Chevy slid over the gravel on the hard shoulder, bumping into the Plymouth with a dull thud.

Clem leapt out of the car and went to the lady.

"Oh God, ma'am, are you alright?"

Ginny sat at the wheel in shock.

The woman got up slowly and brushed the grit from her coat. She stood straight and looked at Clem. She was tall and had a medium build, with dark curly hair that fought to escape from a red head scarf. Her thick multi-coloured coat flapped open at the front revealing a denim dress and rows of beads around her neck. They seemed odd clothes for someone who was probably in her mid to late fifties. She was soaked from the rain. She looked imperiously over the top of large misted-up spectacles.

"Young man, if you and your lady friend want to drive like you're in the Indianapolis 500 then get a better car. Otherwise cut the speed. Okay?" she said. She walked over to Ginny's side of the

Chevy and opened the door. "Are you okay my dear?"

Ginny nodded. She had tears in her eyes. "I'm so, so sorry. I couldn't help it."

"What brings you to these parts?"

"We're trying to get to Albuquerque."

"This isn't the best route. Not at this time of the year. You should have taken highway 80 at Three Ways."

She turned to Clem. "I take it you were navigating?"

Clem held his hands up. "Guilty. Can I help make it up to you by helping you change your wheel?"

"Very chivalrous of you. Yes, you may."

Ginny chipped in as well, and the three of them got the wheel changed in no time. Clem checked the steering wheel on the Chevy and it seemed fine. As the lady loaded her jack into the back of the Plymouth, a squall of rain hit like machine gun bullets.

"You really shouldn't be travelling in this weather, it is just too unpredictable. You must come to my place for the night, I insist."

Ginny started to say something, "Well, I er..."

"I said I insist. My name is Catherine Devine. Devine by name and divine by nature."

Clem looked around him and shrugged, then introduced himself and Ginny by false names: Jacob Arden and Laura Haydon. As Clem climbed back into the Chevy, he wondered about this strange lady. It was perplexing him that she hadn't mentioned car insurance once. But there was nothing for it now. They had to follow her home and think on their feet.

Catherine Devine's Plymouth didn't drive far. After about only a mile and a half she turned left down a winding track shrouded by trees, which led into a flat meadow encircled by wooded hills.

At the end of the meadow, nestling into the hillside was a wooden cabin. The Plymouth drove across the grass, followed by Ginny in the Chevy, and they both parked outside the porch. Lights were on and smoke curled from a small broad stone-built chimney.

Catherine got out of her vehicle and beckoned them with her arm to follow her without even looking around. She stomped her wet boots on a mat in the porch, took them off and went inside.

Ginny and Clem remained in the Chevy. "What do we do?" said Ginny nervously. "I think we should turn around and go Clem, this is crazy."

Clem looked bemused. He knew he had been stupid to agree. Perhaps they could just go in for a cup of coffee and then wish her well? They had to make sure that she didn't report the accident to the police or insurance company. Just then Catherine came to the cabin door, leaned against the frame and half smiled. After a few moments, she straightened up and started to walk towards the Chevy. They wound the window down.

Clem was just about to speak, but Catherine got there first. She had a kind of exasperated, 'I don't have time to talk this through with you' expression on her face.

"Look, I know your dilemma. I've been there – trust me. You don't want to come in because you're afraid that I will find out about your secret. Well you can keep it secret or you can tell me about it over coffee. I'm not going to betray you."

Clem and Ginny were wide-eyed and speechless. They felt stupid.

"So there you go. There's hot water for coffee and I'm just about to cook up bacon. The fire's warm and you can tell me what your problems are – you never know I might be able to help. I'll leave the door open and the decision up to you."

Then she turned and went back into the cabin.

Ginny turned and looked at Clem. "Stay or go?"

Clem was certain. "We gotta stay Ginny. If she's a whacko she could call the police and if she isn't then we lose nothing. Besides," he looked out at the dark rain clouds sweeping over the brow of the hill, "I'm not sure if we're going to make it to Albuquerque in the Chevy.

Ginny pinched his arm and kissed his cheek and they both got out of the Chevy and walked into the cabin.

Even though it wasn't that cold outside, the warmth of the cabin heated by a large log fire hit them full on. Bacon was already sizzling on the griddle of a range in the kitchen area of the open plan room. The smells of burning logs and bacon were pure heaven to their senses. Several easy chairs were arranged around the fire, each covered with knitted throws. The walls were roughly plastered and covered in all kinds of modern art. A large bookcase full of books took up almost all the wall facing them, leaving a little space for three separate doors. One door was half open revealing a bathroom and toilet and the other two rooms were closed and were probably bedrooms.

"Take a seat," said Catherine, "coffee will be ready in a minute."

Clem noticed that she had almond shaped eyes. She was the same height as Ginny and slim. As she handed them both coffee cups, he regarded her hands. Catherine was a very attractive lady, difficult to age. He originally thought she was in her early fifties but the liver spots on her hands suggested someone older. The way she looked at Clem was what he found alluring. She had a kind of knowing smile that stripped away all pretence, because when under its spell, it would be difficult to be anything but absolutely honest. The next question put him right on the spot.

"When I was young, I was a political agitator and always in

164

trouble. I know the in and out of police cells and only age has dented my enthusiasm for a fight. I'm sixty years young and a child of the 60s, for your interest. Now, you guys wanna tell me about your situation?" she turned her gaze on Ginny, who seemed to melt under its power.

After sipping her coffee Ginny weighed up the odds and elected to tell her all that had happened. She and Clem needed someone to help plan their way out of this fix and they introduced themselves to Catherine under their correct names. Ginny told her everything, only leaving out Senator Randolph Kinz's name – she still couldn't believe badly of him, neither could she betray him. As she spoke, it was like recounting a fairy story, it was almost unbelievable. And she found it odd, really odd that Catherine didn't once express surprise or indignation; she just listened and nodded occasionally. She sipped her coffee and when Ginny had finished she looked up.

There was a long pause before Catherine spoke and she had a kind of knowing look on her face.

"That's quite a story. Well, let me see now. The first thing I need to do is to advise you to keep your heads down for a few days. Despite what you say, there's not exactly a hue and cry out there, otherwise your faces would be plastered all over the newspapers and television. But nevertheless, you need to let the world pass you by a little. What's your plan?"

Clem and Ginny fidgeted. Clem said, "Well, we kinda don't have a plan ma'am, er…."

Catherine broke in, "Don't call me ma'am please, I'm not a school teacher and don't run a bordello, it's Catherine if you don't mind."

"Okay, sorry," said Clem, "Catherine. We don't have a plan."

Catherine cocked an eyebrow and swept away to the griddle, returning a few minutes later with a pile of bacon sandwiches.

"Here, some ketchup if you want it," she said, "what have you eaten so far?"

Ginny laughed, "Sausage, beans cold from a tin and cracker, plus some doughnuts."

Catherine put on a pained expression, "Oh no, what have I done, it's gonna be noisy around here tonight."

That broke the ice and they laughed.

The supper plates were cleared away and Catherine made some more coffee. Then she returned, put down the tray and sat down. She paused for a moment, looking straight at them.

"Look, I meant what I said. You need to hunker down for a few days and by the sound of things you need to rest and think a lot. Don't just go charging around aimlessly or you will make all the wrong decisions. But the choice is yours."

Clem got a nod from Ginny and said, "Catherine, that's good of you. But why are you helping us? We just almost trashed your station wagon."

Catherine laughed. "You should see it in daylight – the bump actually improves its looks." They laughed again and Catherine went on. "I knew you were in trouble when I saw you. A sixth sense I suppose. Anyway, I remember needing help in my youth and I got it too. It's nice to repay acts of kindness and I am happy to do that now."

For the rest of the evening they talked some more, but Catherine charged them not to mention any more of their problems. She got them talking about all manner of things and they felt better for it. One of the doors did lead to a bedroom and by midnight they had talked themselves out and were ready for bed. But before they went to sleep they made love again. Gently and quietly.

Chapter 18

E-Day minus 15

Ginny was the first out of bed in the morning and for some reason felt ill at ease, the kind of feeling brought on by severe anxiety. She smelled the freshly brewed coffee and that cheered her up. In the bathroom, she found that Catherine had thought of everything. Spare toothbrushes and cosmetics were laid out ready for use. Afterwards, Ginny sauntered into the large main room at the front of the cabin, looking out of the window she gasped and put her hands to her mouth. The car had gone. She ran to the door, almost tripping over a stool. As she stood on the porch, she heard Catherine come up behind her and turned around.

"A little bit of trust goes a long way. I put it over there." Catherine put one hand on Ginny's shoulder and pointed with the other. "See, over there just behind the tree line. We don't want any nosey neighbours wondering who owns a Chevrolet now do we?"

Ginny felt embarrassed and tears welled in her eyes. "Catherine, I'm sorry. It's because I'm so scared."

Then she turned and buried her head in Catherine's shoulder. Catherine patted and stroked her head.

"Yeah, it must be scary honey. You're a brave kid. Others would have melted I can tell you. Take some time out here at the cabin to relax and get your mind straight. Tell you what, let's go for a walk after breakfast – what do you say to that?"

Ginny lifted her head from Catherine's shoulder and grinned. The weather was clear and bright and the rain had passed. A walk would indeed be a great idea.

Soon Clem joined them and made no mention of the Chevy's absence. Both Ginny and Catherine waited eagerly to see the look on his face. When he failed to notice even after they dragged him to the window, they burst into laughter and swore they were convinced that men were indeed different to women. Clem readily agreed with them.

The sun bathed the meadow in warmth as they left the cabin and followed a trail up the hill. Catherine told them the trail was okay for 'city-slickers' without hiking gear and only about two to three miles. They crossed over a log bridge spanning a creek which drained down from the hills and ascended through the trees and over ground made soft and springy by decades of pine needles. The air smelled of damp and fungus. The sound of water flowing, falling, gurgling and splashing, had an enormously calming effect and Catherine deliberately walked on, leaving Clem and Ginny to hold each other and to be alone for a moment. At a particularly beautiful waterfall they stopped and kissed and Catherine was quite far ahead of them. Then she turned and looked at them quite deliberately and Clem caught her eye. She looked as though she had something to say – it was a weird look.

The trail curved around to the west and they stopped to admire the outstanding panorama. Catherine pointed out the Chiricahua and Anita peaks to the northeast then directed their gaze southwest right down to the desert floor many miles away. A different place, a different climate almost – but scene of their worst nightmares. Already they wanted to stay at the cabin, locked away from the world, forever.

After walking almost around in a circle the trail ended in a mixture of rocks and log falls. They scrambled down until they reached the cabin. It was late afternoon and they felt as though their legs were going to drop off. As Catherine set about preparing the evening meal, she looked around and saw that both Clem and Ginny had fallen asleep in the large cushioned chairs by the log fire.

Two hours later Clem's eyes opened and he stretched his weary limbs. Ginny stirred too. The fire had been stoked and Catherine stood over him, her lovely almond eyes shining and wearing a big smile.

"How about a coffee?" she said.

"Great," he replied, "sorry we fell asleep on you."

"That's okay, what with the fresh air and all that you guys have been through I can't say I'm at all surprised."

It felt good to relax and after coffee came the most marvellous pot roast. When they had finished Clem and Ginny did the dishes.

They sat down and noticed that Catherine had brought out a bottle of Jamesons Irish whisky and three glasses. She had a kind of resigned look on her face. She poured about two fingers each and they drank each other's health.

"So, tell me more about the video your, er, friend, wanted you to make?" she said.

Ginny became enthusiastic. "It was to be a state-of-the-nation video, that's what it was about, from the viewpoint of six teenagers whose fathers are US senators. Not from the so-called adult establishment, mired in false politics and self-interest, but from our perspective, the young people of America. You know? We are the people that really count, the future, Catherine. We wanted to do this so much. We needed to have our say."

Catherine drank her whisky and poured another. Clem and Ginny were hardly into their drinks.

"So you want to do your bit. And you really thought that a video would do that?" said Catherine almost too dismissively for Clem's liking.

Clem answered, "Catherine it's better than nothing, isn't it?"

"Better than nothing? Let me tell you guys, a bad strategy is actually worse than nothing," she said it bitterly and it surprised them.

Catherine looked wistful. "Sometimes, you know, I feel that the wheel has actually turned full circle."

She took a large mouthful of whisky, held it in her mouth and then swallowed it noisily.

"You know what, in 1965 Time magazine called young American people, and I quote, 'a generation of conformists'. Well what about that? Damn. Only the year before, 1964, three young civil rights workers were murdered in Mississippi. They gave their lives for their cause. All around the country the next ten years were punctuated with race riots, anti-war riots and of course the murders of Martin Luther King and Bobby Kennedy in 1968. See now, all that many young American people wanted in those days was an administration that lived up to the promise of civil rights for everyone no matter the colour of their skin, and an end to the Vietnam War. Most of all, they wanted the freedom to express their views. You really think your video would've achieved that?"

Clem heard all she said as though he was receiving a punch to the stomach and Ginny fidgeted.

"I don't for one moment doubt your resolve to change the world guys, but you live in an age of plenty. But don't forget that this has been achieved on the back of yesterday's youth in the face of blood, sweat and tears." Catherine smiled ironically and looked up at the ceiling, "Mind you, many of them are now in the so-called establishment you hate so much. When they were your age they wore Chairman Mao t-shirts, then, guess what? They swapped them for smart, expensively-tailored suits and now they are city bankers and attorneys. I mustn't be sour though. I have to admit that in some ways things have changed for the better."

Catherine stopped and sipped the hot coffee: "But then we Americans are surely the best at moving on aren't we? No one will ever doubt our resolve. Oh no, we put things right when we need to that's for sure. Good old Uncle Sam. But do we ever learn the lessons of history? We can deal with the mega-tragedies and emergencies. When New York's 9/11 horror and the tragedy of hurricane Katrina in New Orleans happened, we just wept, got out our spades and fixed things, then we moved on. We left the devious ones in the US Administration to use the situation to continue to perpetuate all manner of dumb-ass policies. But here's the truth of it guys – real people still suffer."

Clem was watching her mood and expression and said, "So what are you saying Catherine?"

"I'm saying that the government must listen to and work for we the people. Not for me the politician or lobbyist. Do you ever look at a presidential election and wonder what all those people with the funny hats at conventions are cheering about? They care more about the candidate's after-shave or perfume than politics. They care more about going home winners after a good day's campaigning than understanding the true nature of the policies being touted by the candidate. They like winning more than losing and that's what is more important to them. The razzmatazz guys. You know something? In England, there is a park, called Hyde Park and it has an area called Speaker's Corner. You can stand on a box and say, within reason, just what you want to say, without fear of being thought a lunatic or being locked up."

"And?" said Ginny.

"And I don't believe that we can do that here, in this country I love, I really don't," said Catherine, pouring herself yet another large whisky. Her voice was getting slurred but she continued, "You guys think the sixties was the decade of smoking pot and good sex. Well, the sex was good for sure, but there was more to life than that. We could put a man on the moon in 1969, but we just didn't know how to listen to our own citizens, especially not if they were gay, black or shouting that the Vietnam War was wrong. For the next two years, demonstrations at universities led to deaths of our own kids in Berkeley California, Jackson State and Kent State. Damn, our own kids! When the Chinese did that in Tiananmen Square Beijing we called them animals!"

"But Catherine, things did get better, remember, Nixon was impeached when he broke the rules wasn't he?" said Clem.

"Yeah, he was, but it was a close-run thing Clem. A close-run thing where true patriots had to stand up and be counted."

Catherine continued. "Look, I just don't want to see good kids like you believe that your video, whatever, would've changed the world. No way! People don't believe videos, they believe people, especially if you've got bad news to deliver. Trust me that's the way of the world."

Ginny was more perceptive. "You were at one of the universities, weren't you? What happened to you Catherine?" she said.

Catherine smiled softly and her eyes watered.

She said, "Yeah, I was at Kent State in Ohio, with my boyfriend, my most precious boy. And we protested like mad. We yelled for free speech and despised all those who took things at face value and allowed over a hundred thousand of our boys to die in Vietnam without questioning what it was all about. We asked why it was that we were there at all and what we were supposed to be aiming for. We screamed about the darkest evil of racism that remained in parts of America. Then one day we were letting off steam about the US invading Cambodia when Nixon was meant to be talking peace and the National Guard came onto campus. Our own boys! You know what President Reagan is reported to have said when he was Governor of California? He said, 'If there is to be a bloodbath let's get it over with.' And they had their bloodbath. Four dead. Nine wounded."

Catherine took a handkerchief from her sleeve and dabbed her eyes. After a few minutes, she sniffed and continued.

"My boyfriend wasn't killed or counted as one of the wounded, but he was hit on the head by a young fresh-faced National Guardsman who was probably more scared than he was, and collapsed with concussion a day later. He never fully recovered and later took his own life in a fit of depression brought on by the head injury. I campaigned like crazy for a long time afterwards, but my soul was shattered. Civil Rights and peace had been my sword for years now. I dropped out of all that years ago and came here for peace and tranquillity. I never regret it."

Clem and Ginny were quiet.

Catherine smiled and continued, "So, you want to change US politics huh? My, my, the innocence of youth. I've been there, honey, I really have. I will never, ever, lose my burning passion for Civil Rights, this is something that needs constant attention or it will sneak out of the back door and be lost forever."

Clem felt stupid. Catherine frowned, leaned forward and gently touched his shoulder. "Now I need to tell you something. You say you were to make a video in secret at the San Quiller tin mine and then something went wrong and your friends got killed. Did you know that right from the get-go the whole country was looking for you?"

Clem looked surprised, "No, Catherine, what I said was that we had left letters for our parents about what we were doing and saying they weren't to worry. That can't be true."

Ginny shifted uneasily in her seat.

Catherine poured another glass of whisky.

"Clem, the news stations across America reported that you and your friends had been kidnapped. Your parents were on television pleading for your return. The report of the killings is very recent. You can google it all on my computer over in the corner there," she pointed to the far corner of the room where a screen-saver heralded the work of Amnesty International.

Clem was speechless. Ginny turned to him looking guilty.

Clem put his head in his hands and said, "I just don't understand."

Catherine was by now bleary eyed and she stood up unsteadily.

"I'm really sorry. I hope my stories and the plain old truth didn't spoil your evening. But I guess that it has – big time. I'm certain of one thing though, if you are serious about making a stand, make sure you have a plan and you watch your back. Or stay here and walk the hills with me for the rest of your life. Your choice."

She leaned down and kissed them on the cheek, before stumbling to her bedroom.

Her words bounced around Clem's mind and he couldn't resist going to Catherine's computer and googling the mass of information on their case. He was staggered. It was true. As they had begun to make arrangements for the video at the tin mine their parents had been worried sick about their safety. Now everyone thought they were dead. He began to realise that simply going home was not an option. He thought of phoning his parents. But he knew what would happen, his dad would try to play the big Kahuna and fuck everything up. He started crying and Ginny came over and hugged him and tightly buried her face in his back.

They stayed curled up in a chair in front of the log fire, unable to think straight or talk, with chests tight and thumping, until the pink red embers that glowed in the dark, darkened and, like their enthusiasm, slowly died.

Chapter 19

E-Day minus 14

Fred Spiker lifted weights in the mini gym of his Washington home. Pumping iron helped deal with the stress of working for President Brannigan. The job had cost him his marriage. Now, at the age of 54, he began to count the cost. Going to bed and waking up alone, distanced from his children and constantly having to act as an apologist for every two-bit failure of the Brannigan administration and to clear up the shit after every Brannigan gaffe. This was not how he had planned his life to be.

A loyal and high ranking senior official in the White House with a track record for brokering between parties and a can-do attitude towards seemingly intractable problems, he was quickly identified as a man who could deliver deals in difficult circumstances. When the time came, Spiker was honoured and easily enticed to his appointment as White House Chief of Staff by the new president. Since that heady day some two years ago, when he and his wife had toasted the appointment with champagne, life had steadily got intolerable. All those personal qualities that had thus far assured his success in life now worked against him as he became sucked into more and more political problems. He overlooked the issues that really mattered: his home life and integrity. Spiker sacrificed them to the art of compromise and misplaced loyalty. By the time he stopped to think properly about his personal life it had slipped almost unseen through his fingers.

The US had been through a torrid time over the last six years. There was no doubt about that. In particular, Bush's ill-advised and ill-fated adventure into Iraq contributed enormously to the country's woes. It was now a widely-known fact that the war had been deliberately mis-sold to the American people. The consequences of poor post-invasion planning had led to considerable loss of Iraqi and American lives, and a cavalier attitude to human rights, only marginally better than that practised by Saddam Hussein, sullied American claims for democracy. The most notable failure of all though, was not fully understanding, or wanting to understand, the culture and history of the people they were challenging – a history that was five times older than that of the US. Sunni and Shia Muslims had been at each other's throats for over fifteen hundred years; expectations that this would end in a short space of time were naïve and dangerous. Once the conflict had begun it was always going to be impossible for the US to extract itself without further damaging its reputation. It had approached a stalemate. History had shown that stalemates always ended up in a deadly game of strategy and opportunism.

The resulting political pressures damaged Bush's health and he retired a broken man. Or so the official story went. The White House water cooler story was that Bush fell off the wagon and hit the bottle again, big time. And no one in the media noticed. When he was drunk delivering a State of the Nation address, they just thought he was inarticulate and made light of it. But Papa and Mama Bush had stepped in and made an intervention. And in 2004 Dubya had gone back to Texas to convalesce.

Up to the plate stepped Vice-President Jake Brannigan to continue the work of his boss for the remaining two years. Spiker had initially been enthusiastic to join his team, but gradually became disabused of the notion that Brannigan wanted to bring all the conflicts to a halt; quite the opposite in fact. He seemed to relish the discord the more it went on. The Republican majority in Congress had diminished and it was now finely balanced, this led to manufactured headlines and sound bites to gain advantages. Dissenters to public policy were mysteriously outed, citing extra-marital affairs, fraud or alleged homosexual misconduct; Spiker had lost two good friends that way. He wasn't stupid. He knew that they were blameless and this was done, 'pour encourage les autres.'

The White House now resembled a medieval state where dukes, princes, bishops or interest groups lobbied for favours in return for support. But Spiker had to give Brannigan credit where it was due. The President was never ever implicated – this much he had obviously learned from history. One Italian prime minister was later to describe him as 'mani pulite' – (clean hands).

Spiker put down his weights and got off his bench. He towelled himself dry of sweat and walked to the window and opened it. Despite the cold, he breathed in the cool crisp air for a few moments before closing it tight and going to his den.

On his desk was the print out of the draft paper he had written warning Brannigan of the threat from the white supremacist right. A cadre of wealthy young extremists was developing across the US with ambitions of taking over the Republican Party. But Spiker knew Brannigan would dismiss them as a threat and would be arrogant enough to believe that he could harness their energy to his own cause. There was no chance that he would get a debate on that issue. He sat down again and drummed his fingers against the top of the large maple wood coffee table. The remaining paper on the table was written by Dan Quantock of the FBI, the subject of which was the six teenagers, kidnapped by Arab terrorists, who were now all dead.

What was this all about? His heart went out to the parents and families, but something was wrong. No group had claimed responsibility for these terrible actions – no political gain had been made and no conditions had been wrought from the US administration. Terrorists rarely did anything without a clear objective coupled with a blast of propaganda public relations. Also, he was no expert, but the search always seemed more hype than substance. Spiker read the reports again and was still confused. He ran his hands through his hair and sighed loudly.

There was nothing for it but to get to the White House early.

He took one last look at the Quantock report – he must talk to the Head of the FBI, Troy Hammond, because something was not right. He just knew it – but what?

Chapter 20

E-Day minus 13

Clem awoke early. The two days in the cabin and beautiful surroundings were what he and Ginny had needed. But enduring a second night of Catherine hectoring and belittling him over glass after glass of whisky had disturbed him. He threaded himself out of Ginny's grasp and got up off the couch. His body ached with the exertions of another hike the previous day and his knotted position throughout the night. Just then Catherine came into the room holding her head.

"Oh, God, my brain shrank during the night!" she said

Clem wished he could joke back, but his mind was still numb and he just smiled weakly and nodded.

"Clem, I'm sorry for laying so much on you guys. I have a lot of rocks round my heart and a big chip on my shoulder. But I do know what I'm talking about and it just seemed stupid to let you guys wander off aimlessly and possibly into great danger. Let's get some fresh air, shall we?"

Clem nodded. Catherine had been right to tell them about her life to set the scene and give them her assessment of their position. They still had the freedom to come to their own conclusions – but he knew in his heart of hearts that would be useless. Her reading of the situation was spot on.

Clem slipped on a coat and so did Catherine and they opened the door silently and crept outside. After about a hundred yards they sat on a large tree trunk. The early autumn sun was rising slowly and its light was more orange than bright. The hills looked beautiful, with patches of mist like balls of spiders' webs nestling throughout the undergrowth.

They talked for an age and Catherine convinced Clem that he should think of something momentous. The situation demanded it. Safe and yet momentous. He smiled and called her a barnstormer. She retorted that that's what made chicks from the sixties and he should never forget it. It was amusing enough to bring Clem out of his addled state. Catherine smiled at him and left him to his thoughts. When she got to the door of the cabin, she glanced back and saw Clem still hunched up, sitting on the tree trunk obviously thinking about what to do next.

Ginny and Catherine were just preparing the table and the sausage and pancakes lay invitingly in the centre when Clem burst in. He stood in the doorway and gave them the plan. It was audacious, unique and would surely have enormous impact. He had worked at CNN over the summer of his freshman year. He could remember his way around the CNN building in Atlanta and knew how hungry news presenters were for good stories – and this was a good story. He also had a good friend, Jamie Cook, who he could contact and arrange for them to gain entry to the building.

Ginny and Catherine were awe-struck. Catherine quickly retrieved a copy of the Washington Post and turned to the TV listings.

"Larry King?" she said.

Clem looked at Ginny. "No," he said, "he's gonna want to be more politically correct than anyone else. He will want too much due diligence, I can understand that."

"Okay, you can try Aaron Brown's news night, that's damned lively and looks at the day's issues including, let's see what does it say here, oh yes, breaking news and live updates. Or, you can go with, Paula Zahn, her show is great and I watch it all the time. A cut-to-the-chase interview-driven hour. Now that looks more like it?"

Clem's eyes opened wide.

"Hang on, oh dear, Paula is away for a month and has a rookie stand in called Damien Tasker. That's no good then," she said.

Clem jumped up. "No, that's perfect. You know, this guy Tasker will want to make a name for himself. He will jump at the chance of a good breaking story."

Ginny clasped her hands together and said, "That's a fantastic idea Clem, but I don't want to put a damper on it, won't he want to carry out, what did you call it, 'due diligence' too?"

"Yeah, he will for sure. But if someone who works there, someone they all know and like, can verify who I am – sorry, I mean, verify who we are - through personal contact and state categorically that we are alive and well despite all that has been said by the US administration, then I would think that they would find it difficult to say no."

Catherine and Ginny jumped up and cried out loud. The excitement was electric. They hugged and Ginny cried.

After they had quietened down Clem brought them to order. "I need to make a call to CNN." He looked at Ginny: "You still got that cell phone Ginny?"

She nodded. "Clem, I want to call home."

"No, out of the question," he said hastily.

Ginny's eyes welled with tears. "But Clem, they already know that I'm not dead. What's the point of keeping them worried. Why not?"

"I don't care Ginny. The answer's no, definitely no. There will be a tap on the line, we can't risk it."

Ginny reluctantly went to the bedroom and got the cell phone and limply handed it over to Clem. Catherine looked on disapprovingly. Later, she tried to persuade Clem to change his mind, but he was adamant in his view. She explained how difficult it must be for Ginny and that he shouldn't underestimate the shock to both their systems. They had been through a lot together. Her parents must also be suffering as indeed his must. But Clem's views of parents were coloured by his own poor relationship. Having got nowhere, she stood up and went to console Ginny who was outside sobbing softly.

Clem put the cell phone into Catherine's charger and called without waiting for it to fully charge up. He tapped in a number from memory.

Jamie Cook couldn't believe his ears, the reception was very poor but could this really be Clem Johnson? Several times he had told friends of his sadness at the recent news of the callous murder of his young friend who had wanted so much to be a film producer and director. He was stunned to hear Clem's voice. Clem reassured him several times and then took him through the scenario of their escape step by step. Repeating it over and over, until he was sure that Jamie fully understood. He told him never to mention their existence to anyone. When he was sure that Jamie was fully tuned in to the situation, he used his powers of persuasion to draw his friend into helping. He just needed to be interviewed. Live. Jamie promised to do everything in his power to arrange it. They agreed to meet in Atlanta in a cafe just behind the CNN Studio Four building in three days' time.

Clem was elated. It felt good to be in control after being chased, threatened and worried sick about what tomorrow would bring. Ginny came back into the cabin and they embraced. She and Catherine were delighted with the result.

Catherine pecked him on the cheek, "Smart boy. But first we must get to Atlanta. I think we should split up. You should fly from Albuquerque, Clem, and we will drive."

"We?"

"Yes, 'we', this is not going to be easy Clem and you need someone who is not known to authority and who can look out for you. Besides, you need cash and moral support. Now tell me if I am wrong?"

Ginny took Clem's arm lightly. "Mary Poppins knows best I think. She's right Clem. We can't do the first part of the mission on our own."

Clem looked at them both. They were right. He smiled and said, "Okay, it doesn't seem right to put you in harm's way Catherine, you've been great so far. But you're right. Okay then, we're a team," and they embraced together.

"Just promise me," he said.

"What?" said Catherine.

"That you won't burn your bra in public, smoke pot or do a protest sit-down in the Centennial Olympic Park Atlanta. We know what sixties babes are about!"

Catherine grabbed a cushion and playfully hit him several times and they laughed. It was the first real spontaneous laughter Clem and Ginny had experienced for quite some time.

Chapter 21

E-Day minus 12

Quantock had to focus and keep a clear mind. Breathing deeply, he unscrewed the green top on a bottle of sparkling mineral water and washed down an anti-depressant pill. Then he reached into his desk drawer and brought out some white paper and black felt pens.

The two teenagers had not been apprehended, but then he was attempting to find two needles in a giant haystack while keeping the operation low key. Quantock didn't like to be beaten. He drank some more water from the bottle and the bubbles went up his nose. It brought back a sudden memory. He heard the voice of his son saying, "Bubbles go up my nose Daddy!" It made his chest tighten and he frowned and almost snapped the top off the felt pen in his right hand. He shook his head and tried to focus.

The wheels on his executive chair squealed as he pushed the chair backward to get up. He walked across and regarded his chess board. As he looked he experienced a slight pain in his left temple and he raised his hand to rub the spot to increase the blood flow. It was difficult to concentrate. The answer? The answer was not to make a move. It was time to think not act.

Quantock straightened up and walked back to his desk, sat down and took the top off one of the black felt pens. He would mind-map, a technique he had developed where a shape for a subject or problem is drawn first, then around it are sketched or written other words, shapes or pictures that represent the situation. He wrote 'Clem' beside a sketch of a matchstick man. He opened a file on Clem in which all his known contacts had been listed. Gradually Quantock enhanced the map by adding Senator Johnson and words such as, school, friends, the names of the other teenagers, and then he added another matchstick man off to one side, labelling it Kinz. He thought a little more about Clem and his environment, and then started to add more words. He worked feverishly for about an hour and when he had finished the map it had scores of entries. Sitting back, he admired his work, but it took more time to try and link relationships and think about them in some depth. After some time, he then took a separate piece of paper and created a map for Ginny. Then he wrote a list of headings under which he placed actions.

Quantock called in his secretary. She came into the office quickly recognising the tone of his voice, it was clear that today was not a day to mess with Mr D Quantock. He didn't even look up.

"Becky, take this envelope to Jim Rook and tell him to action all the items listed. Then he is to call me when done. But most important, he is to call me about an entry I circled in red. Be real sure to do it now please." He raised his head slowly and she felt the full glare of his eyes. This man could be so unsettling.

Quantock's frown dropped after she left the office. He noticed for the first time that she had a backside that would have stopped the traffic in his day and smiled. He knew how his staff felt about him and that he was not the man he had been before his wife and son had been killed. But then nothing was the same. Sex was the farthest thing from his mind, he no longer drank alcohol and making friends seemed perfectly pointless. He was in a constant state of mourning that occasionally threatened to bring him to the brink of a nervous breakdown; only work saved his sanity. No matter how boring or even exciting – so long as it was work and it meant lots of overtime. At least this Kinz fiasco had added some spice to his life. Which way would this go?

Jim Rook was fully in the picture about Clem and Ginny having survived the killing at the tin mine and being on the run. He saw no reason to doubt Quantock's theory that they were enemies of America who were part of a plot to bring down the President and demoralise the country. He had been doing his own research on Clem and didn't like what he found. Clem's father was almost certainly a closet communist. On Hoover's watch, he would have been impeached. The mother was an anti-war hippie who dabbled with lesbianism and the occult. Clem was heavily involved in communist and anarchist controlled anti-war groups. His Facebook timeline had postings about and likes for almost every radical extremist event in the USA over the last year. He was also friends with or followed some known extremists, including Michael Moore, Sean Penn and Susan Sarandon. Everything about him screamed subversive. Ginny came from more patriotic stock, even though her family were Greek, but it was likely that she was deliberately rebelling against her father. She was regarded as a left-wing firebrand on her politics course who promoted gay rights and feminism. Her Facebook trail and friends evidenced this. So, if the pair of them were not guilty why were they on the run? This was the Patty Hearst story repeating itself. He worked methodically through Quantock's list of Mind Map questions. Three hours later he called his boss

"I've got a name."

Quantock grunted with relief and Rook continued.

"Jamie, Jamie Cook. The boy was a close friend of Clem Johnson's. Now young Clem wanted to grow up to be a film producer or big shot director. Jamie is two years older and works for CNN in Atlanta. Our young aspiring radical film maker managed to swing work experience at CNN last year. My money is on him returning there to do something on air, something, well, revealing, so that he becomes so visible he can no longer be apprehended."

"What makes you think that?" Quantock said.

"It was his girlfriend's remark to her mother. It's in the transcript of the latest phone tap. She said to her mom that, '…you'll be hearing about us soon enough…' Given that they are notorious and newsworthy already that must mean that they plan something big, for wide consumption, something, well, revelatory."

"Outstanding, Jim." Quantock said.

Quantock made another call. "Teddy, it's Dan Quantock. Are you and Cissy up for a little watercolour job?"

There was a pause before Teddy answered in a hostile voice. "What gives you the right to ring me after what you did to me?"

Quantock blinked in surprise. "What have I done Teddy?"

"You ran out on our chess game. You were losing and played chicken. Simply ignored my last move and then nothing."

"When was this Teddy?"

"Last January. That's right isn't it Cissy? Yes, Cissy's nodding. January."

"Hold on." Dan thumbed his Blackberry and chuckled. "12 January. Qc4. Checkmate. You left your king unprotected. I thought the reason you didn't respond was because you were a sore loser."

"I never got that text. Ask Cissy she'll tell you. What? I can hear you, Cissy. No need to shout. Cissy says maybe that was the day my Jap cell phone died. Dang thing went kamikaze on me and torpedoed into the john. The water killed it. Had a helluva job switching all my stuff to a new cell. But this time it was American. Apple iPhone. They call it the Jesus Phone. Fancy that." He laughed.

"It's good to hear from you Dan. But enough of my joshing. Let's talk turkey. What? Be quiet woman. No I'm not going to invite Dan to Thanksgiving. Don't matter how good your corn bread dressing is. I'm talking business."

Chapter 22

E-Day minus 11

Catherine and Ginny drove away from Albuquerque, leaving Clem looking a little forlorn as he turned, waved and then walked towards departures. Ginny waved back. It made good sense to split up. If people were watching out for them they would be looking for a couple, but not perhaps a single young man alone. Nevertheless, he would need to keep his head down.

Catherine drove south along Interstate 25. They would pick up Interstate 20 at El Paso which would take them across New Mexico, Texas, Louisiana, Mississippi and Alabama direct to Atlanta, Georgia. A glance at Ginny was enough to tell her that the next few days would be awkward without Clem beside her. Ginny was subdued and there was a hint of a tear in her eyes. They had built a tremendous bond between them both and had seen more danger in a few weeks than some people ever see in their whole lives. Catherine reached out and touched her hand lightly. but said nothing. Ginny sniffed slightly and turned to look out of the car window.

Catherine sighed and thought about the two seemingly crazy kids with whom she was now entangled. From the time, she first saw them that evening in the rainswept hills near her home she knew they were in trouble. But, above all that, she knew they were scared and it showed. Why not simply pack them some food and send them on their way?

Because it brought it all back to her, that's why. The sinister nature of politics worried her, especially when things happen that you cannot fathom out. Catherine had the feeling that there was more to this than met the eye – all her revolutionary hackles had risen and could not be put back in the box. She reminisced about the old days and the successes and failures as the Plymouth cruised gently along the interstate highway.

Ginny as well as feeling sad, was also feeling guilty. In the middle of the night she had crept out of bed and quietly gone to the main living room. It was easy to locate the cell phone, its green light glowing in the darkness as it charged from the mains electricity. With the door shut tight, Ginny put the throw from the settee over her head and dialled home. Her mother had answered sleepily. It was difficult but Ginny stopped her from talking and asking questions and told her not to worry, it would soon be over. This would be her last call, but they would hear about them soon enough. Her parents were to keep their spirits up – the important thing was that she and Clem were alive, but they were not under any circumstances to call Clem's parents. If they did, then Clem and Ginny's lives could be in danger. She made her mom swear to this, blew her kisses and ended the call quickly. Then she erased all trace of the call having been made on the cell phone records. She hated cheating on anybody, let alone Clem, but when it came to thinking about her mom going through agonies worrying about her, she simply couldn't hold back.

It was nearly fourteen hundred miles to Atlanta and Catherine and Ginny allowed two days to do the trip, exchanging drivers and taking only one short overnight stop. Catherine was worried about the ancient station wagon and hoped that it would last the journey, but was resolved to park up and hire a better car if they had to.

As the journey progressed, Ginny learned more about Catherine's life. An attractive young woman, Catherine had commanded attention wherever she had gone, but her real talent lay in her forensic questioning and the way she managed to undress a political situation exposing its most private and embarrassing parts. She was the scourge of governors, congressmen and anyone in authority who tried to hide information or discriminate against others. She never got over the loss of her lover and never would. Later years in her life had seen Catherine writing papers or books on civil liberties and women's issues and this had suited her.

Her wit was as sharp as a knife and she had a raunchy sense of humour. They stopped for gasoline north of El Paso and as they pulled out of the forecourt Catherine saw some men, stripped to the waist, digging a large drainage ditch. She wound down the window and wolf whistled. When the surprised men looked up and smiled, she shouted, "Nice pecs boys!" They waved and responded with hoots and whistles. Ginny compared Catherine to her mom. They were so different, yet she now desperately needed them both.

They drove throughout the afternoon and much of the evening, eventually unable to go any further they stopped at a small motel over the border into Oklahoma. It didn't do food but a nearby gas station provided hotdogs and waffles. After getting ready for bed they sat and talked more. Ginny envied Catherine's independent nature and self-confidence and yet she detected there was something deeper that was being hidden and not talked about. Rightly, she guessed it was Catherine's loss of her lover that hovered in the back of her mind and drove her on to be the person she was. Ginny talked about her family and how loving and protective her mother had always been. She loved her father deeply, but he sometimes fitted the all-American image of a busy businessman or congressman: no time for family or fun, just work, work, work. She just wished that he would listen to her and understand her more, instead of putting her down.

Catherine smiled and said, "I don't know the context Ginny, but have you ever thought about the world that he inhabits, the stresses and strains and his family background? I certainly think from what you say, that he needs some reconstruction, but if he is daily immersed in wrangles with aggressive men in business or politics, then he is going to bring that stuff back home with him, isn't he?"

Ginny nodded.

Catherine continued, "And you may need to ask yourself why you don't like him questioning you. What makes you so special that you can't take a bit of delving into why you say what you say and getting you to justify what you believe in. Do that without throwing a tantrum and I guess he may just, well, kinda look at his young daughter and realise that what she says is right."

Ginny put her arms behind her head and leaned back, "Wise woman you!"

They had established a good relationship and Ginny felt that she had adopted Catherine as a big sister. She felt good about that.

Teddy and Cissy Warburton had been watchers for the FBI for about twenty years. They were both amateur artists and had a remarkable eye for detail and prodigious memories. Together they were a formidable team. They were both in their late sixties, but their eyesight was as sharp as that of a twenty-year old. The money wasn't great, but it did help to pay the bills and let them work together. It also left time for watercolour painting that they both dearly loved.

Darrel Bremner of Atlanta airport security managed the CCTV cameras and knew Teddy and Cissy very well, they had worked together many times. When they arrived, he knew there was important business to be done and let them both sit at the console. Darrel loved them both. They were real characters. Making coffee and buying doughnuts for them was a joy for him.

"Okay Tedster, what's to do today buddy, who're ya lookin' for?" he said.

"Oh, Darrel, just a couple of wild cats that need to be watched, that's all," said Teddy and he turned to Cissy and winked.

For the remainder of the day they fooled around, but as one joked the other watched the screen, then they would swap positions to give each other a break. This is what made them a formidable team. On twenty such occasions they had spotted fifteen suspects who were watched then later apprehended. They had quite a reputation.

Darrel was joking about baseball and Teddy had turned to joke about the poor performance of his team. Just as Cissy was putting the doughnut to her mouth, she noticed on one of the screens that a child was running across the arrivals concourse straight across the path of an electric buggy carrying disabled passengers. The child tripped and fell in front of the buggy and it looked certain she would be run over. She saw the mother turn, but too late. The doughnut hung barely inches below her lips, she let out a squeal and she froze. Teddy and Darrel looked up. Just then a young man ran at an angle towards the child and dived to save her. She sighed with relief, bit the doughnut and waved to Darrel to zoom in on the action.

"What a nice boy," she said out loud through a mouthful of dough and jam. Then the girl's hat fell off and the boy reached down and scooped it from the ground, looking up and smiling at the mother. Cissy reached for the photographs now placed prominently on the console and said, "Bingo!"

Quantock got the call from Teddy that they had spotted Clem in Atlanta airport. He steepled his hands and revelled in being right.

Clem took a bus to Centennial Olympic Park Drive and alighted at the entrance to the CNN building. He stopped and looked up at the tall building and took several deep breaths to help him gather his wits. Tourists were milling around and talking excitedly. One man, middle aged and slightly balding, stood aimlessly to one side. He was squat and fat, the sort who would look more at home with a six pack, a couch and a television. He looked up at Clem.

"Hi, buddy! Goin' round CNN?" said Clem.

"Yeah, guess so," said the man and he shrugged absent-mindedly.

"Damn, I wanted to do the trip round CNN today, but didn't get a ticket," Clem said.

The man frowned and fidgeted, "I don't have a ticket, but my name's on the Atlanta tour bus list for a guided tour. Came here all the way from Birmingham Alabama. Thing is I'm bored with the whole danged thing. My sister thought I could do with a day out."

Clem pretended to look thoughtful and then said, "Why sir, if you don't mind me saying, we can work something out. I could buy your place on the tour round CNN. That would make me happy, you can have some cash and, well, everyone's happy."

The man started to shuffle left and right.

"How much?" he said.

"Twenty-five bucks?" offered Clem.

The man needed no further persuasion and accepted the cash. They shook hands and Clem joined the throng from the two coaches from Birmingham Alabama as they entered the CNN building.

The tour guide assigned to the group was attentive and answered all the questions. Some of which bordered on the ridiculous, but that was always the way. When the tourists crowded around the newsroom, looking in at the presenters as they delivered their programmes, Clem put up his hand.

"Excuse me ma'am," he said to the petite tour guide.

She nodded towards him, "Yes, sir."

"Ma'am, isn't it a little dangerous for complete strangers to get so close to the presenters, I mean terrorism and all that?"

The tour guide gave a patronising smile. "Well, sir, you can rest assured that the presenters are quite safe. The glass you see before you is reinforced and will stop bullets and a significant blast. The only way into the studio is through a door at either end and this has security guards and screening of bags and visitors. So, I can tell you, sir, Larry King and others are quite safe."

Clem gave her a smile in return. Things hadn't changed significantly since he was last here doing his work placement from university. As the tour guide spoke about the news handling process, Clem watched the interaction between the people in the newsroom. They all had security badges and control was evidently very tight. To one side of the centre of the newsroom he could see a glass partition and behind this was where the guests to the programme sat. He knew this because he had been in that room. It was where guests got last minute touches to makeup and lapel microphones.

The security meant there was no way he and Ginny could burst into the studio, they would have to persuade Damien Tasker, the rookie presenter standing in for Paula Zahn, that their story was kosher and a blockbuster. If on the other hand the rookie wanted to take it through to his producer, they would face problems. They had to take that chance.

Leaving CNN, Clem swung his bag over his shoulder, walked a few blocks down Centennial Olympic Park Drive, turned into a small street and stopped in front of a large 1950s apartment block. He approached a grey door with numerous bell pushes on the frame.

Would anyone be in? He pushed a bell that had a blue dymo tape label underneath it that read: 23c Merric Grabowski.

"Ello?" said a voice with an Eastern European accent.

"Ello," Clem mimicked, "I come for some borsch, the best borsch in the world." Then he returned to his normal accent, "Hi Merric, it's me Clem, open the door, damn your ass!"

"Oh, Clem, but I thought? I come, now," said the unsteady voice.

The door opened and a dishevelled old man peered around. "It's you, it really is!" he said. "Come in my boy, come in."

They both went slowly up the stairs and Clem followed him into his apartment. It was just as he remembered it. Full of mementoes from the man's past. The one that always fascinated Clem was of a young man in Polish Cavalry Officer uniform sat on a magnificent black horse. Underneath was the inscription. "Dla Pulkwownika Grabowski od 25-go Pulku Oficerow Krolewskej Kawalerii, 23-go sierpnia, 1938" (To Colonel Grabowski from the officers of 25th Kings Cavalry Regiment, 23rd August 1938). It was Merric's father and he was immensely proud of him. He listened to countless stories of daring escapades and resistance work against the Nazis. Then after his father died, he learned about Soviet oppression.

They embraced warmly like father and son.

Clem stayed with Merric when he was doing his placement with CNN and they had remained firm friends. He explained the situation, without leaving anything out. When he finished Merric squinted at him. After a while he spoke.

"This is like communist Poland, yes?"

Clem felt awkward, his rational nature wanted to agree and yet his patriotic heart encouraged him to demur, and he blurted, "Not quite Merric, I believe that there has to be an answer, but I just don't believe that Uncle Sam has gone as far as that. For now, I need your help. Two ladies will join me the day after tomorrow and we have a plan. I will need to use both your spare rooms and am quite happy to pay you something."

Merric looked offended and his eyes opened wide, "Certainly not, no, no, no. You are my friend and now so are they." He raised his chin in defiance and Clem knew that it was stupid to argue.

Clem was pleased when Merric started to prepare a Polish stew and not borsch soup which he hated. Merric poured two large glasses of vodka and they toasted each other's health.

The stew was served with some ceremony and Merric clapped his hands and almost shouted, smacznego! It was a delicious meal and more vodka followed. Then Merric put his hands on the table.

"Okay then, you are to meet young Jamie, I remember him. He's a nice boy. But can you trust him?"

"Completely, Merric."

"And what if he is being watched?" said Merric.

"Well, maybe he is, but if that is the case then there's nothing I can do about it. I'll be arrested straight away." Clem frowned at Merric's common sense.

Merric thought for a moment and then said, "When times were bad in Poland during the war we used intermediaries. It sounds terrible, but they were expendable and less of a loss than perhaps a trained agent. I am ashamed to say that children were often used. This is not quite the same thing, but I could get a boy who does errands for me to meet your friend and deliver a note. You should not expose yourself to danger. What do you say?"

Clem thought for a moment. It was a good idea. Merric could watch the cafe from a distance and see the response.

"That makes sense Merric. Let's do it. I'll write the note and you contact your friend." He then sat down and wrote instructions to Jamie. He pleaded with him not to tell the rookie presenter anything at all. Just that he had a news scoop that would shock Americans. He should tell the presenter to list an interview with two college students, Jacob Arden and Laura Haydon, who had exclusive information about an anarchist plot to create mayhem on college campuses. It would be worth it. Then he sealed the envelope and gave it to Merric. They drank two more vodkas to loud proclamations of na zdrowie!

As Clem made his way to bed, his head a little light from the effect of the vodka, he began to feel a touch uncertain about the CNN plan. Would it really work?

Chapter 23

E-Day minus 10

Catherine and Ginny arrived in the evening. When Ginny saw Clem, she flew at him and hugged him tightly. It was such a long embrace that Catherine and Merric moved quietly away to introduce themselves. Over supper they watched the presidential election progress. Brannigan was at a rally in Ohio talking about his father.

"And my daddy said, a woman is better at bringing children up and keeping a home than a man. But when it comes to defending that home, it needs the man. Now my respected opponent looks like a man and talks like a man [much laughter and whoops from the audience] but she is still a woman. The jihadis don't respect her. Hell, they would put her in a burka." He paused dramatically. Thought a while, then silently shook his head. Then he grinned, almost comically. "Mind you I would be tempted to put her in a burka as well, might shut her up. [the audience screamed with laughter]. No, no. Only kidding. The way Muslims treat women is obscene. Totally obscene."

Ginny looked at Catherine, appalled. Merric chuckled. Clem was about to join in when he caught Ginny's glare. "Shocking. That's so, so…outrageous." Clem said lamely.

After supper Clem explained his plan and Ginny was enthusiastic about it. Catherine was less so, but had no better ideas and so she went along with it.

"Let's do it. But we'll need to script what we are going to say because you can bet that after the initial shock, say twenty seconds, the plug may be pulled," she said "so get the message across quickly."

They all agreed and Clem set about his script. He also read the letter that he wanted to be given to Jamie again.

Chapter 24

E-Day minus 9

Kristoff Kalescha was a bright, athletic 11-year old and wanted to be a professional roller-blader, but his skates needed upgrading. Today he smiled more broadly than usual. He imagined himself moving gracefully on new blades, hands behind his back, between the people on the sidewalk, swish, swish…whoosh! Adoring girls from tenth grade watching his every move. The money that Uncle Merric gave him would help him towards his target. He felt very grown up working for his favourite Uncle. Well, he wasn't a blood uncle, it was just a handle that his mother insisted he used out of respect for the old family friend.

His mission was to deliver a letter to a man that would be sitting at a table at the café on the corner of Marietta Street, he could hail him if he wanted. The man's name was Jamie Cook.

Kristoff was to say that a man asked him to come to the café and deliver the envelope to a Mr Cook. He smiled to himself: perhaps there would be another tip?

He arrived at the café with a swish of his skates as he carved a wide semi-circle and quickly noticed a young man with dark curly hair sitting alone near the door. It was him. He was obviously expected and the envelope was delivered without a hitch. Although the young man looked a little surprised, this didn't stop him giving

Kristoff a dollar. As directed, he skated on past the café and did not head anywhere near Uncle Merric's apartment, making a very wide circuit, before finally returning home.

A man reading a newspaper on the sidewalk outside the café spoke into his ear piece "A young boy has just delivered a note to the target. Target is in the café reading the note. Over."

Jamie got up, slipped the note in his pocket and left the café. He turned into an alley, which acted as a short cut to the CNN building. Two joggers in hooded tops came running towards him. Before Jamie knew it, he was bundled against the wall and received a punch in the nose. His eyes were blinded with tears and he felt blood pour from his nostrils. One of the joggers went through his pockets emptying them, before taking the watch off his wrist and the other held him fast. Job done, the men ran away. Some people ran up the alley to help Jamie who had slumped to the ground holding his nose.

The whole incident had taken less than a minute.

Within twenty minutes Quantock was reading the transcript of the note passed to Jamie Cook and smiled.

That afternoon Merric and Catherine went to the same café on the corner of junction of Merrieta Street and International Boulevard and sat close in a corner seat convenient for a good view of the television set on a pedestal above the counter. In view of the café's location and the clientele it was continuously programmed to CNN. They ordered coffee and doughnuts and settled back to watch the Paula Zahn hour.

Clem and Ginny took a separate route to the CNN building. They went up the stone steps and into the foyer and approached the reception desk. Two large security men stood either side of the glass door entrance into the studios.

"Hi, Jacob Arden and Laura Haydon, we are here for an interview on the Paula Zahn show," said Clem confidently.

The receptionist smiled and looked at a list on her desk. It took an age for her to run her finger up and down the list. Clem's heart beat fast and he felt impatient and nervy, and tried to control his anxiety and stay calm.

"Can I have some ID, sir?"

"ID, we, er, well we kinda dashed here real quick 'n don't have any." Clem looked crestfallen and Ginny clutched his arm. The receptionist's brow furrowed. She reached for the telephone and spoke to the producer. After a few seconds, during which Clem and Ginny's hearts beat like steam hammers, she frowned even more and then turned to them both.

"He cleared you," she said with a surprised look, "you have an internal docket for introductions so I guess that will be okay." The look on her face was one that displayed a need for process and procedures and her world had been clearly dented. She was obviously the sort of person who didn't like exceptions to the rules.

"Okay, put these passes on. You have access only to the corridors, bathrooms, and the main canteen in the building and, as you can see on the pass, to studio three. You are expected there fifteen minutes before the broadcast and looking at the time now, you had better hot foot it there without delay."

Clem and Ginny smiled at the receptionist and she managed just a slight tilt of the lips. Elated, they made their way between the two security guards and into the corridor. Passing studios one and two they heard the sound of interviews and music coming from speakers in the corridor. They slowed as they reached studio three, their hearts thumping and chests tightening. Clem looked at Ginny and they gave each other a silent high five, kissed and knocked lightly on the door.

The door opened and a short squat woman with teardrop shaped spectacles peered through the opening. She looked at her clipboard. "Arden and Haydon?"

They nodded. This was rewarded with a jerk of the head to the left. No introduction or guidance just a silent gesture. As they went through, they entered a cluttered, behind-the-scenes area, with equipment all over the place and various helpers and professionals sorting out everything from sound and picture quality on the cameras, to changes to scripts involving intense concentration and frantic scribbling onto running sheets.

"Over here," said the woman, "I'm Irma Glendale, executive producer for the Paula Zahn hour. If you go into this side room here," she opened a glass door to a room alongside the main broadcasting area and pointed, "our makeup specialist will get you ready for the show. It's almost a quarter to five and you should be with the presenter at about a quarter past five, okay?" She left them quickly and without waiting for an answer.

Clem and Ginny nodded and then both went into the allotted room and sat in chairs to have face makeup applied to prepare their looks for the glare of the lights and the intrusion of television cameras into every crevice in their faces.

The clock on the wall ticked away the seconds and minutes with small dull sounds and with each small 'clump' of the mechanism they both felt more nervous. The show had started and they were the second guests to appear. The third guest, a diminutive preacher holding a big bible, arrived and stood to one side waiting to be allocated a seat to be made up.

Then it was time to go. Irma with the tear-drop spectacles opened the door and they stood up to leave the dressing room. Irma stepped back into the dimness of the outer broadcasting area without saying a word. Clem lead the way through the door. They had gone no more than a few paces into the gloom when shadowy, strong hands reached out and grabbed Clem by the arms.

A voice said, "Don't struggle Clem Johnson, we have you under arrest son, it's useless to resist."

Clem's head was ringing as the stress of the moment came upon him in a sudden rush. He couldn't believe it. He struggled, but to no avail, as strong arms held him fast. Ginny was not so constrained. The space in the studio was limited because of the haphazard storage of equipment and files. She was behind and to the side of Clem as he was apprehended, with no one to hold onto her. Wasting no time, she skipped past Clem and his captors and screamed as loud as she could.

Skipping over equipment and hotly pursued by a burly man in a suit, she headed for the presenter's console. Damien Tasker heard the scream and stopped talking; his guest looked around, quite shocked at the sudden noise, his mouth open wide with surprise.

"Stop, I'm Ginny Grivas I'm still alive..." she shouted. But she wasn't close enough for her words to be heard above the melee.

"Ladies and gentlemen, I think we have, as they say, been penetrated," Tasker's voice was sarcastic and his guest smiled wanly, "and we are going to have to take a break."

As Tasker finished this announcement, Ginny realised that she was not going to make the console and let out another terrifying scream. Then she was grabbed and wrestled to the ground and an iron hand clamped around her mouth to prevent further disruption.

A soft drinks advertisement was screened, followed by several others in quick succession.

Merric and Catherine were watching the CNN programme and were speechless. The audible screams were recognisable as Ginny's.

Merric spilled coffee from his cup and Catherine's hands went to her mouth. They were shocked and suddenly very afraid.

Merric and Catherine crashed through the door to the apartment. They slammed the door behind them and breathlessly held each other.

"Oh, my God, oh my God!" gasped Catherine.

Merric was calm and cool. After a few minutes, he slowly pushed Catherine away. "Gather your things we must go!" he said.

"What do you mean? No one knows we are involved and Clem won't inform on you," she said.

"It's never that simple. The state has enormous resources at its disposal. I've been through this in my homeland and I know what I am talking about. Okay, let's go shall we?" He went to a cupboard and took out a large old-fashioned carpet bag then went around his flat selecting clothes, valuables and money that he wanted to take with him.

Catherine threw her few items into her bag. "Are you sure this is necessary?" she said.

Merric smiled. "Okay. Where is your car?" he said.

"A block away."

"Here take this," he said throwing a small car blanket to Catherine. "We'll go to your car and wait. Let's see what we see."

Then he led Catherine down the back stairway, around the parking lot and through a dark alleyway to the main street where Catherine had parked the Plymouth. After putting their bags in the trunk, Merric guided Catherine into the back seat where they both lay low in the seat leaving a slim view of the road outside the apartment.

Chapter 25

E-Day minus 8

Quantock didn't have much time to spare. Clem and Ginny were both safely in custody and he was desperate to track down anyone who had been associated with them both. They had to be isolated. He was pacing up and down the FBI office in Atlanta when Jim Rook came in.

"We've picked up young Jamie Cook. He's pretty scared and shaking like a leaf. If we formally arrest him then there will have to be charges and that's going to be difficult. What shall we do now?"

"I don't know," said Quantock, "if we act too quickly then he will gain strength and plead the Fifth Amendment, call his brief and defend what he did. We have to break that defence."

Quantock paced up and down more quickly with his right hand to the side of his head. Then he stopped, lowered his hand and clicked his fingers.

"Yazoo! That's it Jim. We make him think that he's been duped."

Jim looked askance, "But how?"

Quantock smiled, "Let's cool him first. Usual stuff Jim, lower the temperature in the interview room, give him a few cups of very strong coffee so that the caffeine kicks in and keep him awake and on his own for a long while. Do that first then come back and see me – quick now!"

Jim Rook shrugged his shoulders, but found it easy to respond quickly to a strong leader – there weren't too many around these days. He walked quickly down several corridors to the interview room where Jamie Cook was being held, collected a cup of black coffee from a coffee machine, and then unlocked and entered the interview room noisily. Jamie sat on a light metal and plastic chair at an equally lightly constructed table, his head in his hands.

"Hey, man! What's goin' on? I asked for a lawyer ages ago where is he? Someone speak to me, talk to me, but do something for Chrissake." He sounded nervy and agitated. His nose was very swollen.

"Jamie. So sorry. You must be worried out of your mind – well, I know I would be." Jim put the coffee down in front of Jamie, "Here, drink this it's hot and strong and will do you a power of good."

Jamie gratefully took the coffee and sipped it loudly.

Jim picked up on Quantock's theme and gently led Jamie into its mesh. He put his hands on his hips and said, "Jamie, I gotta say that you seem such a straight kind of guy. I'm, well, just so surprised. This is just so damned serious. Words like treason are being used."

"Treason!" said Jamie, almost spitting out his coffee, "free speech yes, treason no. My God this is stupid."

Jim was satisfied with this response and backed off, "Jamie, I have to go now, I'll be back soon I promise," he said.

"No, don't go," pleaded Jamie, who wanted to talk rather than be left alone with his fears. But Jim left the room and locked the door leaving Jamie with his agitation. He began to walk down the corridor, then doubled back and turned down the heating to the interview room.

Jim entered the temporary office just as Quantock was putting down the telephone. He was smiling. Then he looked at his watch. He explained what he was going to do and Jim grinned broadly and called him a legend. They would wait until three in the morning. It was a slim chance, but might just work. Jim couldn't wait to see this one through – a master at work!

Quantock smiled and turned his attention to the other possible contact, Merric Grabowski a Polish immigrant. He had been the person who had provided Clem with accommodation while he underwent work placement at CNN. How much did he know? What was his role in this stunt?

It did not matter. They would soon find out.

Merric and Catherine were almost asleep when two cars stopped in the road outside the apartment at about half past midnight. The occupants got out slowly, there were no sirens or fuss, just quiet efficiency, half a dozen men fanning out with four entering the apartment block entrance and two standing, looking around. After finding the apartment empty, the searchers rejoined the watchers and they got back in their cars and drove away.

Catherine was shocked. "Oh God. Okay, then, you were right. I am so ashamed! Let's go."

Merric pulled her down below the seat line. "No. Wait."

They waited for about five minutes. Then from about four cars down the street they saw it. A flash of orange light as a cigarette was lit. Merric marked the car in his mind and they both sat back to play a waiting game. The night passed and as dawn broke the street grew lighter and traffic along the road gradually increased as people went to work. Catherine awoke, rubbed her eyes and realised she desperately needed a pee. The diner on the corner was just opening up and she eased out of the car slowly. Merric was asleep. She stretched herself behind a lamp-post then casually walked down the sidewalk towards the diner. After visiting the ladies' room, she bought two coffees to go and a bag of bagels, then paid and left the shop to walk back up the street. As she briskly passed the car that she thought held the watcher, she looked inside. To her joy, she saw that the man was asleep. It had been a long night.

Quickly, she made her way back to the car, stowed the breakfast in the front passenger seat, then started the engine and slowly pulled out to join the queue of traffic. Merric stirred.

"What…?" he murmured.

"Relax. Our watcher is fast asleep and I have our breakfast. Where shall we go now?" said Catherine in a calm voice.

"Oh," he said through dry lips, "head out of town to Washington. I have a friend who lives on the East side. We can stay there until we sort out what to do next. But when you can, please stop? I am an old man and need my breakfast, I have had enough excitement already!"

Catherine didn't smile at this stab at humour. She was worried sick.

Jim broke the news to Quantock that Merric Grabowski had not been apprehended. To his surprise, he simply shrugged his shoulders and said, "Well, you can't win 'em all. My guess is that with his background he will want to avoid all trouble with the state and he will keep his head down until he passes away. He's long gone that's for sure. Anyway," he said, looking at his watch, "it's show-time!"

Jim smiled. This he must see. Everything was arranged and he knew what he had to do. Together they walked down the corridors that led to the interview room. Jim went to the area behind the two-way glass and Quantock entered the interview room.

Jamie looked terrible. Several plastic cups, some a third filled with coffee, lay in a pile in front of him. His nerves were jangling and ragged through too much caffeine, and with hair that was dishevelled and face shiny with grease and a swollen red nose, he looked like a wino. Quantock almost winced at the sight of his dark shadowed eyes, that clearly wanted to close but weren't being allowed to. Yellow bruising was also spreading under each eye from the trauma of the "mugger's" punch,

"Jamie. My name is Dan Quantock. I want to ask you some questions."

Jamie looked up, "Mr Quantock. I have been here for hours, what the hell is going on?"

"Okay. I will tell you," Quantock said, leaning in towards Jamie's frightened face. "I'll give it to you straight Jamie. I have to decide whether or not you are part of a major plot to drive the President out of office by threat and blackmail. Are you the kind of person to propound the merits of an ultra-right-wing, anti-negro, anti-Catholic, anti-Jewish political group that, frankly, should never be allowed to see the light of day let alone get coverage on CNN?"

"What? Clem? All that. Oh no, I just don't believe it," said Jamie, and he began shaking.

Quantock gently put his hand on Jamie's shoulder.

"Look son, did you speak to Clem Johnson?" he said.

Jamie looked at him nervously, then down at the table.

"Why, yes, Mr Quantock, I did."

"How?"

"Well, he was on a cell phone, it wasn't that clear I grant you, but hey, it was Clem – I mean I was sure it was."

"Did you meet him face to face?"

Jamie hesitated, "No. No, I guess I didn't. He sent me a note saying that he had to keep out of sight." Then he rallied his strength. "With all this going on I can't say that I am surprised." He was breathing heavily and Quantock knew that the caffeine was reacting with his tired body. His heart would be pounding and he would feel as though he were hyperventilating. Now was the time to strike.

"I understand your loyalty for your dead friend..."

Jamie broke in, "But he's not dead!"

Quantock continued like a patient parent: "…as I say, to your dead friend. Look, why don't you come with me?" Jamie was confused and stood up unsteadily; Quantock took his arm.

From behind the viewing screen, Jim quickly scrambled out of the side door and made his way down to interview room number three, joining another man at the table. Quantock followed moments later with Jamie who was by now breathing heavily and shuffling along beside him. Instead of going into the interview room they went into the viewing area. Quantock turned to Jamie as they got inside.

"Quiet now. If you make a noise Jamie I'll get very angry, okay?" he said, planting both hands on the table and looking directly into Jamie's eyes.

Jamie paled and replied, "Yes sir, but what…?" he stopped talking and stared at the window in front of him. A slim young man sat with his back to him. He was medium build, say a hundred and fifty pounds, dressed in jeans and a sweatshirt. His fair hair was curly and covered his ears but it was not overly long.

"Clem!" said Jamie softly, and Quantock put his finger to his mouth. He turned up the speaker knob and the sound of voices filled the small area.

Jim was saying, "Come on now, be a man and fess up. You gave it your best shot and failed buddy, there's no sense in denying it. You're a loser. But what the hell did you expect to achieve?"

The fair-haired man snarled his response: "You stupid lickspittle lackey of ZOG. How can you be so ignorant of what is going on in America? The Kikes are in alliance with the Niggers and the Papists, controlling everything. No jobs for white men, our boys dead in Iraq and the rest of the Muslim rat holes. Now the Zionists want a lesbian as a President. Well, fuck that man." Suddenly he stood up and threw his chair across the room. An armed guard grabbed him around the middle and grappled him to floor. Jim sat patiently. The boy carried on shouting, "You can do what you like to me G-Man, but when bombs go off and blast your ass to heaven you won't be laughin' then. We have a hundred Timothy McVeigh's out there."

Before he could continue, the guard wrenched the boy's head around and Jamie's jaw dropped.

It wasn't Clem.

Quantock led Jamie back to the interview room. When he got back there the air con was adjusted to a warmer level and a plate of sandwiches was waiting on the table along with some orange juice. After one hour, Quantock had the boy eating out of his hand. Jamie accepted that he had been duped and felt stupid. He would resign his job that morning and move on. There was nothing else to be done. Quantock stopped him and offered to mediate with CNN bosses. He would say that it was a government sting to catch a particularly vicious group of individuals bent on mayhem and that Jamie had no option but to comply and, under threat of prison, keep it all a secret. The rookie CNN presenter would also be exonerated. Jamie was relieved and thanked him profusely. Quantock let him leave the building and Jamie waved as he crossed the road, happy to be an American and so well looked after by agents like Quantock!

It didn't take long to talk to the key players in CNN and explain the situation. The story for popular news consumption was to be that some kids tried to get up to political mischief, but they were stopped and given a talking to. Everyone agreed to move on and Quantock was pleased to close down the incident.

Then he called the President's office. At the end of the brief call, he added, "Sir, they will be held safely. Yes, sir. Yes. Absolute safety."

Chapter 26

E-Day minus 7

Clem didn't like to swallow the tablet and he coughed when the water was poured down his throat. But then he liked the injections even less. It was impossible to prevent the medication being administered and over the next few days he would move in and out of sleep and feel that nothing mattered whatsoever. He tried to focus on his surroundings, but it was difficult. His vision constantly swirled like the ebb and flow of a tide; each time he wanted to crawl onto a tempting calm shoreline the scene tilted and wouldn't stay still long enough for him to gain some balance. The lighting was low and the sheer net curtains covering the windows billowed in the wind allowing an occasional glimpse of green grass and clumps of shrubs with autumn colours. As he moved his head a middle-aged woman in white uniform came over to his side.

"You okay honey?" she said.

"Where am I?"

"You're in hospital and the best thing for you is to get some rest. Don't do any thinkin'. Don't do any moving around, you'll only fall over. It is in your own interest to just stay quiet and calm. If you don't then I'm gonna have to give you some more medication," her face was warm and yet her voice had a stern tone.

"Are you a nurse or a prison warder?"

"Now honey, you're letting your mind get excited. I told you not to do that!" she then reached in to a tray and took out a syringe. Clem paled and knew what was coming. Then he felt a slight prick and his ears heard the sound of rushing like a subway train and he was suddenly elated and transported to unconsciousness.

David Weinberger, Director of the CIA, and Troy Hammond, Director of the FBI, met at a neutral location in Washington, each accompanied by an aide they could trust. The location was a small residential hotel used as a front for clandestine meetings of all kinds. An unseen hand closed the large oak door to the dining room where they were seated at a glass table. There were several bottles of mineral water, a small icebox and six tall glasses on the table. The room was decorated in bottle green wallpaper and was dimly lit by several retro cylindrical wall lights. The scene resembled a Mafia meeting between two clan bosses and their minders. The air was electric and tense.

Weinberger started the discussion. "I don't get it. Six teenagers, each a son or daughter of a prominent US senator, are kidnapped by two ex-Blackwater operatives; why? Your man, what's his name? Quantock, that's it. Your man catches up with them following an unspecified hunch and despatches them both without mercy. It seems we are to believe that our boys could have been in the pay of jihadi terrorists seeking to hold the nation to ransom." He paused and took a deep breath before continuing.

"I know that the two boys concerned could be, er, how shall we say, a little undisciplined at times, but there is nothing to suggest that they would go Benedict Arnold on us."

Hammond sat impassively listening to the opening remarks. He frowned and responded. "Okay. Try this for size: one of the girls had been sexually assaulted, raped in fact, and the report said, let me see I have it here." He flicked through the pages of a report in front of him, "Ah yes, here it is, Ralph Anderson was known to have a voracious sexual appetite and a drug habit, as well as a record for being erratic and violent. We know about an incident in Thailand, but the details on file have been redacted. Anderson's DNA was matched to the semen in Senator Dempsey's daughter's body and his blood tested for cocaine. So what the hell makes you love these guys so much?"

Weinberger bristled and fidgeted. "For the record Martin Gonzalez has never been in the employ of the Agency and Ralph Anderson left in 2003. But they have done important service for America and they are on the jihadi most wanted list as a result. The jihadis wouldn't want to turn these guys; they would behead them publicly on YouTube. And something stinks about the set up. Who's ever heard of jihadis hiding out in the Arizona desert? They would stand out like crows at a fancy birds's show. This simply doesn't smack of Al Qaeda or any other group. They would've captured the kids, dressed them up in orange jump suits, sat them in front of a video camera and threatened to slit their throats. Then they would have sent copies to every dumb ass organisation willing to show the film on prime-time TV news channels. Wouldn't they? This smacks to me of being a false flag operation. And I tell you this. My people are fed up to the back teeth and mad as hell with getting the blame for everything that goes wrong in the security world. We're not going to take it anymore."

Weinberger sat back exhausted, breathing heavily almost as though he had gone ten rounds of boxing. There was silence. Too much for the CIA aide who, exasperated, blurted out, "I think we've wasted our time, sir"

The FBI aide smiled sarcastically, causing the CIA boy to yap: "What the hell are you smilin' at Hoover boy?"

"Cut it out the pair of you," said Hammond. "If this is the way that two agencies act towards each other, then America's in a worse state than I thought." He turned to Weinberger, "I hear what you say David, it just takes my 'Hoover' brain a little longer to figure out what's going on. Now I suggest we send these two boys out of the room to sort out their differences, whilst you and I continue?"

Weinberger readily agreed and the aides left the room after being made to shake hands. When the door closed both men took off their jackets. Weinberger went to light a cigar and Hammond stopped him. "I would be grateful if you wouldn't smoke, if you don't mind?"

Weinberger smiled and couldn't resist making a barbed remark, "Ah yes, the President thinks it good sport to smoke his cigars at meetings to annoy the anti-smoking brigade. Doesn't seem to respect anyone does he? Except of course, Sadie Burrows. But then she can moisten my cigar any day!"

Hammond ignored the coarse remark. "Look David. I don't like this any more than you do. I have my own suspicions. We should work together on this or we'll end up pitching each organisation against the other and that's counterproductive. I can see by your expression that you know more – so tell me."

The atmosphere softened and Weinberger poured some water into a tall glass and helped himself to some ice.

"You're right. I do have some more information. We both know that a deep clean team went to clean up a mess in Arizona."

"Sure, so what?"

Weinberger continued, "Well one of the cleaners was in Desert Storm with Martin Gonzalez. After the war, they went their separate ways and then, bang, this guy ends up cleaning up Gonzalez' body in Arizona. Well, he told us that the bodies were recovered from a small hotel in the town of Benson. We followed this up. One of our agents, a pretty girl, very persuasive and likeable, visited the hotel and spoke to the clerk. She failed to get anything out of him. In fact, he was so uncommunicative that she was convinced his life had been threatened. Undeterred, she carried out exhaustive checks and guess what? Two teenagers were seen in the company of a man resembling Mr Dan Quantock. Your man, Troy. She also checked out all the automobile rental agencies and, strike two, she found that Clem Johnson had used his credit card to hire a vehicle and that the FBI had been informed of this."

He put his hands together and stared at Hammond.

Hammond frowned, "David, the kid's belongings were left open to the world at the tin mine for quite a period and it is just possible that someone stole Johnson's wallet and used the credit card?"

"Yes, it is just possible. Trouble is Troy, you don't believe that."

"I don't know what to believe David. We have to be frank with each other. This is not easy. The man you speak of, Quantock, is now quite highly placed and has the ear of the President. All work involving the investigation into the whereabouts of the missing teenagers has been undertaken by him and he answers directly to the President."

"You mean…"

"I mean nothing, David, nothing until I can put together all that you have given me and followed up on my own investigations," said Hammond.

"Okay, Troy," said Weinberger. "I'll wait until I get an update from you. And if you need any extra collateral it's yours."

"Thank you, David, much appreciated," said Hammond.

They shook hands.

Chapter 27

E-Day minus 6

A pale platinum sun was rising over the Potomac as Merric and Catherine were welcomed into Merric's friend's apartment in George Town, Washington. It had been a long drive, going around in circles to shake off anyone who might be following, although they checked several times and knew they weren't. The traffic was heavier than usual and in a funny sort of way they felt safer because of this. There had been nothing, absolutely nothing on any of the news channels about Clem and Ginny's antics on CNN except for brief cheerful laughs from presenters about teenagers gaining access to play a prank on a rookie presenter.

After Merric had introduced Catherine to his friend Rosa, she left them to talk. She owned a small cake shop in the local area and had laid out some pastries. A plate was laid with babka, or grandmother cakes, small, rich and bread-like, formed in a bundt, a shape reminiscent of a woman's skirt, and szarlotka, which was apple and cinnamon cake. Despite the wonderful aroma of the pastries and coffee Catherine didn't have much of an appetite and just picked at them. Merric on the other hand still remembered the poor times in Poland and distraught or not, held to the notion that the body must be fed.

"What on earth has happened to the kids?" asked Catherine.

Merric chewed the remainder of a babka cake and swallowed some coffee. After a while he answered.

"Kto wie? Who knows? They will be somewhere. Somewhere out of sight. No news on the television, Catherine, means that no one really knows about their situation and that they are, how would you say? Non-people." He looked glum.

Catherine's eyes welled with tears and she felt her throat closing with anger and frustration. There really was nothing that she could do. She descended into a depressive state, put her elbows on the table and her head in her hands. Merric finished the other babka.

Catherine raised her head. "Merric. We are missing our duty, our definite duty. We have to tell Ginny and Clem's parents that they are still alive. Ginny's mother does know that she was not killed and must be beside herself with worry."

Merric clucked his teeth. It was true. They did have a duty to advise a worried mother. But there were dangers and for a start both parents' houses would be bugged and watched.

"Catherine," he said, "we should contact Ginny's mother first. I know of Clem's father and he is a dumb guy, really dumb. The boy told me much of his life and relationship with his father. This man will make instant trouble and this will do us no good. He will consider himself to be a distressed father approached by two charlatans who want to get money out of a grieving family. No, from what I hear, Ginny's mother is the best bet. She has at least been contacted already and knows that her daughter didn't perish in the tin mine in Arizona. But if we do this Catherine, we have to plan it carefully. No contact by telephone at all you understand? Although I am, to all intents, a fugitive and how would you say, am in the frame now, the authorities probably do not know anything about you. But I must repeat, no telephone under any circumstances, please."

Merric paused for a second and Catherine interjected. "Merric you are so right. I have to get to talk to Ginny's mother, somehow. And I will need to start," she looked sideways towards a personal computer on a sideboard near the window, "on the net."

John Zirl had only been in the CIA for three years. He had majored in Criminology at university and then joined the Washington DC police department, making the rank of sergeant after four years. He had then applied and got the job as special agent in the CIA and after an 18-month training programme was able to take to the field. David Weinberger had taken a liking to him and John had a feeling that he was giving him help with his career. Now he was being asked to take on a very delicate investigation which involved the FBI. John knew there was bad feeling between the CIA and FBI. There was a terrible atmosphere between them and it had to be fixed. John's mission was to make covert contact with Senator Grivas. Thanks to plants he had in the FBI, Weinberger knew that only four bodies had been found in the Lynchburg case, the other two, the FBI claimed, were buried deep in the San Quiller tin mine following a roof fall. He also knew that teams of FBI special agents had been detailed to watch Senator Grivas and Senator Johnson and their families. Finally came the intel from an FBI informant that two teenagers had not been murdered at all and were being held in an exclusive private mental health facility in north east Washington.

Zirl stood by the stage in the Alumni Hall of the University of Pittsburgh listening to Senator Grivas and his Democrat challenger make their election pitches to a packed audience. He calculated that the number of red and blue placards were about equal. The speeches ended to tumultuous applause and Grivas came down the stairs shaking hands with well-wishers. Zirl held his hand out and Grivas grasped it. "Senator Grivas. Well done, sir. You must remember me" said Zirl loudly.

Grivas smiled and Zirl could see that he was trying to check his mental database of names. Zirl leaned forward. "I'm a friend of Ginny. Ron Grainger. Here's my card. Ginny is alive. Don't acknowledge what I am saying. Just phone me as soon as you can. I'm on your side. But if you want to save Ginny don't say a word to anyone. Just phone me. "

Grivas took the card and Zirl disengaged. He said loudly "You got my vote, sir!" and supporters nearby cheered. Senator Grivas smiled broadly and carried on shaking hands

Grivas was escorted to his car. The driver stopped reading his newspaper and called out.

"Home Senator?"

"Yeah, home. Straight away and no diversions," he replied.

Once in the car he took out Zirl's business card. His throat thickened. He had been hard on his wife when she said she had been called by Ginny. He accused her of hallucinating or to have talked to con-merchants. They had a terrible argument with the both of them ending in tears – not something that came easily to the tough Senator Grivas. Perhaps she had been right after all? He rang the number on the card.

Catherine had googled Mrs Angela Grivas and amongst a wealth of useful information had come across her election calendar. She now drove north, to Marple Township in Pennsylvania, which sat between the state capital Harrisburg and Philadelphia, and where the Grivas' had a house. Mrs Grivas was due to open a charity event at the local children's hospital.

A collection of stalls and tents, laid out in the hospital's grounds, was doing a steady trade and the smell of toffee apple, candy floss and hotdogs drifted in the chill autumn air. Catherine wandered around, browsing the stalls but scoping the crowd for the sight of Mrs Grivas. Then she saw a woman dressed in a beige woollen suit, cream blouse and with matching crocodile shoes and handbag being ushered from the cake competition tent. It was unmistakably Angela Grivas. She stood slightly to one side of a group of women, occasionally responding to a remark, but otherwise remaining sealed up in her own company, looking slightly aloof and detached. But then she had a lot on her mind, thought Catherine. She walked towards her and stopped several feet away. Perhaps she could do this without saying a word?

Catherine looked steadily at Mrs Grivas and after a while, Mrs Grivas returned her gaze. At first, she looked away. Then, on seeing Catherine's persistent gaze she turned her head back in her direction. Catherine raised an eyebrow. Mrs Grivas tilted her head slightly, but continued staring. Then she slowly started to walk towards Catherine; bingo!

"Do I know you?" asked Mrs Grivas. Her expression was frozen, completely without emotion.

Catherine put out her hand and Mrs Grivas took it, "No, but I do need to talk to you," she looked around her, "about Ginny."

She lifted her head slightly and replied, "What about Ginny?"

"She called you twice, once from Benson and once from my place. Does that mean we can talk some more?"

This time Mrs Grivas put her hand to her mouth. Her voice faltered slightly and eyes welled, and she said, "Yes, I think we should."

Catherine was gentle with Mrs Grivas. She touched her hands frequently as they sat drinking coffee at one of the several untidy tables in the refreshment tent, and she explained exactly everything that Ginny and Clem had told her and what she saw in Atlanta.

Angela Grivas' eyes widened and big tears fell down her cheeks. After five agonising minutes, she composed herself. She needed to stay calm and understand that Catherine had seen Ginny and she was alive. She was alive!

It was a complicated scenario and Mrs Grivas was uncertain as to what to do next. It was confusing and she felt impotent, but she had to control her emotions, stay calm and be responsible. Catherine told her that no undue fuss should be made without thinking the situation through. Angela agreed. They hugged and exchanged cell phone numbers.

Senator Grivas was waiting for his wife when she came in. He dragged her unwilling and angry into the garden sun lounge at the bottom of the garden saying they needed secrecy and he had heard something he didn't quite know whether to believe. He was so wound up he wouldn't let his wife get a word in edgeways. But Angela Grivas won the day, because she burst into floods of tears and she recounted her meeting with Catherine Devine; when this double confirmation sunk in, Nick Grivas broke down. They wept and clung to each other. When they were calmer, they focussed on their situation and the need for secrecy even in their own house. Double confirmation, their daughter was, after all, safe and well, surely now they could believe that everything was going to be all right?

He hugged his wife and said, "Let's get our daughter back. And I tell you this for nothing – somebody will pay for this. I swear it."

PART FOUR

AMERICAN CARNAGE

"A good plan violently executed right now is far better than a perfect plan executed next week."

General George S Patton

Chapter 28

E-Day minus 5

Senator Grivas was in no mood for anything other than straight talking. He was met by the man purporting to be Ron Grainger at a selected rendezvous and allowed himself to be driven to another location. They both got out of the car when it stopped in a small courtyard at a townhouse south of the city. The house had been fitted out as an office and Grivas was led to a small conference room. Another man was there and he shook the senator's hand introducing himself with a smile as John Smith, another CIA agent.

"Senator, sit down please," said John Zirl aka Ron Grainger. "I know that you are worried sick regarding the whereabouts of your daughter, so I'll waste no further time. One of our agents thinks he may have found out where she is being held." He then clicked on a laptop and said, "Watch this."

Video footage played on a nearby screen and showed the surrounding area of Montrose Park mental health facility. Then it slowly moved towards a wooded area. The camera moved through the wood and stopped short of some railings. Slowly some leaves were moved and what appeared to be a large white building came into view. The video cut to a shot of some French windows. The telescopic lens was of a very high quality, because it zoomed in a long way and still provided a crystal-clear picture. As it did so it focussed on a female form in a dressing gown sitting in a chair.

Senator Grivas instinctively leaned forward and said out loud, "It's Ginny, I know it."

The video was freeze-framed.

Senator Grivas quickly stood up. "Okay, that's it, I want my daughter out of there, now. Let's go, what are we waiting for?"

Zirl spoke calmly, "I'll tell you Senator. We are still assessing the dangers of alerting those who are holding her. We can get her out without harming her, but we will lose the opportunity to surprise those who organised this terrible thing. We also need to flush out the source of all this trouble. This situation is bigger than your daughter sir. It is of national importance. We need you to trust us."

Senator Grivas sat down again and said resignedly, "Okay. As long as this does not put my daughter in any more danger than she has been put in already. I can't put her through any more. But I am also madder than hell. There is an implication that my house and phone may be bugged – me, a senator! How does this happen? Who breaks rules like this?"

The two men sitting across from him looked at each other before responding, "Senator the guilty will be brought to justice. I promise you."

"I just want you to get my daughter out of there."

Coffee arrived and Zirl outlined the escape plan. The nursing staff shift at the hospital changed twice a day. An agent planted on the inside would administer a drug to Ginny It would have a devastating effect on Ginny's facial skin, turning it into a flaky and spotty mass. This would be distressing for her, but the effects were temporary and it would allow a substitute to be put in her place at just the time of the change of nursing staff. She would then be smuggled out and back home. This time there would be no hitches.

230

They would go back for Clem when it was all over and they had achieved the element of surprise. Then and only then would they get to the bottom of the situation. They also had to work quickly to meet a deadline that was closing.

The presidential election was due in eight days and postal voting was well underway.

Senator Bobby "Bubba" Johnson, played "Strange Fruit" on his saxophone in his den. Tears rolled down his dimpled cheeks. Next door in her therapy room his wife sat cross legged surrounded by candles and crystals meditating. Her face was also wet with tears. Different rituals of grief at the loss of a beloved child were also painfully played out at the homes of the Dawsons, the Danberrys, the Dempsters and the Masters.

Angela Grivas invited Catherine to her Washington house. In the kitchen over coffee and baklava, she explained slowly and clearly that she and her husband were contacted by the CIA about Ginny and Clem. Catherine had been right; her lovely daughter and Clem Johnson were alive. Angela explained to her that the agents understood that Merric and Catherine would be suspicious. The agents wanted it known that they fully understood how the pair felt about authority, but that they should be reassured because Senator Grivas and Angela were acting as trusted third parties. Catherine had no other option than to offer her full support.

A medium sized cleaning truck drove along an avenue of tall chestnut trees, the remaining leaves were different kinds of red brown and wet with the morning mist. Then it slowed down in front of the gates to the Montrose Residential Clinic. The driver showed the correct papers and was waved on by the security guard.

The cleaning company often used different staff and so it was no surprise to see new faces. The truck went to the rear of the main building and three people, two men and a woman, dressed in green cleaning fatigues and the driver got out. They unloaded two lockable boxes on wheels, five by three feet in size. The tallest of the men, nicknamed Shorty, tapped lightly on the side of one box and got a light tap from inside in return. They looked at their watches; it was nine in the morning.

"Hi, you guys new here?" said a voice from the direction of the rear door. They jumped at the unexpected intervention.

"Oh, jeez, sorry you made me jump," said the woman. "Yeah, we're a new team. I'm the supervisor, Martha."

"Okay, for what it's worth your friends usually stay for coffee and doughnuts afterwards, but don't tell your administration – they pay for the extra time. See you later?" said the male nurse.

Martha winced inwardly and thought, "Ooh, great. Not." But she smiled and said, "Sure that would be great, thank you. We'd better get on with the job. See you."

The team had been briefed meticulously; today the wing where Ginny Grivas was housed was scheduled for a clean-up. They pushed their wheeled boxes and equipment through the institution.

The doors to the wing they were to clean were guarded by a reception desk. Martha approached the receptionist and showed her ID and the receptionist pressed a button to open the doors. The team passed through. Martha turned to a male member of the team. "Okay Tyrone, you start here."

Tyrone set to work. After a while, at the time of the staff shift change, he saw two nurses approaching. He bent down to his metal box and pulled a pin at the base of the box and the doors flew open. All manner of equipment fell out including several containers of cleaning fluid. The floor was deluged with different colour liquids, brushes and containers, right in the path of the nurses.

One of the nurses lost her temper, "Oh man, my damned shoes, these are just clean on today, you horses' ass you. My God look at the mess!"

Tyrone knew his script. "Well, ma'am," he said in a slow drawl, "no need shoutin' at me, this ain't my fault. I don't make the damned boxes." His voice grew shrill and angry. "You try livin' on the peanuts I get using this crap and see how you like it. You ain't got no call shoutin' at me like that."

Then the shouting match escalated with each accusing the other of being unreasonable. The noise could be heard back down the corridor and Martha the supervisor wasted no time at all. She rushed into Ginny's ward, and then slowed as she approached the armchair in which Ginny had been placed for the day. Ginny looked in a terrible state. The drug smuggled into the hospital and placed in her drinking water by another operative a few days earlier had done the trick and her face was a mass of flaky skin and red weals – she was hardly recognisable. Martha bent down and whispered in her ear.

"Don't worry. You are gonna be quite safe soon."

But Ginny couldn't really take anything in. The drugs being administered to keep her docile were very strong. Martha produced a syringe and calmly emptied the contents into Ginny's arm. It was a mild sedative to put her into a shallow sleep. Shorty opened the main body of the steel box and out sprang a young woman in a towelling robe. She had Ginny's build and hair colouring and face was covered in flaky skin and red weals. She waved her hand in front of her face indicating that she had found it hot in the box. They removed Ginny's dressing gown and night shift and the girl put them on, handing her own robe to be put on Ginny.

Shorty then reached down and lifted Ginny's body gently off her chair. Martha dressed her in the towelling robe and together they placed her into the padded interior of the steel box on wheels. After making sure the drug had worked and that she was quite asleep and her body was in a comfortable position, the box was locked. Martha looked at her watch. The CIA operative had survived because she was able to breathe through a tube, but Ginny was unconscious and would not be able to do so effectively.

"No more than thirty minutes at the outset. After that she runs out of clean air!"

They both touched the shoulder of their companion to be left behind then made for the scene of chaos at the entrance doors.

Other nurses going off shift had stopped to watch the row. When Tyrone heard the squeaking of the wheels on the first steel box and the tap, tap of the shoes of his comrades coming down the corridor he stopped yelling. Martha barrelled up through the spectators and snapped: "Tyrone, what the devil have you been doing and why are you yelling at these nurses?"

"Those boxes are lethal," said the younger of the two nurses, "I'm calling the health and safety supervisor and both of them will be impounded, right now, that's what. I'm not having this crap again."

The situation was now getting serious and Martha had to think quickly. At first, she said nothing and glared at everyone. That silenced them all. Then she walked towards the metal box on wheels and knelt down. She went straight to the pin that had been used to eject the material and theatrically got down on her knees to inspect its housing. Standing up she turned towards Tyrone and frowned.

"How many more times do I tell you Tyrone? This pin is a safety pin. It is used just in case little children get inside the box and cannot get out. You pull it and everything flips apart. Good for the kid whose life it saves, bad for a pair of nurse's shoes. The pin should be secure, Tyrone, secure. Not hanging like a donkey dick ready to be pulled by some fool like you!"

Her voice rose and the nurses physically recoiled at the admonition. They almost felt sorry for Tyrone. He sheepishly looked down and said, "Yeah, I remember now. I'm sorry. Can I pay for the shoes?"

The atmosphere changed now that the nurses gained support from someone of their own gender. Then, pleased that they had been vindicated, they thanked her, waived the cleaning bill for the shoes and moved on. As Shorty and the driver cleaned up the mess, Martha and Tyrone pushed the metal box with Ginny up to the doors and rang the intercom. "We're just packing up now. Can you let me through me please?" The doors swung open and they passed through. At the reception desk Martha handed over a completed worksheet, with the areas they had cleaned checked off. She then set off with Tyrone back to the truck.

The chastised Tyrone nudged Martha and said: "Golly gosh Martha, you know what? You're quite frightening when you get one on. I'll give you damned donkey dick when we get back to base."

She smiled and knew she'd take some joshing for that bit of quick thinking.

All of the team were back in the truck within ten minutes. Ginny had now been in the box for twenty-one minutes. Just as they were about to drive off a chubby administrator tapped on the window and they heard him say: "Hey, you guys, what about your coffee and doughnuts?"

Martha wound the window down. "Oh heck, we want to, but we're running late. Real sorry, next time perhaps?"

The administrator looked crestfallen. "But I ordered them specially. Wait here, won't be long."

Martha tried to say "No, really, it's okay…" but the administrator was already hurrying away. It was too risky to drive away. They had to wait.

The minutes ticked by. When it seemed as though they were going to have to run for it, Martha told Tyrone to open Ginny's box and let some air in. Finally, the friendly hospital administrator waddled around the corner with a big bag of coffee and doughnuts.

"Here y'all are. We have high standards of hospitality here. Have a real nice day," he said.

Martha took the package and smiled her thanks. She tapped her driver and they drove to the main gate. As they slowed, a stern looking guard stepped out in front of the truck and waved them down. He walked to the passenger window, tapped it with his hand.

"Okay, vehicle search!" he said loudly.

They all let out an audible groan. Then the guard smiled and let out a loud guffaw.

"Golly Moses, I love doin' that to new cleaners. Never fails! Off you go now boys and girls," and he waved the truck on laughing wildly like a maniac, "see yo'all next week".

A little way down the road the driver looked at Martha and said, "Well at least somebody got some kicks out of today!"

Ginny was beginning to regain consciousness and the mixture of drugs in her body left her confused and unfocussed. The team bathed her body with cool flannels and gave her plenty of water to drink. After a short journey to a safe house on the East Side, she was unloaded carefully from the truck and taken inside. As she was helped into a bedroom kitted out with medical equipment she could just about make out two figures. Then she heard their voices. Even through the mist and with hearing that was dull and full of echoes she recognised them as her mother and father. Tears flowed and wet her cheeks. Then her parents were with her hugging her tightly, all three of them crying and trying to talk.

Later that day Ginny asked to see Merric and Catherine and they were brought to the safe house in a car with its windows obscured by tinted glass. More hugs and tears followed. But it was clear that Ginny was very tired and they left her to sleep.

In the sitting room, Zirl, Nick and Angela Grivas, Merric and Catherine made small talk. Zirl coughed as a sign that serious discussion was to begin.

"Senator Grivas has kindly agreed to take forward the next stage of our plan to bring the bad guys to justice. He will be delivering a lecture tomorrow on what America owes the Greeks at the Institute for Democracy in Washington. It's non-partisan and Judy Woodruff, who presents the CNN television programme, 'Inside Politics' is chairing it. If Ginny is up to it, the Senator will present her and expose the murderers on national TV."

Nick Grivas nodded his agreement. Angela and the others looked worried.

Zirl put his hands together and frowned. "There will be some risk to Ginny. We suspect that the murderers will be at the event. We will have men there to mitigate this threat, but…"

Catherine cut in. "You need a diversion. Make the murderers think Ginny is going to be somewhere else."

Merric clapped his hands and they all looked at him. "Aha!" he shouted, "My thoughts exactly. The FBI could not find me. They searched my apartment, but we were gone, poof, gone! So, they must believe that I know something. In which case, I go to a hotel and organise a press briefing. It is that special time is it not? When foreign journalists are looking for stories, especially those that relate to the presidential election."

Merric sat, with hands outstretched, eyes wide open and appealing.

The senator looked at Zirl and said nothing.

Catherine spoke up. "I could help too. Ginny and I are about the same size. With make-up and sunglasses and trendy clothes, I think I could pass as her from a distance. The FBI won't be a hundred per cent sure it's me but the whole set up will scream that I am about to spring a live exposé. It will buy time for the main event."

Zirl smiled. "Merric, Catherine, I like your plan."

Angela smiled and went to kiss Merric and hug Catherine. Nick Grivas shook Merric's hand.

The girl in Ginny's bed space in the hospital waited two hours before making herself known to the staff. She produced papers to prove that she was not Ginny Grivas but an investigative reporter and advised all those she spoke to, to release her as soon as possible because her location was known to a wide variety of government and newspaper agencies. The matron had the unenviable task of breaking the news to Quantock.

Chapter 29

E-Day minus 2

Quantock was at the White House incandescent with rage; his heart was racing and his fingers tingled. Ginny Grivas had been sprung with such ease it had to have been done with help from people on the inside and he strongly suspected the involvement of the CIA. He phoned his CIA chess buddy, Alvin Studebaker to sound him out and was told that he was not available. To make matters worse, Merric Grabowski, Clem Johnson's Polish friend, was determined to have his day at a press interview to be hosted in a Washington hotel, the Quo Vadis, and Quantock did not know what he would reveal. It occurred to him that this was probably the best time and place for Ginny to be brought out of hiding, into the press glare. But he also suspected that Senator Grivas was now in contact with his daughter and Grivas was also giving a speech at the Institute of Democracy at the same time which was being televised by CNN. Ideally, he needed to watch both of them, but he didn't have the resources to do both properly. He would think on it.

He walked head up, down the long corridor to the President's Oval Office, having advised him of the situation earlier during an edgy telephone conversation. Confidence was his stock in trade, but he was going to have to call on every ounce of this if he was to survive the week or even the day. He reached the door to the office and was met by one of the President's executive officers who announced him. This was followed by a shout from the President, "Get in here Quantock!"

Quantock closed the door behind him, it felt heavy in his hands and the atmosphere of the room was warm and cloying.

"Mr President," he began, "I have to say…"

"You have nothing to say, nothing, Quantock. For the record, I know nothing, you understand me, nothing? I don't know of the Kinz scam, the existence of the remaining two teenagers from the tin mine fiasco. I … know … goddamn … nothing. Do you really understand what I'm saying to you?"

The President's face was red with apoplexy. There were beads of sweat on his brow. The veins in his temple were standing out.

Quantock paled and nodded, not with fear or fright, but with the sick feeling of failure and humiliation. At least he was suffering this in private. He chose silence. The President continued.

"I want you to fix this situation, Quantock. Do you hear me? You will fix this situation or I will fuck you. And I kid you not. You will be truly fucked. The election is four days away. Four days for you to fix things."

By now Brannigan was leaning over the edge of the table and pointing a nicotine-stained right forefinger at Quantock's face. He was shaking with rage. Without ceremony or waiting for an answer from Quantock, President Brannigan waved his hand unceremoniously towards the door. "Now go. Fuck the fuck off and do your fucking job!"

Quantock left the room. He was determined to beat this set-back. He had always come out on top and nothing was going to stop him this time. In the car, he received a text. "Company is arranging for Aphrodite to bare all at Quo Vadis."

On reaching his office Quantock called Jim Rook.

"Hi, Jim, it's Dan. I need an Iranian speaker for a meeting with a contact tomorrow. Doesn't your greenhorn Salim Kennedy speak Iranian?"

"Farsi. Yes. Salim does. His mother's Iranian."

"Good. Send him to see me. Immediately."

"Yes, boss," said Jim. He put the phone down with a click and Quantock was left listening to the mesmerising dial tone that mixed with the thump of his heartbeat. He lowered the telephone onto the cradle, held it there for a few moments, and then quickly dialled a number.

"Robert. Hi, long time no speak. Yeah, just fine, listen, I need a TV quality camcorder that can be used to record a few things at a public meeting. You know the type, robust, decent carrying case with lots of pockets and of course easy to use." He paused as he listened to the response, then continued. "Thanks buddy, I'll collect it from the store today, just put my name on the label. I'll sign for it."

Quantock drummed his fingers on the desk. Then he reached for his cell phone rather than using the internal landline and whilst thumbing through his Filofax he dialled a number. It was answered after a few minutes.

"Sean. It's me, Dan Quantock. Listen you renegade Irish bastard, I'm in a hurry. I need something from you. A product. Czech. Similar size to a standard video cassette for a news-quality camcorder. I need it by tomorrow. When you've delivered it, you forget that you gave it to me, right? You forget – completely! If you don't deliver you will never see daylight again. You'll be handed over to the Brits and a message will be sent to your old comrades in Belfast, that Mad Dog is home and waiting to be put down."

Sean promised on the Blessed Virgin and his mother's life that he would deliver and Quantock believed him. He began to feel a lot better and the pain of President Brannigan's fierce admonition receded slightly.

He walked to his chessboard and reached down for the black queen, lifting it up and hovering over the centre of the action on the board. He carefully checked all the angles several times, and then firmly put the chess piece in place.

Chapter 30

E-Day minus 1

Foreign journalists packed the foyer of the Hotel Quo Vadis, bustling and talking, hoping for some excitement. They were all junior reporters, the more senior journalists were on the road following the election campaign or the tin mine murders.

There was a queue for coffee. None of those present knew what to expect. This old Polish émigré had called for the world's press to be available to listen to something that would be of special interest to voters in the presidential election. It was rumoured that someone from the CIA had been ringing editors telling them to send someone to cover it. It was all very mysterious. He might be a nutcase, or he might have something interesting, what was it to be?

Three newspaper reporters from Eastern Europe laughed and joked with some of the other reporters and were clearly not taking things too seriously. Several young English television and newspaper journalists had a strange way of sitting together and yet appearing totally separate, conferring with craned heads, then springing apart like repelling magnets.

A journalist from Austria turned to Eva Markel who worked for Der Deutsche Zeitung and said, "After this, shall we take some time out for a good American cocktail. I know a good bar quite close by?"

Eva blanched. The man was over forty years old and married. She was twenty-eight and ambitious for her first big break. The last thing that she wanted was to get involved with an over-sexed and over-weight married Austrian. She looked at him and shook her head. Then she took out a business card and held it tightly in her hand. Maybe this crazy Pole had more to offer than her dubious colleagues realised. It was worth a try. She shook her long curly black hair loose and settled back in her seat to wait.

Salim Kennedy looked around him. It felt strange to be in a room with so many foreigners, Russians, English, Germans, Chinese and others. He enjoyed taking in the differences of the characters. Although, he thought, there were times when he himself felt foreign. America was a culturally mixed country, but the events of 9/11 had left people suspicious of cultures that they did not understand. His mother was Iranian and father Irish American, but Salim's looks were distinctly Middle Eastern.

He wanted to question the assignment. It seemed stupid. But Quantock had cut him short. He was told to shut up and listen. The only thing that Salim should be interested in was following Quantock's instructions to the letter. No, absolutely no, deviation. He was to get to the press conference early and choose a seat close to the front and set up his camera on a tripod. But then came the odd part. He wasn't to record the words of the Polish émigré, Merric Grabowski. But he was told to hold the recording until a young woman, about five feet six inches tall, with long black curly hair, joined Grabowski. This was the important conversation. It was likely that she would emerge suddenly, but it was not known where from. It was simple really, even for a young rookie FBI agent like Salim. He checked the view finder of the camera one last time to make sure all points around the podium were covered and sipped a cup of sweet black coffee. This was exceptionally boring work. He sighed deeply.

At the edges of the room, five CIA field officers, posing as journalists scanned the audience. Back-up teams waited in an adjacent conference room and at the front of the hotel. They were under instructions to shoot to kill if they made contact with armed assailants.

Catherine and Merric peeked from behind a dark curtain. Merric smiled broadly causing his face to look even more lined, like an old, shrivelled-up apple. Catherine's face on the other hand looked beautiful. She had carefully applied make-up which took decades off her age and was dressed in some clothes she had bought for Ginny. A pair of trendy sunglasses balanced on her head. Merric felt that he was falling in love.

"There are lots of people. It is a good turnout. They all want some blood to take to their editors. We shall give them some excitement, eh, Catherine."

He reached for her hand and she took it. "Yes, we shall Merric, we shall. Now let's run through this again. You go and make your statement about being a proud American especially what it means to be free in a democracy. Give some of your past history, your experience of rotten state organised policing and rigged government administration. Your belief in democracy needs to come out too. Then you make some comments about your childhood, Poland under the Nazis then the Russians, then move on to observations of America and how you feel about the politics of spin doctoring information cloaking it with deceit and manufacturing issues, you know the sort of thing better than I do. Then go on to say you have some fears for the future if ever that evil is allowed to manifest itself into American political life."

Catherine was gentle and crafted each sentence slowly so that the old man would understand what needed to be done. He fiddled with his notes, pretending not to be nervous.

"You then move on to say that you have evidence of something rotten. At this point I come out to join you. You don't introduce me, but you go on to talk about Ginny Grivas, and, well, you know the rest."

Merric smiled, "Yes, young lady, I copy. I understand what needs to be done. We're almost there. I must confess to being a little excited myself. It beats playing chess with my friend Constantine Cariocas at the local bar. Besides he cheats. Today, Catherine, we don't cheat."

Catherine looked around the curtain again, and then at her watch, "We'd better move, it's full and almost two o'clock. Now off you go, Merric, quickly!"

Merric looked at her a little nervously and said, ""Uwazaj na siebie!" That's Polish for take care of yourself. You are a lovely lady, I wish I were twenty years younger, Catherine."

She smiled and touched his face with her left hand.

He got up, turned on his heel, gathering some papers that he intended to put in front of him on the desk to make the scene look more business-like. The papers included innocuous information on holidays to Greece, some sports reports and the latest results of the World Chess Championships; that made him chuckle. Then Merric stopped, stood up straight, took several deep breaths, composed himself and walked out from behind the curtain, which flapped dramatically around him. There was a hush as he moved towards the podium at the front of the room. As he passed Salim, Merric dropped some papers and bent down to pick them up. Salim caught his eyes, old, grey and yet very bright and alert.

Just then Eva Markel saw her chance and she darted out of her chair two rows behind Salim and thrust her business card in Merric's jacket pocket. She smiled at him. Merric thought her quite beautiful and he returned her smile, taking her soft hand in his. She led him to the podium and whispered in his ear. Salim panicked.

He dropped his hot coffee over his trouser leg, but didn't feel it in his excitement and haste, and was relieved to quickly find the record button. A quick glance in the view finder and Salim pressed the button.

The explosion was deafening. A bright flash and a tremendous blast wave engulfed the crowded room.

Debris from broken glass, furniture and mangled flesh flew everywhere. For a few moments, afterwards there was an eerie silence, punctuated only by the sound of small particles falling to the ground and the ring of the hotel fire alarm system. Then through the smoke came the moans and cries of pain and anguish from those injured, but still alive.

Catherine was on her knees and bleeding from a dozen cuts on her face and hands. Her face was ashen and tears were forming in her eyes. She stared through the smoky gloom, but couldn't even see where the podium had been. She had been blown sideways as she stood behind the curtain. Where was Merric? Who had done this? Why?

When he got the initial report by text, even Quantock shuddered at his handiwork. But it had to be done. All the loose ends had to be tidied up. Jim Rook rushed into the room.

"My watchers have spotted a young woman with Senator Grivas in his car. She answers to the description of Ginny Grivas. Jesus Dan, I thought she was in custody. What's going on?" he said.

Quantock was nearly sick. "What? Are you sure?"

"Sure, I'm sure."

"Treason is afoot Jim. Treason. The Company has gone rogue. It's Dallas and the Grassy Knoll all over again. There's been a bomb attack on the Quo Vadis Hotel. Dozens killed. It's got CIA written all over it. We're in the middle of something far, far bigger than I thought."

Rook looked at him open mouthed. "What do we do? Does the Director know?"

"We cut the heads off the hydra, Jim. Me and you. We need to get Ginny Grivas back into custody. She is the key to this. Have you got your gun?" Rook nodded and slapped his side. "Right, get a car. Grivas is speaking at the Institute of Democracy. Ginny must be going with him."

Jim hurried away. Quantock opened a cabinet and took his Glock, checked its magazine and slipped it into the underarm holster he wore under his jacket. He removed a second, smaller, slimmer handgun, a 9mm Ruger which was wrapped in a handkerchief and he put this in his side pocket.

Senator Grivas' car stopped outside the Institute of Democracy building. Several people with press badges converged on him; they didn't even notice Ginny in the back of the vehicle wearing a blonde wig and sunglasses. The CIA man John Smith sat next to her. A small dark haired woman with a prominent nose clutched her clipboard and got to the senator first. Her shrill voice grated on his ears.

"Senator, there are lots of mixed messages coming out of Pennsylvania. Brannigan is behind in the polls but you are in front. Why do you think that is?"

Although his nerves were shredded, Nick Grivas had to remember that this was his day job and he gathered his strength for an answer. He patiently addressed the question. "Well, ma'am, I think it's still too early to call it on this election. The polls don't always get it right. The important thing is that everyone gets out to vote and be part of this great democratic system of ours. But tonight, I'm going to be talking about how my forebears in Ancient Greece brought democracy to the world. "

As other journalists shouted questions, the unmistakable figure of Fred Spiker strode through the entrance towards them. Spiker and Grivas shook hands warmly. "I'm looking forward to your speech, Nick," he said. "It's often good to remind ourselves of what a precious commodity democracy is." Spiker escorted Nick Grivas into the building. Ginny waited for a few moments before quickly going up the steps with her escort, John Smith, and following her father until Spiker separated from him.

When she reached her father, he hugged her and said, "We're in the Lincoln Room. We have to be calm. If I'm a few minutes late Judy Woodruff, who is organising the event, will understand. Okay, let's walk around the long way. That will help your nerves."

He bent down and kissed her forehead tenderly. "I love you honey, you're brave and principled and I am a dumb father never to have noticed that before."

Ginny looked up at her father, "Love you too Dad."

Grivas turned to Smith. "Can you give me a few minutes with my daughter?" Smith reluctantly agreed. Together they walked hand in hand through the outside corridors, past busts of Pericles and Plato, Tom Paine and Thomas Jefferson, FDR and JFK. Nick Grivas gave a running commentary on how ancient Greece influenced them all. Ginny just wanted the event to be over. She was tired but was glad to be with her dad; she felt safe. They walked for a few minutes along some dimly lit corridors, and then came across several people crowded around a television set in a side office. One of them looked up, "Hey, Senator Grivas, sir, isn't this just awful?"

"Oh, hi Mike, isn't what awful?"

"Sir, you haven't heard? There has been an explosion at the Hotel Quo Vadis. Some Polish guy was killed, along with dozens of others, including foreign journalists. They reckon it was a terrorist attack."

Senator Grivas turned and saw Ginny's face. She was as white as a sheet, put her hands to her mouth and let out a noise resembling a muffled scream and a groan. She cried out, "Merric, oh dear God, Merric, and Catherine," she put her hands to her mouth and her eyes welled with tears. Then she fainted.

Grivas and some of the younger men picked up Ginny's limp body and carried it into the side office. They laid her gently in a large armchair. Grivas said desperately: "I need to get help. Can you keep an eye on my daughter?"

"Yes, sir," one of the young man answered and Grivas raced down the corridor.

Minutes later, an older man entered the side room. "Everyone leave please. I'm a doctor. The senator's daughter needs space and peace. I will stay with her." The young men obeyed and left.

Quantock stood looking at Ginny. She was certainly a pretty young girl. He remembered her naked body in the hotel room in Benson. It was going to be such a waste to mankind, but it had to be done. He reached into his left-hand pocket and brought out the Ruger wrapped in the handkerchief. From his holster he removed the Glock and released the safety catch.

Ginny's eyes half opened and she turned her head from left to right. Then she stared at the shape in front of her as it came into focus. Ginny recoiled in horror and tried to sink into the armchair. Her eyes bulged and her jaw dropped.

"Nice to see you Ginny. My, my, you and Clem led me on a hell of a chase. You know that? Well here we are and it all has to end my child," said Quantock.

"You killed Merric and Catherine and all those poor people. God knows how many more in your rotten life. Why?"

"Why? Now that is a good question. Why do doves cry? Why are there wars? Why are there corrupt politicians? Why do people on drugs drive cars that kill innocent mothers and children?"

Quantock paused for a moment as if thinking twice about something, and then he quickly threw the Ruger automatic to Ginny. "Here catch this!" he said.

A gentle lob and the handgun detached from the handkerchief and fell towards Ginny. She instinctively put out her hands and caught the pistol and as she did so she rolled it into her right hand, holding it out in front of her. Almost instantaneously Quantock brought his handgun to the ready position.

Just as he was about to fire he felt a metal gun barrel jam into his right temple.

"Drop it!" said a harsh and authoritative voice.

Surprised, he slowly lowered the handgun and let it fall to the floor. Turning around he saw that it was Jim Rook.

"I told you to wait in the fucking car, Jim! The bitch is armed. She was going to kill me."

As Quantock tried to move away, Jim held his collar and pressed the barrel of the gun into his neck. Quantock was transfixed.

Then another voice said, "Hello, Dan. The game's up you piece of shit. Jim, good job done. Cuff him."

Quantock stared in amazement. It was Troy Hammond. They eyeballed each other with mutual contempt.

"You look old and sick Quantock," Hammond said. "You're going to be a lot older and a lot sicker when we've finished with you. And then I'm going to bury you." He turned to Jim Rook: "Keep him here until we can get him out without anyone seeing him. Ginny, come on honey, get over here and let's get you outta here and home."

Ginny was led out of the room and taken with her father to an FBI Cadillac.

Hammond stayed behind and made a call. "David, Troy here. You're a lying two-faced bastard but I suppose you've got to be to work at the Company. Quantock has been taken down. Time for your people to rescue Clem Johnson and take care of him."

He snapped his phone shut and looked in on the Lincoln Room. Fred Spiker had agreed to stand in for Senator Grivas and was speaking about the need to be vigilant to stop tyrants abusing democracy. Hammond watched for a minute or two and saw excited journalists tweet on their phones. He smiled and walked on. The media would be sure to say that Spiker's lecture indicated that something was rotten in the House of Brannigan.

Back in Quantock's office the evening routine was going on as usual. A cleaner vacuumed the woollen carpet and as she moved in front of the desk she knocked the chess pieces off the coffee table and onto the floor. Already fed up with having to tip-toe around the chess set each day, she picked up the pieces one by one, putting them into a large brown envelope. Then she put the envelope on top of the chessboard after giving the board a quick dust down. She was in such a hurry when she left the office that she didn't notice that she had stepped onto the black king, breaking it into pieces and crushing it into the carpet.

Chapter 31

E-Day

The presidential election was neck and neck. Polls put the Democrat candidate Hillary Clinton ahead by two-three points and the media believed that Brannigan would be badly damaged by the Quantock atrocity. Clinton, out of respect for the victims and their families, refused to make political capital out of the tragedy and Brannigan was able to make the headlines on election day by attacking the Chinese and promising to save millions of American jobs.

With voters queuing at the polling stations, the great and the good of the Grand Old Party went onto a war footing. Kinz's Arizona Gambit and its terrible consequences were pieced together. Under interrogation by his former colleagues, Quantock revealed everything he knew and provided copies of letters and other details from his office safe. He also produced a copy of Kinz's letter to the President and this was damning proof that the President did know of the scam's terrible outcome and had unwisely tried to use it for his own aggrandisement, happy to reap the benefits of the political fallout. Brannigan was normally fearless even when confronted by his deceits. However, in the face of mounting evidence of his part in the affair and under sustained pressure from Spiker who knew where other bodies were buried, he agreed to step down whatever the result of the election, stating that it was for reasons of ill health. But he insisted on a proper transition plan and secrecy.

Chapter 32

Quantock was washed and hung out to dry, long before his trial.
The media bought into the story of him being a psychopath. The
shooting of the killer of his wife was re-enacted and Bill Clinton
and the Democrats were blamed for not prosecuting him. Stories
were also spread about how he went on a killing spree at Waco.
Quantock's medical records and psych assessments were leaked.
Particular attention was paid to the type of anti-depressant he was
secretly taking, especially when a journalist got a lucky tip-off that
Kinz was on the same medication. Experts queued up to say that
psychotic episodes could be a possible side effect. Shares of the drugs
company making the tablets plummeted. The point was made time
and time again, often with the help of handy self-surveys, that it
was often very difficult to spot a psychopath.

Kinz, as a war hero, received more sympathy. Experts highlighted
grief at the death of his wife as a possible major factor affecting
his judgement.

The US forces on their way to Saudi Arabia, the Gulf and the
coast of Syria were stood down. But not before Israel had taken the
opportunity to bomb a Syrian anti-aircraft missile installation on
the Golan Heights.

In the interests of the nation, Senator Grivas had to agree with his
Republican peers that the best way of safeguarding the American
political system was to say nothing about Brannigan's actions in

relation to Quantock's crimes and Kinz's suicide. Grivas then had to persuade Ginny. He took her to the Kellari Taverna on K Street, where the owner, Stavros, knew her and fussed over her. Over a shared seafood platter, Grivas praised her intellect and knowledge of the principles of justice and apologised for his patronising and condescending attitudes of the past. He asked her to look at the case dispassionately. The crime was committed by Kinz, Quantock, Anderson and Gonzalez. Brannigan did everything in his power to save the kids and bring the criminals to justice but he was betrayed. He was wrong to withhold evidence and burn Kinz's suicide note and for this crime he was willing to pay a very heavy price in relinquishing his dream of being president. He was also wrong to use the atrocity to help him in his election. But if that was a crime, nearly every politician in America would be guilty of it. The most criminal act of recklessness would be to cheat the American people of their democratic choice at a most critical time in the nation's history. The result had to be respected. Nothing good could come from hounding Brannigan. For the first time in ages, Ginny felt respect and even love for her father. He was right.

Ginny met with Catherine for lunch. And after hugs and tears she explained in confidence about the plan and why she supported it. Catherine cried and sadly shook her head. She wanted to ask Ginny about Merric and what he would have wanted but she held her tongue. At the end of their lunch, Catherine promised to stay in contact with Ginny and warmly embraced her as she left. But inside she was seething with anger. After paying a visit to Clem, she returned home.

On 20 January 2009, the United States of America installed its first woman president. On 30 January 2009, Catherine Devine was killed by a hit-and-run driver on the mountain road near her cabin.

Chapter 33

Two years since Jake Brannigan had stepped down as president on the eve of his inauguration on health grounds. Some insiders said Brannigan had stepped down just as the postman arrived at his door with and envelope marked, 'Justice – Open Carefully'. But most commentators praised him for his honesty and courage. Two years since America had its first female president. As vice-president designate, Sarah Palin had succeeded Brannigan and, after a legal challenge which went all the way to the Supreme Court, had been installed. Two years since the US and world economies experienced the biggest financial crash since 1929. Two years since a wave of riots spread across America and showed no signs of diminishing.

Attorney Lee Finch reached the plateau in good time from Colorado Springs. The snow-clad Rockies to the right of Highway 67 glistened white in the bright sunshine. It sure was a gorgeous place, he thought. The countryside was empty except for snow-draped brushwood and cacti. He had passed only one other vehicle in the last fifteen minutes. The ADX Florence facility came into view on his left. Through a high chain-link fence protected by security lighting he caught glimpses of a well-ordered collection of squat red-brick buildings nestling down in a fold in the ground while around and above them a series of twelve imposing white cylindrical gun towers loomed. Lee turned onto the slip road to the main entrance. A sign with white letters reversed out of red warned "No trespassing. Federal Bureau of Prisons. Federal Correction Complex Florence. 24 Hour Area Security". Another sign directed him to the visitors' car park. This sign also carried a warning not to approach the guard shack. Finch parked his car, grabbed his brief case and walked to the single-story reception building. He had a feeling his every move was being watched by CCTV cameras and by the gun towers. An officer holding a pump action shotgun was visible behind the window of the guard shack. Finch was buzzed into reception and a guard behind the glass-screened counter asked for his visiting order and driving licence. He was then buzzed through a side door and asked to remove any metallic items and put them in a plastic tray and to hand over his jacket, briefcase and shoes. After passing through the metal detector, a second guard frisked him and a third guard allowed a sniffer dog to inspect him.

Welcome to the Supermax, Finch thought. The Alcatraz of the Rockies. Over four hundred of the worst criminals incarcerated here for life. It wasn't just mass murderers, gangsters and foreign and domestic terrorists held here. There were also former servants of the USA. The spy and renegade FBI agent Robert Hanssen was serving fifteen life sentences for selling secrets to the Russians. But Finch was here to see someone even more notorious. Former FBI Agent in Charge, Dan Quantock. Sentenced to thirty life sentences for organising the kidnap of six American teenagers, the children of US senators, and the murder and mutilation of four of them. Guilty also of the murder of a Native American and two ex-Blackwater accomplices. Guilty of causing the death by explosives of a young FBI agent, a Polish émigré and sixteen others in Atlanta and the wounding of another of thirty-five. Guilty of the attempted murder of a fifth teenager and the illegal incarceration of a sixth. Guilty of using his position of trust to pervert the course of justice.

In the Supermax, Quantock had few rights. Locked down for twenty-three hours a day in a seven-by-twelve-foot coffin of a cell. Bed, table, stool and shelf made of concrete and a stainless-steel toilet pan. For entertainment, a black and white TV showing pre-recorded religious and educational programmes. Taken in shackles for one hour's exercise in a cage in a concrete tank the size of a swimming pool. Denied any sight of the outside world. Denied visitors. Denied a normal life. But Quantock did have a right to see his attorney, albeit very rarely and for specific legal reasons. Today Finch had been allowed access to discuss new evidence with Quantock which could form the basis of an appeal.

Finch was escorted to a sealed booth for the interview. A glass screen separated his side of the booth from the prisoner's. He took papers from his briefcase and a notepad and laid them on the counter in front of the glass. The door to the other side of the booth opened and Quantock shuffled inside. The guard removed his shackles and closed the door. Quantock smiled grimly. He had aged dramatically in the course of just a few months. His cropped hair was white and his skin grey. It looked like he shaved that morning but had done it very badly. His skin had shaving cuts and there were clumps of bristles which he had missed with the razor. He had lost weight and his khaki shirt and trousers hung off his thin frame. His shoulders were stooped. Even his eyes looked like they were dying. Quantock sat down and picked up the telephone receiver. Finch did the same.

"How are you doing, Dan?" he asked gently.

"They won't let me have a chess set."

"I know. It's against the rules."

Quantock shook his head sadly. "It's not right."

"How about everything else. You getting enough food?"

"Don't care about food."

"Now about this new evidence. Can you give me some more detail?"

Quantock lowered his voice. "It was the jihadis. They substituted my medication. They used a mind control drug on me. I can prove it. I read up on it. Kinz was a jihadi. He was a secret convert to Islam. He controlled me. He knew my weaknesses. The jihadis in this prison are trying to control me. I hear them tapping at night. The preacher on the TV is also sending me secret messages. He wants me to convert to Islam."

It was a bright sunny day and Clem had just finished his video shoot in the garden. Plumes of black smoke rose lazily in the sky from the riots in Mount Pleasant on Washington's North West side. Clem put his camera down on top of a pile of equipment that carelessly lay around him and sat down in a canvas chair that someone had labelled: "Boss." It was the end of a tough recording session. His head ached. Where was he? Oh, Philadelphia, that's it, Philadelphia. Yesterday it was Pennsylvania, before that Wisconsin and before that…well, he just couldn't remember. The subjects of his video had been hard work as usual. They were always hard work and had to be persuaded to talk; this annoyed Clem. Surely, they had something to say? Why did they just sit there and need so much encouragement? Faces, dumb-assed faces, always the same? The left side of his face twitched uncontrollably.

Clem was proud of his video company. Perhaps it had played its part in the reformation of government afterwards? Everyone told him that this had been the case; well everyone he knew anyway. He wanted to be one of the very best at producing 'fly on the wall' documentaries, exposing corruption and maladministration in government as well as business. Clem accepted that big business continued to provide the lifeblood of US capitalism, but his mission was to make social responsibility part of the American Dream. His video of that title would be dedicated to Senator Randolph Kinz. Kinz would like that. It was just taking a bit of time that was all.

Sometimes he heard Kinz's voice, as clear and loud as anything, but he wasn't really sure. He heard a lot of voices. It only happened when he had a headache or he got upset. He felt agitated today. His mind was in a whirl; it was always in a whirl these days. President Palin was visiting the shoot today, or was it next week. Why couldn't he remember? He must be ready to meet her. He began to brush his clothing with his hands and straighten his hair.

Just then Ginny Grivas walked through the French windows across the lawn, accompanied by a young black nurse in a starched white uniform and sensible shoes. A middle-aged man in a recliner on the lawn looked at them, grinned and then wolf whistled. Clem stopped rubbing his head, looked up and laughed nervously.

"That's Joe the Plumber for you." he said loudly as Ginny approached. "A normal red-blooded American. You betcha."

He shuffled forward slowly, squinting, with his hand outstretched for a handshake. His dressing gown fell open and his slippers flip flopped on the floor.

"Madam President. I'm so glad you made it, so very glad," he said.

As Ginny reached him he fell to his knees and buried his face in her stomach. She was never able to convince him that she was not the president and her stomach never failed to knot up when she was with him. She stroked his hair and face gently, softly, until he quietened down. Ginny was now an experienced senior case worker for the American Civil Liberties Union and was able to schedule regular visits to see Clem. Nothing. Not riots or weather would ever stop her visiting Clem.

The nurse reached for a syringe and Ginny glared at her and said: "It was the drugs that did this in the first place, does he have to have more?"

The nurse shrugged and reluctantly moved away from them both.

Ginny held Clem's head as she had done on every visit for almost two years now, each visit unrecognised or not remembered and always confused.

She cupped his head in her hands and whispered in his ear. "The American Dream is doing okay, Clem, just okay, don't you worry." Tears rolled down her cheek as she said it.

****

READ MORE LANCE CLARKE

Laka Stvar

Jane Kavanagh has a point to prove. Burnt out from spying on the IRA, she is keen to show herself as a capable agent in war-torn Bosnia. Her mission: to investigate a drugs trail and locate a Serbian war criminal. The challenge turns out to be more difficult than she expects and pushes her further than any other mission she has ever done. But she has to succeed, for herself – and for the innocent children of war.

"The authoritative descriptions of the mood and attitude of the characters are highly evocative of this terrible period in recent history."

Not of Sound Mind

A psychotic episode can happen to anyone for any reason. In Essex someone is committing horrific murders. But who is doing the killing and why? The police are taunted and the issue becomes a national concern as the public question the effectiveness of the Government on law and order.

"A circus of obsessions, insanity, exhibitionism (political too) throughout all the levels of the population of Essex."

Know Thyself

A collection of self-discovery: stories of humour and darkness, greed and awakening; each tale with a woman as the protagonist. Sci-fi, horror, adventure and fantasy – read these stories and find out: do you know thyself?

Visit: www.lanceclarkewriter.co.uk

Printed in Great Britain
by Amazon